Warning at One

The Lois Meade mysteries by Ann Purser from Severn House

MURDER ON MONDAY
TERROR ON TUESDAY
WEEPING ON WEDNESDAY
THEFT ON THURSDAY
FEAR ON FRIDAY
SECRETS ON SATURDAY
SORROW ON SUNDAY
WARNING AT ONE

WARNING AT ONE

Ann Purser

This title first published in Great Britain 2008 by
SEVERN HOUSE PUBLISHERS LTD of
9–15 High Street, Sutton, Surrey, England, SM1 1DF,
by arrangement with The Berkley Publishing Group,
a division of Penguin group (USA) Inc.

British Library Cataloguing in Publication Data

Purser, Ann
  Warning at one
  1. Meade, Lois (Fictitious character) - Fiction 2. Cleaning
  personnel - England - Fiction 3. Detective and mystery
  stories
  I. Title
  823.9'14[F]

  ISBN-13: 978-0-7278-6692- 9   (cased)
  ISBN-13: 978-1-84751-099-0   (trade paper)

All Severn House titles are printed on acid-free paper.

Typeset by Palimpsest Book Production Ltd.,
Grangemouth, Stirlingshire, Scotland.
Printed and bound in Great Britain by
MPG Books Ltd., Bodmin, Cornwall.

For Matthew, who gave me a good idea

Warning at One

One

In the stuffy back bedroom of number four in a terrace of small red-brick Victorian houses, the old man, who had been born in that same room seventy-eight years ago, opened his eyes and saw a grey dawn over the roofs of Tresham, his hometown in the heart of England.

"There 'e goes, bless 'im," he muttered, as he turned over and pulled the covers over his ears. "Cock-a-doodle-doo, my dame hath lost her shoe, my master's lost his fiddlin' stick, and don't know what to do!" The old man's voice was croaky, but he could still hold a tune, and he chuckled at the bawdy innuendo of the old rhyme.

It was five o'clock in the morning and the town was asleep. At least, it had been asleep until the old man's splendidly feisty cockerel had begun his noisy alarm. His voice was piercing, as it was meant to be, and all along the terrace the inhabitants groaned and put their hands over their ears or pushed in their earplugs.

The old man's name was Clement Fitch, and his neighbours in number five had moved out several weeks ago. They were driven out, they said, by that sodding bird crowing its head off underneath their window. They had complained to the owner, Mrs. Lois Meade of the village of Long Farnden, but she had done nothing about it. It was rumoured that as well as running a cleaning service, New Brooms, she was also a police informer—not for money, but because she enjoyed snooping into other people's business.

Lois Meade had not at first been interested in looking into the problem of the crowing cock, until she was warned by her tenants that if it didn't go, they would. So they went, and spread the story as widely as they could, even getting their photograph in the local paper. As a consequence, new tenants had been slow in coming forward. Nonexistent, in fact.

Lois, who was Tresham born and bred, had moved into the

village of Long Farnden with her husband, Derek, a local elec-
trician, some years ago. They had three grown children, none
living at home, and Gran kept house now that Lois had a business to run. She had in fact thought carefully about the old
man, and decided to do nothing about it for the moment. His
family had lived there for generations and her sympathies
were with him. And anyway, the sound of a cockerel was
preferable to the never-ending revving of cars that edged
through the narrow street, a shortcut to the nearby supermarket.

Besides, the old man was frail, and would probably soon
snuff it, Derek had said, then the problem would solve itself.
Maybe Lois could give the cockerel a home? Gran had
exploded at this idea, and said that as long as she was house-
keeping for them, no feathered alarm clock would be welcome
in their garden.

Now, as Lois drove down Sebastopol Street in Tresham to
New Brooms' office, she was reminded of their empty house.
Derek and some friends had won the lottery jackpot, and he
and Lois had bought the little house as an investment and
source of income. She didn't like to think of it not earning
its keep, and resolved to call in on the old man to talk about
the cockerel. But first, the office.

"Morning, Hazel," she said as she walked in. Hazel was
one of her original staff, and now manned the office whilst
her toddler, Elizabeth, spent the day with one of her two
grandmothers or with Hazel's old friend Maureen, who lived
next to the office.

"Morning, Mrs. M," Hazel said, using the name adopted
by all Lois's cleaners. "How's things?"

"Difficult," replied Lois, "unless you happen to know a way
of silencing a crowing cockerel?" She saw Hazel, who was
the wife of a young farmer, raise her eyebrows, and added,
"And no, I can't kill it. It's not mine. Belongs to old Clem
Fitch who lives next door to our house in Gordon Street. Our
tenants left, complaining, and the agents haven't been able to
find new ones. All because of the cockerel. I wondered if the
vet could operate and remove whatever it is."

Hazel laughed. "I doubt it," she said. "You could ask, but
be prepared for a dusty answer!"

"Give me the phone, then," Lois said. "And no sniggers
from you, please."

The vet's receptionist seemed to be having trouble with her reply, and said if Lois could hold on, she'd go and ask. Lois could hear voices, then a hoot of laughter, and then the girl returned to the phone. "Um, you still there, Mrs. Meade? Yes, well, the vet says if there is a way, he's never heard of it, and if you'd like to bring the bird in, he will deal with it so that it'll never crow again."

"Thanks for nothing!" said Lois crossly, and cut off the call.

"No luck?" Hazel said, and thought it tactful to change the subject. "We've got a new client, referred to us from your house agents. In Gordon Street, on the other side of the road from Clem Fitch. Bigger houses that side. It's a new owner, an elderly lady with failing sight, and she'd asked the agents if they knew anybody who could clean for her. Naturally they mentioned New Brooms. Do you want to call in on your way home?"

Lois said that it fitted in well. She was going to see Clem anyway, and could do both. Then she settled down with Hazel to go through the post and any messages that had come in.

Two

By the time Lois knocked on the front door of number four, Clem had been up for hours, had had his usual cursory wash, and gone out to feed his cockerel before fetching the morning paper from the corner shop.

The bird's territory was an old, brick-built outhouse which had once been the two-hole lavatory for the six houses in the terrace. Children were put in together, and sometimes man and wife. The shit-cart, as it was universally known, had come once a week to empty the buckets, clanging its way along the street at an early hour, accompanied by a foul but familiar smell, and awakening the residents just as Clem's cockerel did now.

Clem had cleaned out the outhouse, but kept the two-hole seat, its surface polished smooth by countless bottoms. He used the cavity as a store for the cockerel's grain and mash. With wire netting filched from the dump, he had made a frame that fitted over the open door during the day, and the bird had grown to a good size, roosting on top of the crossbeam in the roof. Iridescent feathers gleamed in the sun, and his comb and wattles were bright scarlet. He was a very handsome fellow, and Clem was as proud of him as if he had been his only son.

Now Clem opened his front door a couple of inches, and said, "Yes?"

"Good morning, Mr. Fitch," said Lois. She was prepared for a cool reception, and was certain that Clem knew exactly who she was.

"What d'you want?" Clem answered. He had a good idea of what she wanted. The people next door had done a runner, shouting at him that his ruddy cockerel had driven them mad. Nobody had come in next door since, and he was half expecting this woman's agent to pay him a visit. Now he was faced with the woman herself. Ah, well, he was too old a hand to be bullied by a woman.

"Can I come in for a minute?" Lois said. "There's something I want to ask you. Won't take long, but it's beginning to rain and I'd rather not stand on the doorstep."

"You could try saying please," grumbled the old man, and opened the door just wide enough for Lois to squeeze by him. She wished she had taken a deep breath before entering, enough to last her for the whole conversation. There was a fire smouldering in the grate and the close atmosphere was heavy with whiffs of old, unwashed clothes, frying pans never cleaned, the same fat used over and over again, and an all-pervading smell of mice.

"Go on, then," Clem said, "say what you come for." He was determined to make her introduce the subject. At this point, unfortunately for Clem, the cockerel decided to crow loudly, though it was now the middle of the day.

"That!" said Lois, smiling in spite of herself. "That awful row is what I've come about. You have to admit, Mr. Fitch, it's got a powerful voice!"

"Glad you like it," said Clem, folding his arms challengingly. "Pretty good, ain't it?"

"Maybe to you, but not to your neighbours, and not at five o'clock in the morning."

"Not in winter, it's not five. In winter it's much later. 'E don't like the dark, doesn't old Cocky. Mind you, 'e knows when the day's breaking much sooner than the lazy sods living in this terrace."

Lois tried another tack. "Can I see him? He sounds like a wonderful bird. Maybe he needs a wife, and somewhere to run about?"

I know what you're up to, said Clem to himself. You're goin' to say why don't you find him a nice home with hens and a yard for exercise? Well, hard luck, missus, there's bin others tried that, and I've got an answer.

On cue, Lois said, "I happen to know a farmer would give him a good home. Hens and a field to chase 'em in. He'd have a great time, Mr. Fitch." She knew as soon as she'd made the suggestion that Clem had set himself against it. He was keeping his cockerel, even if it meant him moving in with it and barricading the door.

"Could you think about it...please?" said Lois, making for the door. She was feeling breathless, and needed some fresh air. "I'll come back in a few days. I don't want to cause you any trouble with the authorities an' that. But something's got to be done, Mr. Fitch. Think what'd be best for Cocky. Cheerio," she added as pleasantly as she could, and made a quick getaway.

The house across the way had a name as well as a number. Double-fronted, and with three scrubbed stone steps, Braeside was one of several detached houses in the street, and the date, carved in the stone lintel above the door, indicated that it had been there before Clem's terrace. Lois imagined the furore that must have followed the plan to build workmen's houses opposite the solid citizens of Tresham in their superior detached residences. Nothing changes, she thought as she stepped up to the front door and rang the bell.

It was a while before she could see, through the frosted glass panel, a woman's shape approaching. The door opened, and an elegantly dressed person, holding a white stick and wearing dark glasses, said, "Good morning. Mrs. Meade, is it?"

Lois said yes, it was, and she had an appointment for twelve o'clock. Was she too early? If so, she would be quite happy to wait in the car. There was a distinctly regal presence about Mrs. Imogen Blairgowrie, and Lois reacted accordingly. Blimey, I nearly curtseyed, she said to herself as she followed the woman into the comfortable, sunlit sitting room at the back of the house.

Mrs. Blairgowrie turned to Lois and indicated a chair for her to sit down. "I am still getting used to the geography of this house," she said, "but it is beginning to feel like home. Do you know, Mrs. Meade," she added in a friendly, confiding voice, "as soon as the agents told us the name of the house was Braeside, I knew it was the one for me. My son was with me, of course, and insisted on asking all the right questions. I was concerned only with what seemed like a nice warm feeling here, and the Scottish connection. We are a Scottish family, you see."

Lois nodded, and realised the old lady was waiting for her to respond with similar details. "Fine," she said. "I'm glad you like it here. I was born in Tresham, but now we're in Long Farnden, not far away. New Brooms has been going for several years, and we've got a good reputation. The agents said you'd like some help in the house? All my cleaners are thoroughly reliable, honest, and discreet." She always said this, getting it out of the way at once.

Mrs. Blairgowrie nodded approvingly. "Very necessary," she said. "Discretion is vital when someone has access to everything in my house. And, of course, now that I cannot see so well, it is even more important."

"If you'll forgive my asking, Mrs. Blairgowrie," Lois said tentatively, "do you mind telling me just how much you can see? I really need to know, so I can tell my cleaners to give you the best possible help."

"Almost nothing," the old lady said airily. "Just vague shapes, and very little colour. Best to assume I can see nothing," she said.

Days and times for the cleaners were fixed, and Lois got up to leave. Mrs. Blairgowrie rose at once. She's pretty good on her pins, thought Lois, and when she stood back to allow her new client to lead the way to the door, she marvelled at the sure way she moved out of the door and into the passage.

"Goodbye, then, Mrs. Meade." Mrs. Blairgowrie smiled. "I shall look forward to meeting you again." She shut the door, and Lois walked across to her car. As she drove home, she thought of Clem and the cockerel, and of her new client. Who should she send to work at Braeside? It needed some thought.

If the old lady really could see next to nothing, it would have to be a nimble, observant person. Bridie, perhaps? Or Bill? It would be a pleasant job. No problems, as far as she could see. Then she had a quick picture before her of the blind, upright figure walking firmly to the front door, minus her stick, finding the small Yale lock at once, and stepping back with complete confidence to allow Lois to leave.

"If she's blind," she said aloud, "I'm a banana."

Three

"I went to see a new client this afternoon," Lois said. She was leaning against the Rayburn watching Gran wash lettuce at the sink.

"Thought you were going to sort out the cockerel man." Gran shook the lettuce and put it into a whirly plastic drier.

"I did go, but I haven't sorted it. For one thing, the house stank. I had to get out before I was suffocated."

Gran scoffed. "Don't be so silly, Lois! If you'd lived where I did when I was a child, you'd know——"

"——what a smelly house really was," completed Lois. "I expect you're right, but when I was a child on the Churchill housing estate in Tresham, you probably remember there was no wallowing in pig muck, so I'm not hardened to it like you."

"Well, that's enough of that," said Gran firmly, vigorously chopping up tomatoes. "Now tell me sensibly how you got on."

Gran still had the power to make Lois feel eight years old, and she obediently told the cockerel story and how she was convinced nothing was going to persuade the old man to get rid of it, unless forced to by the cops. "And I'm not prepared to go that far, Mum," she concluded.

Gran nodded. "Quite right, too," she said. "Something'll turn up, anyway. I'm not sure Derek's right in saying the old boy'll snuff it. That wiry sort live long. Anyway, what about this new client?"

"A blind woman. Mrs. Blairgowrie."

"Mrs. who?"

"Mrs. Blairgowrie. She's Scottish, and lives in a house called

Braeside. Opposite old Clem, which is handy."

"Braeside?" said Gran sharply. "One of them detached villas? That rings a bell." She paused for a second or two, then turned to face Lois, leaning her back against the sink. She wiped her hands on her apron, and added, "Now I remember. Braeside was where there was that murder, years ago. Old man murdered his young wife. Stupid old fool thought he could keep her happy, and o' course he couldn't. Not even with all his money. She played around and he found out. Strangled her. He was strong enough for that!"

"Mum! When was this?"

"Oh, years ago. Back in the thirties. Nineteen thirties! It was all over the national papers at the time. Quite famous, Tresham was, for a while."

"What happened to the old man?"

"Hanged, o' course. They did in them days. And right and proper, too, in my view."

Lois took a deep breath. "And Braeside? I suppose the old story's been forgot."

Gran shook her head. "Never forgot," she said. "For one thing, it's known to be an unlucky house. Nobody stays there for long, and usually something bad happens to them. That's why it goes for much less than the others along there. The story's still around, however hard the estate agents try to keep it quiet."

Lois looked at the clock. "Derek'll be home soon," she said. "Better go and get cleaned up for tea. Anything I can do, Mum?"

Gran did not answer, but her silence was eloquent. Lois vanished upstairs.

A while later, the television in the sitting room might as well have been playing to an empty room. The three people in front of it were asleep. The telephone rang loudly, and all three awoke with a start. Lois was first on her feet, and went out into the hall to answer it.

"Mum?" It was Douglas, Lois's firstborn. He worked for an IT company in Essex, and seldom came home. But he was assiduous in keeping in touch via e-mail and telephone, and Lois always thought of him as her most dutiful child. Josie had her own little empire at the shop, and this took all her time. They saw little of Jamie, the youngest, who was a musician and found it impossible to get away.

"Are you all right?" This was always the first thing Lois said to Douglas, and the answer was, with luck, "Fine, Mum. How're you and Dad?" This ritual over, he would come to the point. This time, he had something really important to say.

"I've made a decision, Mum," he said. "I've thought it over carefully, and decided to give up this job and come back to Tresham. Still some jobs in IT going there, and I'd really like to be nearer home."

"Ah," said Lois, remembering the last time he had mentioned it. Derek had not been exactly overjoyed, saying that Douglas must not think he could come back to Long Farnden and expect his mother and Gran to welcome him with open arms. They had more than enough to do already. Nor should he expect to move into their Tresham house for a peanut rent.

Douglas was still talking, and Lois concentrated. "Last time I spoke to Gran," he said, "she mentioned that you were having trouble finding a tenant for the Tresham house. If so, could I be your tenant?"

"I'll call your father," Lois said, passing the buck without hesitation.

"So what did you tell him?" Gran said as Derek returned to the sitting room. She was very anxious that Douglas should be encouraged to move nearer to his family. In her view, all children should stay within shouting distance of their parents, for the mutual benefit of all concerned.

"Don't pester, Mum," Lois said. "Derek knows best where his sons are concerned." She didn't believe this for one minute, but knew how irritated Derek would be by mother-in-law interference.

Derek nodded. "Quite right, me duck," he said. "I told him straight. If you want to live in our house, I said, you pay the going rate and go along with all the rules and regs. O' course I said it nicely, and made sure he knew we'd be pleased to have him close by."

"Huh! I should think so, too," Gran huffed. "I should've thought that with all that money the pair of you have got in the bank—"

"Change the subject, Mum," Lois said quickly. They were treading dangerous ground. Derek—and she herself to some extent—was sensitive to any suggestion that they should change their careful habits just because they had won the lottery. It was up to them what they did with it. And, as Derek said often, they never knew when they might need a lump sum in an emergency.

Four

Clem sat in his battered chair by the front window, peering from behind grey net curtains at the street outside. The windows themselves were filmed over with dust, and would have been ample protection for him to watch without being seen, but the need for a concealing curtain was deeply ingrained. His old mum had always had thick lace curtains. She stared out of the same window, watching the world go by and commenting on its foolishness to anyone who would listen.

In those days, of course, most of the women in the street would sit outside their front doors and gossip, keeping an eye on the children playing tag and hopscotch with little fear of traffic. No longer, thought Clem. The best he could do was watch people in cars going to the supermarket and the occasional resident leaving his house early in the morning and returning in the evening. The narrow street was lined with parked cars, and frequently there were jams and hooting horns and symptoms of road rage reaching Clem even when he was out in his yard attending to his cockerel.

But now there was something new. The house opposite, Braeside, had stood empty for six months at least, but now someone had moved in. "Looks like just one old lady," he muttered, disappointed that it was nothing more exciting. A tall, heavily built man in his middle years came and went at odd times, bringing bags of supplies and taking out bundles of letters to the post-box on the corner, but he obviously did not live there.

"She don't 'arf write a lot o' letters," he said to Satan, as he cleaned out his shed and gave him fresh grain. "Do you reckon that's her son?" Satan cocked his head on one side, straightened up, and crowed derisively. Then he flew up to his perch and sat there, hunched up resentfully, and stared at

Clem.

"What d'you want then, Cocky?" Clem said. He remembered the Meade woman offering the bird freedom and a harem of hens. Was that what his best friend wanted? Clem felt a pang of guilt, but smothered it quickly. No, the splendid cockerel was happy enough. He'd pine away and turn up his toes if he was miserable. Birds were like that. He remembered his old mum had a budgie that she doted on. When she died, no matter what Clem did, the budgie pined, wouldn't eat, and eventually Clem found him one morning lying on his back with his legs in the air.

"There wasn't nothing left of 'im. Just a handful o' feathers," he had said to his neighbour. The neighbour was dead now, and Clem refused to think maybe his turn would come next. The new chap was a rotten substitute. He was never seen, kept his curtains drawn, and not a sound came through the wall. A dead loss, Clem considered. And o' course, the other side was empty. Was it really Satan that put off a new tenant? He didn't believe it. A sensible person would come along soon.

Nothing interesting was happening over the road, and Clem thought he might as well make himself a cup of tea. But as he got up to go into his kitchen, a young bloke carrying a bag of what looked like tools walked up to the front door of Braeside and knocked. Clem sat down again, and moved the net curtain a fraction of an inch to one side.

After a minute or two, the door opened and he saw the old lady standing there, holding on to her stick. He'd seen her in the little square of front garden with a white stick, and assumed she was blind. She was smiling, and stood back to let the man walk in, and then the door was shut. Clem hadn't seen him parking a car or a van, and supposed he'd left it in the supermarket car park. Everybody did that, even if they weren't going in to shop.

Clem went off to make tea quickly, so that he could get back to his observation post as soon as possible. He wanted to see the man coming out, when he could nip out of his front door and watch where he went. Maybe get a clue to what he was doing over there. Might be one of them what preyed on old ladies, he thought.

Mrs. Blairgowrie led the way to her kitchen, and sat down

by the scrubbed wooden table. "Now," she said, "why don't you sit down while I tell you what I want done. What was your name again? Mrs. Meade did tell me, but my mind is like a sieve these days. Old age is a wretched thing!" She laughed and pointed to a chair.

"I'm Bill Stockbridge, and I've worked for Mrs. M and New Brooms for quite a while. I also work at the vets, so I don't do cleaning work for as many hours as some of the girls, but I love it. I get teased a bit, as you can imagine, but I'm used to that. I can assure you I'll do a good job. And," he added, "I won't sit down, if you don't mind. Mrs. M has strict rules, and we're allowed a coffee break halfway through the morning, if convenient for the client."

"Oh, yes, that'll be fine, if you could make it yourself, and one for me, when you're ready. As you've probably been told, I am nearly blind and not too good with kettles and boiling water and so on." Her voice was hoarse, as if she had a bad sore throat. Bill could see what she meant by the wretchedness of old age. He wondered briefly how she managed when left alone, but listened carefully to her instructions and then set to work.

The house was dark and stuffy, but clean. Bill looked around and thought how nice it would be if the whole place was given a coat of sparkling white paint. Open a few windows, too. They were streaky on the outside, where a lazy window-cleaner had done a bad job. Inside they were dusty, and he began to clean them, planning to suggest he bring a ladder and do the outsides as well next time. Mrs. Blairgowrie had mentioned her son, who lived a few miles away and came in regularly. He brought her shopping and an hour or two of companionship. He obviously didn't do much else.

The furniture was an odd mixture of old and new, some well-made and some gimcrack. Bill polished a large dressing table, carved intricately around the mirror, with bevelled glass and drawers that opened and shut as if on silk. It wouldn't do for me, he thought, but it must have cost a packet when new. Could be picked up for a song now, he reckoned. Then he moved on to a bedside locker that had clearly come flat-packed and was held together with glue. The front of the little drawer drooped to one side where the peg holding it had broken.

"The whole place," Bill said to his wife, Rebecca, that evening, "looked like it had been bought from secondhand shops in a job lot. The old lady can't see much, of course, but I reckon she's used to a better kind of life than Gordon Street. There are good bits here and there, but it's a right ragbag otherwise."

They sat with supper trays in front of the television, with the sound turned down low. Their small daughter, Louise, was asleep upstairs, and they were anxious not to wake her. She went to playgroup every morning, while Rebecca taught part-time in Waltonby village school, and Bill filled every hour of his day with hard, physical work. Both had valued their quiet evenings, uninterrupted by a small girl wide awake and raring to go, and now both realised that soon their nights would once more be disturbed by a new member of the family.

"What's she like, this Mrs. Blairgowrie? Isn't that the name of a place in Scotland?"

"Yeah. She's Scottish, though the accent seems more like Irish sometimes. She's okay. Followed me about for a while. Checking up, I suppose."

"That's odd," said Rebecca. "How could she check up on you if she can't see?"

Bill shrugged. "Dunno," he said. "Not my business really. I just do the job as well as possible. I expect Mrs. Meade will want to know how it went," he added, and right on cue, the telephone rang.

"Thought you might ring," Bill said. "It all went well. Funny place, though." He told her about the furniture and about Mrs. Blairgowrie following him around. Lois asked him rather sharply if he'd noticed anything strange about the house itself—the atmosphere—was it welcoming?—that sort of thing.

"Not like you to be worried about atmospheres, Mrs. M!" He laughed. "Anyway, men don't notice such things. I leave that to the girls. It's a straightforward job, and the old duck was very pleasant when I left. Thanked me a lot. Said she looked forward to seeing me again. In a manner of speaking . . ."

Five

In his chilly, sterile house, Detective Chief Inspector Hunter Cowgill looked wearily through the Daily Mail whilst he ate his porridge and toast. He hated porridge, but his late wife had insisted that it was good for his cholesterol level, and so he was in the habit of soaking the oats in water overnight and boiling up the sticky mess next morning. A little salt was the only flavour he added. His wife had been a porridge purist.

Once or twice lately he'd stretched out a hand to take down a packet of Chocopops from the supermarket shelf, but her stern face had appeared before him and he'd withdrawn hastily.

And here's me, he said to himself as he forced down the last spoonful, legendary villain catcher, a hard man among hard men, still nervous of his dead wife. He sighed, and carried on reading, mostly the crime reports, but occasionally allowing himself a quick glance at the newspaper's page three girl.

This reminded him of Lois Meade. Not that he'd ever seen her in the nip, worse luck, but a chat with her might cheer him up. She was one of his most useful informers in that area of the county, though he could not really call her an informer, since she had refused money for snooping—as she called it— from the beginning.

"Hello, Lois? It's—"

"I know who it is. What d'you want?" Lois was in the middle of calculating wages, and she frowned.

"And how are you?" Cowgill continued, smiling. Still the same Lois, thank goodness. He hadn't any particular crime to discuss with her, but some suspected villainy, and keeping a conversation going was part of his job. "How is the business going? I drove past New Brooms' office yesterday, and several cars were parked outside. Looked good."

"There're no parking restrictions, are there?" said Lois defensively. "So what else?"

"Nothing like that," Cowgill replied, "but I have heard there's a proposal to restrict Sebastopol Street to residents' parking. Hasn't gone through yet, though. I'll keep you informed about that."

"Is that what you rang about?" Lois said, trying desperately to remember where she had got to in her columns of figures.

"No. It was nothing specific. Just wondered if you had anything to report. Anything we could nip in the bud before it became a major problem. You know the kind of thing. Gangs of yobs—sorry—gangs of disillusioned young people suffering from boredom and lack of parental love. Stealing from old people, breaking windows, crashing cars, generally causing mayhem. Any of those?"

"Not a lot in Long Farnden." Lois grinned reluctantly. He could be quite a funny old trout. "Mind you," she added, remembering the hit-and-run merchants who'd mowed down Dot Nimmo, one of her team of cleaners, "mind you, I reckon Tresham has more than its fair share of thugs. Them back streets—plenty of trouble there. But still, you'd know all about that."

"Only too well," Cowgill said. "Well, anyway, Lois, keep in touch. Let me know if you have any problems with the office in Sebastopol—or your little house in Gordon Street. It's quite a colourful area around there. I expect you've seen the local?"

"How did you know I've got a house in Gordon Street?" Lois said sharply, ignoring his question. "No," she added, "don't tell me. Cowgill has eyes everywhere. The scourge of the shires, they call him. By the way, here's something you won't know. My Douglas is coming back to this area—may take on the Gordon Street house."

"A wise decision, from what I hear."

"Is there anything you don't hear?" said Lois, scarlet with fury. "I'm busy," she added, "so don't bother me again unless you've got something important to ask." She replaced the phone before he could answer, and glared at her computer screen. She accidentally touched the wrong key, and the whole lot went blank.

"Bugger it!" she exploded, and decided to go down to the shop to cool off and have a word with Josie.

Long Farnden's narrow main street was busy this sunny morning. The old ironstone houses glowed on either side, and the nice old man from Beeches Farm was sweeping mud off the pavement. Lois saw Rebecca Stockbridge with a couple of schoolchildren from Waltonby heading for the shop, and they met at the steps.

"Morning, Mrs. M!" Rebecca said cheerily. "Say good morning to Mrs. Meade, children," she added, and they dutifully chorused their greeting.

"Going shopping?" Lois asked. She knew there was no shop in Waltonby. "Something special on at school?"

Rebecca shook her head. "No, we're just doing a bit of practical arithmetic," she answered. "Luke here has a shopping list, and Kate has a purse full of money. I often do this with the children, and Josie knows the routine. She lets the children add up the purchases and pay the bill. I stay in the background. You'd better go first, Mrs. M. We might take a while!" She moved the children to make way, and Lois said casually, "What did Bill think of Mrs. Blairgowrie?"

"Didn't he tell you?" Rebecca had overheard the conversation between Bill and Lois. Why was Mrs. M asking for more?

"Oh, yes, he did. But he sounded like he'd been a bit uncomfortable at first. No worries, Rebecca. I shall see him later."

Josie was sitting on a high stool behind the counter, reading the local paper. She put it down and smiled warmly at her mother, and at Rebecca and the two children. "Who's first?" she said. Before Rebecca could speak, Lois said that she had one or two things to talk to Josie about, and the children could go first.

By the time Luke had filled his basket, and with Kate had added up the total in their heads, getting it wrong several times, and had then handed over the right money to Josie, Lois had cooled down and collected her thoughts. She waved to the children as they crossed the road to Rebecca's car.

"She's a nice woman," Josie said. "How's their little girl doing? I don't see much of her. Most of the time Rebecca comes over here from Waltonby after school."

"She's fine. Now, I've got news for you. I'll give you three guesses."

Josie smiled. "One, Douglas is coming back. Two, Douglas is getting a new job, and three, Douglas wants to live in your house in Gordon Street. Right?"

"How the hell did you know all that?" said Lois, completely

flattened. First Cowgill and now Josie, knowing all her business. She began to wonder if she was bugged.

"Douglas told me, o' course. He phoned me after he'd spoken to you and Dad. I hope you'll make him pay the proper rent. No special rates for favourite sons."

Lois sighed. "Josie, dear, have you forgotten how we helped you buy this shop? But no, Dad has already told Douglas. No favours. He'll be earning a good screw, anyway, and can well afford it." She walked up to the counter and picked up the local that Josie had been reading. Splashed across the front page was a picture of the supermarket at the end of Gordon Street. All the big windows along the side approach had been smashed, and workmen were clearing away the broken glass and putting up boards into the empty frames.

"Hey, Josie, look at this!" she said, and began to read. It had all happened in the middle of the night. A gang of youths was suspected, but the police were not sure. It was not the usual theft of alcohol and cigarettes, and of course all the money was locked away. The police were puzzled. Food had been stolen, but not luxury items. Basics, such as bread, milk, fruit, sugar, tea, and coffee, had been taken in large quantities. Empty trolleys were left in the car park, neatly stacked in a row.

"We are anxious to hear from anybody living nearby who heard anything at all unusual," the police reported. "Meantime, we are following up several leads. There have been a number of similar thefts around the county."

"Nasty," said Josie, frowning. "And very close to your house. No wonder it's difficult to let property round there. What with crowing cocks and gangs of thieving louts, I reckon our Douglas might change his mind. Unless, of course, he gets a reduction—"

"That's enough!" Lois said. "Just give me a loaf, and I'll be going. A lot of paperwork to get through before lunch."

"Oh, dear," said Josie to her empty shop. She could almost see a black cloud hanging over her mother's head as she marched back up the street towards home. Who'd rattled her cage this morning? Josie tidied the shelves after the children's assault, and the answer came to her. It'd be Cowgill, wanting Mum to help him again. "Trouble afoot," she sighed, and arranged her face into a smile for the vicar, who bounced in for his usual pound of Cumberland sausages.

Six

By the time Lois reached home, the village gossip network had been busy. Gran greeted her with the supermarket story, and tut-tutted about the state of Tresham these days. "Not like it was when we lived there," she said. "People up on the Churchill don't dare to go out of their front doors at night now. Do you remember how it used to be, Lois? All of us friends. It was a community in them days. All helped one another."

"Rubbish," said Lois, still full of irritation. "It was just as rough as it is now. That Robertson family round the corner from us, always one of 'em in the nick. And the rest doin' their best to live up to his example. And don't you remember fireworks night, when old Mrs. Williams had a firecracker shoved through her letter box, and had a heart attack from fright? You got a short memory, Mum."

Gran stared at her. "What's eating you, Lois? You're like a bear with a sore head this morning."

Lois slumped down on a kitchen chair. "Oh, I don't know, Mum. Just when everything seemed to be going along steadily, suddenly it's all changing. Old Clem and his cockerel, Douglas moving back, Bill not tellin' me everything about that blind woman. And now this trouble at the supermarket. Shall we be able to rest easy with Douglas living in Gordon Street?" She got up and stared out of the window at the garden. Her small white dog was squatting seriously on the grass.

"That's the last straw!" she shouted, and began to laugh hysterically.

"What's funny, gel?" Derek had come in through the back door, and joined Lois at the window. "Might be funny to you," he muttered, "but I'm the one to clear it up."

Gran looked from one to the other. "Time for a coffee," she said. "Sit down, both of you, and let's get this Douglas thing straight. I won't say a word, except this. Whatever you do about him and the Gordon Street house, you'd better agree on it, else we'll never get any peace. Go on, sit down, Lois.

And you, Derek. I'll take mine to the front room."

"Your mother," said Derek, and paused. Lois looked fiercely at him. If he was about to criticise her mother, she was ready. Nobody but herself was allowed to do that, she thought, not strictly accurately.

"Your mother," repeated Derek, "is one o' the best. Got more common sense than the rest of us put together. Now," he added, "about Douglas. I wrote him a letter last night, and you'd better read it before I go to the post."

He got up and reached behind the clock on the shelf over the Rayburn. He handed her an envelope, and she opened it. It was not a long letter, and the story of the supermarket robbery had been cut out from the newspaper and enclosed. Derek had set out the terms of letting, added the agents' particulars, and said that if Douglas would like to take the house, he should get in touch with the agents and then be treated like any other tenant.

"Why've you said that?" Lois asked, pointing at the letter.

"Best way to avoid family argument, I reckon," he said. "We won't have nothing to do with it, except I expect you'll want to help with curtains and furnishing, an' that. Otherwise, the business side of it will be between him and the agents."

Lois sat for some minutes in silence. She was confused, wondering how Derek could be so hard-hearted. Then her thoughts cleared. He was right. There could be endless trouble, with her being unable to forget she was Douglas's mother, and Derek... well, not hard-hearted so much as hard-headed. She nodded. "I agree," she said. "Much the best. Now, I'll go and get the exiled Gran. Not so sure you're right about her, though. She can be a right old bag, bless her."

Derek pulled Lois to her feet and gave her a hug. "We got a lot to be thankful for, me duck," he said. "Let's not rock the boat..."

She looked at him sharply, but said nothing. Derek was no fool, and could read her mind. He knew, she was sure, that Cowgill was hovering again.

In Gordon Street, Hunter Cowgill walked slowly, looking up at the solid semi-d's on one side and the humble terrace on the other. Rich man in his castle, poor man at his gate, he thought, and smiled at the memory of his childhood Sunday school. They still sang that verse then, he thought. Now it was more likely to be the poor man in the castle. Not that there weren't still plenty of people living below the poverty line, driven to crime to keep afloat. But usually driven by drugs or drink or gambling.

What a world, he said to himself, as he walked back again and began knocking on doors. He would not as a rule be doing the legwork on this, but he had a special interest in Gordon Street. Lois was his special interest, and he wanted to keep a close eye on this one.

"What're you selling?" Clem had opened the door about six inches and peered through at this tall man in a suit and mackintosh. The man fished out an identification card, and Clem's heart gave a jolt. Police. So that Meade woman had reported the cockerel. Rotten trick! Somehow he'd not thought she was that sort. Well, he was wrong.

"May I come in a moment, Mr. Fitch? Just one or two enquiries. It's about the supermarket burglary."

Clem heaved a sigh of relief. "Nothin' to do wi' me," he said, but he opened his door wider and admitted Cowgill.

Their conversation was brief, but whilst Clem told him that he heard nothing, saw nothing, and was dead to the world until six o'clock in the morning, Cowgill looked around the grubby, untidy room.

"Do you have any family living in Tresham, Mr. Fitch?" he said. Clem nodded, and said that his daughter and her husband—"No good, that one"—had two children and lived up on the Churchill estate.

"I expect you see a lot of them, then," Cowgill said innocently.

Clem shook his head. "Once or twice a year. I keep meself to meself, mostly. Mind you," he said, brightening, "me young granddaughter—she's nearly twenty—has started work up the road in the supermarket and pops in quite often. Lovely girl, she is."

"Good," said Cowgill. "She'll keep an eye on you, then." It was meant to be a joke, but said in his chilly voice it sounded to Clem like a threat.

"Don't need no—" At that point, a piercing crow from Satan filled the house. Cowgill looked through the open door to the kitchen. Clem held his breath.

"He's in good voice," said Inspector Cowgill with a faint

smile. "Thanks, Mr. Fitch. I'll be getting on. Thanks for your help." And he let himself out of the front door and closed it quietly behind him.

Seven

The curtains in Braeside were drawn, and Cowgill looked at his watch. Someone should be up and about, surely. He knocked. Nothing happened. He knocked again, louder. Loud enough to wake the dead, he thought grimly. He looked up at the bedroom window and saw the curtains twitch. Someone was there, then. He knocked a third time.

This time there was movement in the house. He could hear the tapping of a stick, and then locks being turned and a bolt drawn. The door opened, and a grey-haired woman stood there, her dark glasses slightly crooked and her long cardigan fastened on the wrong buttons. She held a stick, and seemed to be peering over his shoulder.

"Yes? Can I help you?" she said, and her voice quavered, husky and nervous.

"Sorry to disturb you, madam," Cowgill said in his best friendly policeman voice. He held out his identification, and realised she did not see it. Of course. What a fool he was! She was blind.

"So sorry," he said, "I didn't know you were...er...I'm from the police. I wondered if you could spare a few moments to talk to me. Is anyone in the house with you?" he asked.

"There's nobody here at present," the woman said politely. "By the way, my name is Mrs. Blairgowrie. And, as you have obviously noticed, I am blind, to all intents and purposes, so I can't ask you in. I have to be very careful. Now, let me think. There's Bill, my cleaner from New Brooms. He will be here tomorrow. Could you come back about twoish tomorrow? He'll be here then."

"Thank you, Mrs. Blairgowrie. So most of the time you are alone here? No permanent companion or lodger? We have to ask, you understand."

"I've only just moved in," she replied. "At the moment I am alone. But my son visits, though not on a regular basis. I never know when he's coming, but he would not neglect me."

Bill from New Brooms, eh? Hunter Cowgill smiled to himself. That's my girl. Never misses a business opportunity. Well, this particular household he could leave to Lois. He must speak to her about it.

"You've been most helpful, Mrs. Blairgowrie." He tipped his hat, not caring that she could not see him. A real lady, if ever he saw one.

In the little house next to Clem's—not Lois's, but the other side—all was silent. Old shutters, the wood split and paint peeling, were still doing the job they were meant for, keeping at bay the outside world. The skinny, middle-aged man, incongruously dressed in jeans and T-shirt, his scrawny arms folded tight across his chest, sat in an upright chair in the corner of his empty living room. He had seen the policeman trawling the street, and had not answered the knocking at his door. He knew it was a cop. You could tell them a mile away, smart mackintosh and hat notwithstanding.

He grinned to himself. He went over the sentence in his head, editing it, wondering if "notwithstanding" was the right word. Once a writer, always a writer, he thought. With the minimum of movement, he turned to look at his bookshelves. They were packed with paperbacks and a neat row of hardbacks bearing his name. The most colourful furnishing in the room. Whatever might happen to him, these books were his legacy to a wife and family no longer in touch with him. He had sinned against them, and was not forgiven.

The knocking began again, and this time there was a shout. "Police! Open up!" He went wearily to the door and opened it. "Yes?" he said in a quiet voice.

The formal questions were asked, the negative answers delivered in a monotone. He was neither helpful nor obstructive. He saw the policeman looking round at the empty room. One chair? Was that enough? He wondered if he would be asked to give permission to look upstairs. But this could tell nothing about the burglary, and anyway, there was nothing to find. One bed. One cupboard and a mirror on the wall.

When the door closed behind the cop, the man relaxed and took out one of his books. He never tired of reading his own writing. He was taken back to the time when he was full of ideas and a moderate success. But he did not wish to reflect on what he had become.

Lois took the call when she was out walking Jeems. The water meadows were lush and green, and she was glad that she could release the little dog from her lead and see her tear away towards the river, without worrying about trespass or encounters with amorous suitors. Jeems seemed to attract them from miles away. As I did once, Lois thought. She grinned. She'd had enough suitors in her day, but Derek had always been the serious one. And the most persistent! Now she looked at her mobile phone with renewed irritation. Not exactly an amorous suitor, but close.

"Not you again!" she said. "Are you at a loose end? No crimes to solve today?"

Cowgill answered her briskly. "A little job for you, Lois, if you have time. I believe Bill Stockbridge is cleaning for a lady in Gordon Street? Living at Braeside?"

Lois sighed. "Correct. What about it?"

"I've called on her today, making enquiries about the burglary. She's blind, as you will know, and seems to me to be very vulnerable. There's a son who visits, apparently. I need to know who he is, what he does, and how often he actually visits her. She's obviously nervous, and I don't want to frighten her with uniformed officers. I would expect her to be nervous, but not to be trembling violently as she shut the door. Looks like something not quite right there."

"You could go back yourself, couldn't you?" Lois was disconcerted, remembering her own unease.

"I could, but the easiest thing for her would be for you or Bill to find out during the course of conversation."

"And, you forgot to mention, she's likely to talk to us more than she would to you or one of your plods. I'm not happy about asking Bill. I'll think about it."

"I'm afraid I need a definite answer, Lois," he said in a softer voice. "If you'd rather not, I have to do it another way."

There was a pause, and then Lois said, "Leave it with me, then. I'll be in touch."

"Tomorrow? I believe Bill will be there in the afternoon?" Cowgill realised he was pushing his luck.

"Whenever," Lois said firmly. She pushed her mobile back into her pocket, and hurried to catch up with Jeems, who was peering suicidally into the river. "Here, Jeems—look, here's the ball!" She threw the multicoloured ball to send Jeems spinning off in pursuit, and bent down to see what had caught the dog's attention. Something dark and formless, wrapped in ballooning plastic, had floated up against the bank. Lois's heart lurched, and she picked up a willow stick lying in the grass.

"Hey! Mum!"

She was startled by the loud voice, and nearly tipped into the river herself. It was Douglas, running along the river path towards her. "What on earth are you doing?" he said.

"You made me jump," she said, breathing hard. "Here," she added, "look at this. I was trying to hook it out. What is it?"

"Looks like a severed head to me," Douglas said carelessly, and was alarmed to see his mother's reaction. "Only joking, Mum!" he said quickly. "Here, give me the stick."

They heaved the object out and onto the grass. Douglas poked at it, and began to laugh. "Read the label, Mum," he said, and pointed to a soggy white paper attached to the plastic. Lois looked more closely, and read, Multipack Best Pork Chops. Guaranteed Organic.

"Yeah, right, but is that what's inside?"

"D'you want to look?" Douglas began to slit open the plastic wrapping. Lois nodded and watched as a dozen or more sodden pork chops fell out onto the grass. Jeems was on them in seconds, grabbing one and taking off at high speed.

"Better go after her," Lois said, recovering her equilibrium. "She'll heave it up in the kitchen else." She watched as Douglas chased across the field, and returned more slowly, dragging a furious Jeems behind him. What on earth were a dozen pork chops doing floating down the river? She looked again at the label. The best-before date showed clearly as being a couple of days hence, so they hadn't been chucked out beyond their sell-by. In any case, who would chuck them in the river for all to see?

"Ye Gods," said Douglas, puffing and red-faced. "I'm glad I decided to live in Tresham. Long Farnden's too racy for me!"

Lois kissed his cheek. "What're you doing here, anyway, love? We didn't know you were coming..."

"Had to go up to Birmingham. I decided to come off the motorway, and clinch my tenancy with the agents."

Lois thought of Derek's letter, not yet in the post. "Well," she said, "we'd better be off home and get some tea. Gran'll be pleased to see you... but I suppose you called there first?"

"Yep. She told me where you were. Just as well I found you, before you fainted away at the sight of twelve drowned pork chops."

"Enough of that," Lois said. "Anyway, what shall we do with them?"

"Throw 'em back? Fishes might be glad of them."

"No... better not. Wrap 'em up again, and we'll think what to do."

Lois had had a sudden picture in her mind of piles of food loaded precariously into supermarket trolleys in the middle of the night. Big multipacks of perishables, mysteriously taken, for no immediately apparent reason. She looked again at the label, but the rest was blurred and unreadable.

Eight

Clem Fitch's old wall clock had been in the station waiting room when they began to demolish it. Locals had protested, trying to hold on to the comfort of the roaring fire made each winter evening by Clem, who took a pride in keeping his passengers warm. He had worked for the railway most of his life, and when he retired he was presented with the old clock, inscribed with his name and dates of service. "Couldn't have given me nothing better," he had said in his short speech of thanks. They had toasted him, and wished him a long and happy retirement, and then promptly forgot all about him as the new glass and steel station building, with no trace of a fireplace, went up in a matter of weeks.

He looked at the clock to check when it was time for Susie, his granddaughter, to finish work at the supermarket. Then he would keep watch by the window for her bright figure, clicking along on her high heels, stopping at his little wrought-iron gate, and shouting cheerily for him to open his door.

There she was! He was at the door before she opened the gate, and prepared to give her a big hug. "How are we today, me darling?" he said, and she extricated herself tactfully, wishing Granddad would occasionally take a bath.

"I'm fine. Can I make you a cup of tea? I've brought some sandwiches, just past their sell-by. Perfectly good cheese and pickle. Okay?"

Clem licked his lips. He cared nothing for sell-by dates, and followed her into the kitchen, where she filled the kettle and unwrapped the sandwiches. He stretched out a hungry hand, but she tapped him lightly and said, "No, wait for a plate, Granddad! Mustn't let standards slip. At least, not while I'm here."

He looked fondly at her slim back and long, shapely legs. Her hair was natural blonde, and she wore it straight cut, like a pale Cleopatra. She had dark blue eyes and used very little makeup. She reminded him so much of his late wife that he swallowed hard. Please, God, he said irrationally to himself, don't let anything bad happen to her. If asked, he always said he was a devil worshipper—and that devil was Satan!

"There we are then," she said, putting the mug of tea and plate of sandwiches on a plastic tray. "You can eat them in your chair, while I tell you what exciting things happened today in Tresham's poshest supermarket."

She rattled away, mentioning names of new friends made among the staff, telling tales of complaining customers and lecherous men who sidled up to her when she was stacking shelves.

"Honestly, Granddad," she said, "you wouldn't believe what 'orrible blokes we get comin' in."

"Was it one of them what done the burglary, d'you reckon?" Clem said, scooping up crumbs from the plate and licking his fingers.

She shook her head. "No. It was a big job. Well-planned, our manager says. All so neat and careful. He said he almost expected they'd left the money at the checkout! But o' course they didn't. Police have been sniffing round ever since, but I reckon they've not found nothing. I asked one, and he said they were following up several leads. Have you finished, Granddad?" she added. "I got some bananas, too. I know you like a banana."

Clem refused flatly to have his banana peeled and cut up on a plate. "What's good enough for monkeys is good enough for me," he said, holding it in his hand and taking bites.

When she had gone, blowing him a kiss from the gate, he felt the sun had gone in, and he shivered. I suppose, he thought, one of these days they'll put me in a home. But not yet, he vowed. For one thing, what would happen to Satan? In his son-in-law's cooking pot for sure. No, they'd have to carry Clem out feet first before that happened. He took a handful of stale bread crumbs from his chipped enamel bread bin and threw them into Satan's house. The bird pecked at them greedily. Just like the toys you swing round and hens peck at a wooden board, Clem thought. He smiled. He remembered buying one for Susie when she was little. He hoped he would still be around to buy another one for his first great-grandchild, whenever that might be.

As he turned to go indoors, he heard the rusty squeal of his reclusive neighbour's back door. He stopped and pretended to fiddle with Satan's water bowl. Don't even know 'is name, Clem said to himself, but he straightened up and said "How do?" to the skinny man. It was unusual to see him out during the day.

"All right, thanks," the man replied, and made for the corner of his tiny yard. He carried a kitchen bin, which he tipped into the recycling box. All paper, as far as Clem could see. And empty orange juice cartons, loads of 'em. They won't take them, the old man chuckled, not with them lemonated surfaces. He clucked a goodbye to Satan and went back indoors.

Susie walked into the kitchen where her mum was frying sausages. The smell was good, but Susie wished they could occasionally have something else for tea. She handed over a pack of four steaks and offered to cook them tomorrow to give Mum a rest.

"Put them in the fridge, dear."

Susie did so sadly, knowing that when tomorrow came the steaks would have mysteriously disappeared, and sausages would be on the sizzle when she came home from work.

"Is our tea nearly ready, Doll? I'm starving." Tony, Susie's dad, had come in and peered at the blackening pan. "How did y' get on today?" he added, giving Susie a peck on the cheek. "Getting used to it?"

Susie nodded. She was fond of her parents, in spite of their limitations. She knew that though they might have sausages for tea every day, and no fresh vegetables ever appeared in the house, her mum and dad would always be there, fighting her corner when necessary, and always protesting that she was right, even when she was wrong.

Doll dished out burnt sausages, baked beans, and oven chips, and put a new bottle of tomato ketchup on the table. "There you are," she said. "Get that inside you and you'll be fine."

"How's it going, then?" Tony said, slipping half a burnt sausage onto Susie's plate. "Any nearer catching them burglars?"

Susie shook her head. "Don't know," she said. "The cops are still everywhere, asking questions. Most of us have already told all we know, which ain't much, and we're getting fed up with it. If you ask me, it was outsiders. Thieves from somewhere else, come off the motorway and finding the nearest supermarket. Then they're off up the motorway again, leavin' no trace. I doubt if they'll ever get them."

Tony frowned. "It don't make no sense," he said. "Not considerin' what they took. There wouldn't be no resale value to them groceries. Bottles of wine and spirits, yes, but flour and sugar? Tea and coffee? No, I reckon it was something unusual. And locals, too, with inside knowledge."

Doll was not interested in the burglary. She was not interested in anything very much, except her job delivering parcels for the local network company. Heavy packages of magazines, mail-order items of every sort, even quite small packs being sent by courier now that postal charges were up again.

She changed the subject. "Did you pop in on Granddad?" she said. She was really pleased that Susie had started this visiting, since it saved her going into town several times a week to see her lonely old dad. "How was he? All right? Not too bothered about anything?"

Susie said that he was fine, but that his house was filthy. He needed someone to give it a good turnout. "I could help you this weekend, Mum. It's my free time. Shall we go down and give the place a good scrub?"

Doll answered that she would be very busy delivering, Saturday and Sunday. She couldn't possibly fit it in. But she reckoned that Granddad wouldn't be cross with Susie for turning him upside down. "I'd just get an earful," she said.

Tony grunted. "Huh! The old bugger could do it himself if

he'd get up off his lazy arse. Don't ask me to help, Susie. I'd tell him a few home truths, and that's for certain."

Susie sighed. Ah, well, she could spare a few hours. She considered he was a nice old man, but she knew it was no good arguing with her dad. "I'll get some cleanin' things, then," she said. "Probably go down next Sunday."

Nine

Bill Stockbridge was working at the Cullens' house in Blackberry Gardens when Lois called him on his mobile. The Cullens' son, Ben, had been one of Lois's team for a while, filling in time between university and finding a job in his field. This had finally come up, and he'd moved on. He was engaged to Floss Pickering, another of the cleaners, and they were to be married shortly.

Lois's periodic reshuffling of the team had put Bill into Mrs. Cullen's house, and he liked it there, chiefly because she worked full-time, and so he had the house to himself one morning a week. He could clean the whole place thoroughly with no interruptions, and this was rare among the clients of New Brooms.

"Hello, Mrs. M. How are you today?"

"Fine, thanks, Bill. All well in Blackberry Gardens?"

Ben said all was tickety-boo, and he would be finished shortly.

"I'm just checking about tomorrow, Bill. You're at the new client in Gordon Street in the afternoon, right?"

Bill confirmed this, at once on the alert. Mrs. M knew perfectly well where he would be tomorrow afternoon. She had the schedules, after all. He waited. From long experience and the sound of her voice, he knew that there would be something else.

"I've been thinking about Mrs. Blairgowrie," Lois said. "She's very vulnerable, isn't she. And this burglary business in the supermarket...Some nasty characters about in that part of Tresham. Does she talk to you about being alone in the house?"

Ah, thought Bill. Now we're getting there. "Not so far. But

I agree with you. She'd be helpless if someone broke into her house. It'd be a doddle for a thief. On the other hand, we know that, but maybe not too many other people do. She says her son comes and goes. Still," he added, "if you'd like me to find out a bit more to make sure she's safe? Perhaps suggest one of them alarm things old people hang round their necks? She could press a button for help then."

Lois was silent for a minute. Bill waited. "Good idea," Lois said after the pause, "very good suggestion. And maybe you could find out some more about her son. How often he visits, where he works, that sort of thing. For her sake, of course. So that we can get hold of him quickly if anything happens to her. I feel a bit responsible, to tell the truth, although it's not strictly part of New Brooms' service. See what you can find out, Bill. And be tactful. We don't want to alarm the old thing, do we?"

Bill said he would be extra careful, and would be in touch if he could find out anything more from her. For her own safety, of course.

"I'll let you get on then," Lois said. "Oh, and could you give me a ring after you've finished at Gordon Street tomorrow? Set my mind at rest. You know how it is."

Bill was now pretty sure he knew exactly how it was. Mrs. M was on the warpath again. Poor old Derek.

Douglas Meade had gone back to his flat in Chelmsford, thinking he could write the report on his visit there, send it off to the office, and then call it a day. He checked his messages and swore. There was one asking him to be sure to contact his boss as soon as possible. He made the call and waited for the boss's dim secretary to put him through.

"Ah, Douglas, thanks for ringing in." His boss was in his early forties and so slavishly followed the current image of a successful executive that Douglas sometimes thought he was a secret clone, with thousands of others, planted by some evil power to take over the world.

"Something wrong?" Douglas said politely.

Something could have been wrong, but it was difficult to tell, being so well wrapped up in jargon and ambiguity. "We have been looking at your details on file, Douglas, and see that you have two weeks' holiday still to come. Now, we also know that you have given notice to leave, and are quite prepared to work out that notice. But I and the MD have been discussing your loyalty and willingness to take on board any old bag of snakes whilst you have been working here. We would like to show our appreciation, Douglas."

Not a gold watch, surely, thought Douglas. But no, the voice on the other end was becoming lyrical.

"Your blue-sky thinking approach has been enormously helpful. Wonderfully encouraging! So it is with reluctance that we shall have to wave you off on your journey to what we are sure will be the top of the pile. Douglas, my friend, we here at what we like to think of as your career big-school, are going to make sure you are suitably rewarded financially, and also have time to settle in the Tresham house, get back into the old country, before starting at the new job."

He paused, and Douglas rapidly disentangled what he'd said.

"You mean you're turfing me out sooner? When?"

A fit of coughing erupted from his boss, who finally said, "Soon as you like, old chap. End of the week?"

"Won't that leave you in a mess?" Douglas decided to make him suffer.

"Oh, well, nice of you to consider that. But no, we have a new man coming in. Not, of course, in your league, but we hope to groom him for stardom in due course . . . So shall we say end of the week?"

Douglas put him out of his misery. "Fine. Suits me well. I have to go back to Tresham tomorrow, in any case. Something urgent has come up. Then I'll be in the office after that and can tidy things up."

He made himself a coffee, and sat down to think. So, that was that. He was not surprised. The cutthroat atmosphere of the place had been a constant warning to watch out. Someone always anxious to step into your shoes. Well, the job he had in Tresham should be a gentler kind of place. Probably not such good prospects for making money, but a better pace of life all round. He finished his coffee and lifted the phone to ring Lois. He could move into the Gordon Street house much sooner, and she and Dad would probably be glad about that. For one thing, he thought wryly, he could start paying them rent.

"Hello, Mum?" He never knew whether it was Lois or Gran,

their voices being so similar.

"Who else?"

Now he knew it was Lois. He told her the gist of his boss's telephone call, and said as far as he was concerned it suited him well. He would have time to move into Gordon Street, furnish the place and get everything organised, before he started at the new company. In fact, he'd decided to be back in Tresham tomorrow to check one or two things, but wouldn't have time to come over to Long Farnden. "Might as well start as we mean to go on," he said. "Don't want to get in your hair."

So he had been hurt by Derek's attitude, Lois thought. But she said only, "What about money from the old job? You gave the proper notice. They can't get away with that."

Douglas explained. "They'll pay me up to the right date, Mum. They just want to get this new bloke in, and get me out so's I don't poison his mind against them."

"Don't be ridiculous, Douglas. Of course they don't think like that." Lois thought of her own New Brooms. The team were like part of the family, even awkward old Dot Nimmo, who had survived through thick and thin, and mostly thin, to be a loyal member. She knew for a fact that each one of them would stand by any of the others if they needed help.

"Ah, well," said Douglas, "New Brooms is not exactly the murky world of big business, Mum dear. Anyway, I'll be in touch and keep you up to date."

Huh! thought Lois crossly. Was she seeing another side of Douglas? The slick businessman, with a patronising air for those less experienced than he was? Well, sod that for a game of soldiers! She'd show him.

Ten

The next day, Mrs. Blairgowrie heard the doorbell and looked at her watch. "Oops!" she said, and walked through to open the front door as far as the chain would allow. It was almost certainly Alastair, but you never knew.

It was not Alastair. She knew that as soon as he spoke. It was an old man's voice, with a local accent, and from behind her dark glasses she blinked. "Who are you?" she said cautiously.

"Yer neighbour, miss," Clem said. "You must've seen me around." He realised what he had said, and corrected himself quickly. "At least, you'll have heard my cockerel wakin' yer up in the morning."

"Ah, yes," she said. "A lovely sound, a crowing cock. Reminds me of my childhood in Scotland. Can I help you, Mr....er...?"

"Fitch. Clement Fitch. Everybody calls me Clem. I just come over to see if you need any help. I've lived in Tresham man and boy, and all them years in Gordon Street in the same house. Not much I don't know about Tresham and Gordon Street."

"How interesting!" said Mrs. Blairgowrie. "I'd ask you to come in for a cup of tea, but I'm expecting my son any minute. He keeps an eye on me and does my shopping."

"I seen him, miss. Tall, dark chap with glasses? He don't live with you, then? How do you manage, you bein' er...um ..."

"Blind?" said Mrs. Blairgowrie in an amused voice. "Well, I manage quite well. I have to be very careful, of course, and not let any strangers into the house. But I have my wireless for company, and the telephone, of course. Do you have family in the town?"

Clem shifted from one aching foot to the other, and wished she would ask him inside, regardless of the imminent arrival of her son. He told her about his daughter and son-in-law, the lazy sod, and his lovely granddaughter, Susie. "She calls in to see me, and sometimes does a bit of shoppin' if I'm not feeling too grand. I'm sure she'd do the same for you."

"How kind!" said Mrs. Blairgowrie.

She's a really nice old duck, Clem thought. "We'll have to think of a way of you attracting my attention," he continued. "I don't always hear the phone if I'm out back with Satan. I know!" he added, with sudden inspiration. "You hang a scarf out of yer bedroom window, and I'll know yer want some help. Have you got an orange one, or a good bright colour like that?"

Mrs. Blairgowrie would not have been seen dead wearing an orange scarf, but she was touched by old Clem and his kind concern. "I have a dark red one. Would that do?" she said.

"Not too dark?" said Clem, and Mrs. Blairgowrie replied, "Blood red, Clem. Should be good for the job. Now, if you'll excuse me, I must put food in the oven for my hungry son. He's always starving! Some boys never grow up, do they. Goodbye."

Clem went back across the street, pleased at having made contact with this nice woman. When they got a bit more friendly, he'd ask her over to his house. Mind you, he thought with a chuckle, he'd have to get Susie to come round and give the place a good cleanup first.

As he reached out to open his front door, a car drew up outside and Clem withdrew his hand. Then he began to fiddle with a mouldy-looking hydrangea in his square inch of front garden, keeping an eye on the car. His old mum used to say curiosity killed the cat, but Clem thrived on it. He straightened up to say good morning to the young man locking his car with a clunk.

It was Douglas, and he had seen the old man once or twice in his yard, tending the noisy cockerel, but now he saw an opportunity to talk to him. He intended to get on well with all his future neighbours in Gordon Street. He might even start a residents' association...

"Good morning! How're you, Mr.... er..."

For the second time that day, Clem said his name was Clement Fitch, though most people called him Clem.

"Glad to meet you, Clem," Douglas said, stretching out his hand. Clem knew his own hands were far from clean, so ignored the gesture. "You movin' in next door?" he said suspiciously. Was this a cockerel-loving tenant, or would he be like the others, causing a lot o' trouble for nothing?

Douglas nodded. "I intend to be here from the weekend," he said. "New job in Tresham. I've been in once or twice with Mrs. Meade. She's my mother, by the way."

Oh, sod it, thought Clem. Mummy's boy! Still, that Mrs. Meade hadn't done nothin' about reporting Satan. Leastways, he hadn't heard nothing since she came callin'. And that cop had seemed to admire the crowing, hadn't he? Should he mention it to this chap, or wait until the complaint came?

"And in case you were wondering," Douglas said, "I've

heard your cock crowing, and it doesn't bother me in the least. It'll be very helpful when I have to get up early! But seriously, Clem, you needn't worry about that. By the way, my name is Douglas. Now, I must just check one or two things in the house, and then be off back to the office. See you soon, eh?"

Clem breathed in heavily. "Right-o then," he said, deeply relieved. "An' if you want any help movin' in, I'm always around." He watched until Douglas's door closed, and then turned his attention to his other neighbour. Curtains drawn across as usual. A glimmer of light showed that the recluse was at home. It was a situation which annoyed Clem more than anything. Fancy living in a terrace and not knowing the man next door! Any normal bloke would be friendly, have a chat now and then. With both of them living alone, they could be real mates and help one another. The recluse must be lonely, hardly ever going out, and then never looking anywhere but straight ahead, making it very obvious he didn't want contact with anybody. Clem shrugged. Ah, well, this Douglas seemed friendly enough. And her over the road, she could be a very interestin' neighbour, given time.

Clem limped into his house and through to the yard. "Hello, me ole beauty," he said to the cockerel. "How's Satan—ready for a bit o' bread? Sorry I ain't got any sinners for you today," he added, and cackled loudly.

When he had finished checking smoke alarms and light-bulbs, Douglas took a last look around and locked up. He looked at his watch, and saw that he still had time for another job or two. What should he do? Mum's cleaners were coming in for a spit and polish before he moved in. Maybe he'd introduce himself to the others in the terrace. He walked swiftly along, finding nobody at home at the other houses, except the one the other side of Clem. He could see a light through a chink in the curtains, though no one answered his first knock. He knocked again, and this time a voice shouted from the other side of the door that nobody was at home, and would he kindly bugger off.

Charming, said Douglas to himself, and as he came out of the little garden, Clem's door opened again. "Yer won't get no joy there, Douglas," he said. "The man don't 'ave nothin' to do with nobody. Bit of a mystery, if yer ask me. Still, when you come to live 'ere, you might have better luck than me. Mind you, I reckon somebody like that ain't worth knowing." He raised his voice to a shout on this last sentence, intending the miserable sod next door to hear.

Douglas smiled and nodded, then got back in his car and drove off, reflecting that living in Gordon Street was going to be even more interesting than he had thought.

Eleven

When Bill arrived at Braeside, Mrs. Blairgowrie opened the door as he was walking up the path. She was smiling, as if she recognised him.

"Good afternoon," he said. "How did you know it was me? You must be telepathic!" He laughed, to show it was a joke. Well, that was Mrs. M's first question answered. The old lady could see enough to know he was approaching. But then she scotched this. "I heard the gate click open," she said sweetly. "When one faculty fails, our others become sharper, to compensate. Anyway, I was expecting you," she added, and beckoned him inside.

He followed her into the kitchen, and almost immediately she told him that her son was due to call in sometime soon. "He telephoned me this morning," she said, "but must have been delayed. He's a very busy man, and we mustn't delay him. I am sure you can keep out of his way. Oh, that sounds so impolite," she added anxiously. "I just meant that he can be very impatient, and it is best to accommodate him as far as possible."

"That's fine," Bill said. "I shall be invisible. Please don't worry. Now, I'll start downstairs so that when he comes I can be out of the way in the bedrooms. Does your son have far to come?" he added innocently. She said that he lived about ten miles away, which was far enough to mean a special journey to see her.

"Does he have a family?" Bill sorted out his cleaning materials, careful to keep his question a casual one. Mrs. Blairgowrie shook her head. "No, he lives alone, like me," she said. "I wish he would find a nice woman to marry. He doesn't seem to enjoy himself much. No hobbies, and never brings a friend with him. I worry about him sometimes."

"I expect you'd like grandchildren...Is he your only child?"

"I'm afraid so. And yes, I would like grandchildren to indulge! Still, it's not too late. He may surprise me yet."

"Well, I must get on. I can skip my tea break if it is easier for you."

"How kind. Let's wait and see when he arrives. His food is ready, and if I'm making a cup for him, you shall certainly have one, too."

"I expect he'll make a cup for you," Bill said, and left her smiling at him as he went off into the parlour, as she called it, a room at the front of the house, overlooking the road.

Here it was perfectly clean and tidy, and Bill was pretty sure it was seldom used. A very pleasant sitting room at the back of the house was obviously where Mrs. Blairgowrie spent most of her time. A stack of audiobooks by her chair wobbled every time he dusted, and she had a smart new radio within reach. She seemed to have an unexpected taste for thrillers! Even so, he thought, she must be bored sometimes, a lady with her lively mind. He had moved on to dust a row of ornaments—strangely unlike what he would have expected to belong to Mrs. Blairgowrie, most of them being crude figures of children and animals. The sort of things you might pick up at a jumble sale. He shrugged. No telling what people liked. He had learnt that from his considerable experience with New Brooms. The thought gave him an unpleasant reminder that he had to speak to Mrs. M very soon.

A car drew up outside Braeside, and Bill busied himself near the window but out of sight. A tall, rather overweight man got out and approached the gate. He had horn-rimmed glasses and his dark hair had been slicked straight back over his large head. His suit was dark and well-cut, and he had the air of a man in a hurry.

The doorbell rang, and then straight away Bill could hear a key turning in the lock, and the door opening and closing.

"Hello? Can you hear me, Mother?"

Bill heard the man give a short, barking laugh, and then Mrs. Blairgowrie came into the hallway. "Ah, there you are, Alastair," she said, her voice husky and quiet. She added quickly, "My cleaner is here, but he has been kind enough to say he will work round us, and not intrude."

Their footsteps disappeared into the sitting room, and the door was shut firmly.

Bill decided to go upstairs. The sound of the cleaner humming over the carpets would probably annoy the impatient Alastair. He felt sorry for Mrs. Blairgowrie, who must look forward to her son's visits. But when he came, he was clearly always in a hurry to get away again. Poor old thing. He did hope she would make some local friends, and wondered whether to suggest a few organisations in the town which would welcome her. He knew there was a club for blind people somewhere. Mrs. M would probably know. He knew she was in the Tresham office this afternoon, and he could call on his way home and speak to her.

A sudden loud voice startled him. It came from the sitting room below, and was certainly not Mrs. Blairgowrie. Why on earth would her son be shouting at the poor old thing? Bill wondered whether to go down and investigate. But that would probably make things worse. He listened carefully as he went about his work, deciding that if it should happen again, he would go down with a convincing excuse to interrupt.

The next thing he heard was the sitting room door opening, and heavy footsteps in the hall. "No, I can't stay. You know bloody well I can't! I'm the one who's answerable for mistakes. So for God's sake, get it right next time." There was no answer from Mrs. Blairgowrie, and Bill waited until the front door banged behind a departing Alastair.

"Bill?" A tremulous voice called to him from downstairs. "I think I would like a cup of tea myself now. Would you be kind enough to make a pot for the two of us?"

Bill washed his hands quickly in the bathroom and went downstairs. He found Mrs. Blairgowrie sitting in her chair, her face white and her eyes closed. She had taken off her glasses, and her hands, usually so calm and capable, were trembling.

"Are you all right?" Bill said. "Was that your son? Has he gone?"

"Tea," said Mrs. Blairgowrie in a small voice. "Would you be so kind?"

Lois was still in the office, chatting to Hazel about new clients and orders for cleaning materials, when Bill walked in.

"Hi, Bill!" Hazel said. "Nice to see you. How's the family?"

Lois nodded a greeting, and wondered what could have brought him in this afternoon. "Nothing wrong, I hope, Bill," she said. He looked uncomfortable, and said no, not really, but he wondered if he could have a private word with her.

"Right," said Hazel, pretending to be offended, "I know when I'm not wanted. I'll be upstairs checking stocks. Then we can do the orders when our Bill has had his private word."

"What is it, Bill?" Lois was really worried now. "Nothing wrong with Rebecca?"

"No, no. Well, not in that way. The thing is, she's—that is, we—are expecting another baby."

"Bill! That's wonderful! But why are you looking so miserable? Isn't that what you wanted?"

He nodded. "Yes, we planned it. But there is a snag. A pretty big snag." He hesitated, and Lois waited quietly. She had an inkling of what was coming, but hoped against hope that it wouldn't be that. It was.

"The thing is," Bill continued, "Rebecca's going to give up work altogether now, and that means her salary will go. And I have been offered a full-time job with the vets and a big increase in what they pay me. I'm afraid it means..." He trailed off, and Lois took over immediately.

"You will have to leave New Brooms," she said sadly. "I knew it would happen one day. We've been really lucky to keep you for this long. I've relied on you for quite a lot, as you know. I shall miss you, and so will the others. But family comes first, as Gran is always telling me. When d'you think you'll go?"

"I can carry on for a couple of weeks, if that's all right with you. Then the vets need me urgently, as one of their lot has left already and they're up against it."

"All right, then. I'll start advertising straightaway." She tried to smile at Bill, but found it difficult. How would she ever replace him? He had been her steady rock in so many ways, and she could not imagine ever finding anyone like him. Well, she supposed the best thing would be to go for somebody completely different. She stood up and gave him a warm kiss on his cheek. "Well done, Bill. I was an only, and I'd have really liked a sister. One-child families are not a good thing. Ask Gran!"

Bill gave her a reciprocal kiss and a hug, and with a manly nod turned and went rapidly out into the street. Lois watched him go and sighed. Why did things have to change? It was certainly all change at the moment, what with Douglas coming back and being their tenant, and all not well with Josie and Rob, and Cowgill chivvying away at her again, as if expecting her to help with a crime that was yet to happen. There was a bit of a puzzle with that burglary at the supermarket, and the floating pork chops. But that surely wasn't it? Time for a talk with him. Then there was the new client at Braeside. Bill was going to tell her something about Mrs. Blairgowrie, but he must have forgotten. No wonder, really. She would remind him later.

"Hazel!" she yelled up the stairs. "You can come down now. Bill's gone, and I need a coffee. D'you want one?"

At this point, the telephone rang. It was Bill. "I'm just around the corner in my car," he said. "I forgot to tell you about Braeside. There's quite a lot to tell, so will it wait?"

"Sure," said Lois. "Oh, and by the way, is the good news public knowledge yet—can I tell Hazel?"

Bill was silent for a minute, then he said, "I'd really like you to tell the girls, Mrs. M. I'm not much good at that kind of thing. And anyway, it's not all unalloyed joy, is it? See you. 'Bye."

Twelve

After Bill had gone, Mrs. Blairgowrie had sat for a long time looking out of her window into the garden. Had this move been a mistake? Maybe, but it was no good looking back to the old life. She reminded herself who she was now, and what she had to do. In the past, she had always prided herself on looking ahead and knowing when and how to make things work for the best. She had been on her own for a long time now. No family, no sisters to confide in. There was Alastair, of course, but she didn't count him. Especially after today. She'd never had many friends, and some of them were dead and some out of reach for long periods of time.

She had got up, put on her dark glasses, and opened the door into the garden. It was a mess out there, with old kitchen equipment dumped by the back fence. Why were rusting old fridges such a depressing sight? It had been a nice garden once. A garden seat stood crookedly on three legs, and under the aged apple tree the remains of a rabbit hutch suggested that once children had lived here happily. The grass was long around her ankles and, aware of overlooking windows, she had felt her way to a crumbling stone bench by the house wall, and gingerly sat down.

It would be nice to have a pleasant garden where she could sit in the summer. She could bring her mobile phone out here so that Alastair could get hold of her if he needed to. Perhaps Bill would help? Or maybe old Clem over the road? But no, he would be too nosy. Not that there was anything much to see. All the information she needed was held in her head. She had always been good at that. No sign of Alzheimer's, the doctor had said. Still, there wouldn't be, would there?

Lois arrived home in Farnden just before five, and told Gran about Bill calling in at the office. She didn't tell her any more than that, wanting to be spared for as long as possible the accusations that were bound to follow. She hadn't valued Bill enough, hadn't paid him enough, had pestered him to help her with Cowgill's stupid cases. Of course the chap would feel he had to go, especially with another mouth to feed. So Gran would say.

Still, reflected Lois as she made herself a cup of tea, her mother had always made it plain she considered cleaning was a woman's job, so with luck she might think Bill had come to his senses at last. No fault of Lois's, then.

Unexpectedly, Lois felt her eyes prick with tears. She was tough, she knew, and reckoned she could cope with anything that might have to be faced. Not so much with New Brooms, of course, but when carrying out Cowgill's assignments she had been in danger more than once. Although she was careful not to involve Bill too closely, he had always been there in the background, a strong, fearless young man. She realised he had been like a safety net for her. Always at the end of a mobile, sometimes sympathetic and at others critical, but always honest and straightforward, and prepared to help. Not easy to replace these days. She sighed, and went through to her office to prepare an advertisement for the local paper. She couldn't specify gender, of course, not these days, but intended to look for another man. Some of her clients couldn't be trusted with the girls.

She looked at what she had typed, and frowned. "Damn it all!" She erased it, and typed, Wanted—Bill Stockbridge clone. Terms: anything he wants. To start immediately. Then she erased that, and began again. When she had composed a reasonable, politically correct advertisement, she sent it off to local papers. She felt as if Bill had gone already, and had left a big gaping hole behind.

Her door opened and Gran appeared, looking tentative. This was unusual, but what she said and how she said it was even more so. "Sorry to interrupt," she said, "but it's nearly teatime. Derek phoned earlier when you were out, and said he'd be back around now. Much more to do, ducky?"

Lois was alarmed. This was so unlike her mother that something serious must be afoot. "You all right, Mum?" she said.

Gran nodded. "Fine," she said. "Cottage pie and carrots for tea. Your favourite."

"Oh, blimey!" said Lois. "What on earth is up? You're being much too nice to me. Got me worried, Mum."

Gran came further into the office and shut the door behind her. "Sit down, dear," she said. "I just need to give you a bit of support. I am your mum, after all."

"Get to the point, Mum," Lois said.

Gran took a deep breath. "I know about Bill," she said. "About the baby, of course. But I know about the other thing. About him leaving."

"How do you know?" Lois asked, and her mother brushed the question aside with a wave of her hand.

"Never mind how I know. I do know, and I also know how much Bill means to you and New Brooms in general, an' how much you'll miss him and think there'll never be anybody like him. I'm sorry for you. That's why I'm being nice, and why I've made cottage pie for tea. And there's Derek just coming in the back door, so tidy up, Lois, and come and eat."

She disappeared fast out of the office, and left Lois feeling stunned. What a day! Gran's loving reaction to the news was almost more difficult to cope with than Bill's resignation. But she switched off her computer, straightened a pile of papers, and went through to the kitchen feeling somehow restored.

Derek was much more pragmatic. "That's life, innit, gel," he said. "Workers come and go. Bill's stuck it out longer 'n I thought he would. He's a great bloke, I reckon. But he was sure to be off sooner or later. Nobody's irreplaceable. You'll find another, me duck, just as good. Different, o' course, but just as good. Got your ads in the local? Sooner you get some applications, the better."

"I'm getting another bloke, whatever you say. Can't say so in the ad, but it's worked so well up to now. Keep your ears open, Mum. It seems nothing's secret from you. Spread the word. And you, too, Derek. Always better to get somebody who's recommended than a perfect stranger."

"Second helps, Gran?" said Derek, holding out his plate.

"Lois first," said Gran, who up to now had always believed the working man took priority.

"Ye Gods," said Lois. "Keep it up, Mum. I might grow to like it."

Thirteen

Bill's wife, Rebecca, had been thinking. She knew that Bill planned to tell Mrs. M about leaving, and she felt bad about it. It had been her decision. They had talked about it endlessly, with Bill saying he knew the vets would give him more work and he could be there for evening surgeries, when cleaning was finished. Mrs. M was always flexible, and anxious to make it possible for him to do both jobs. He could increase their income whilst Rebecca was having maternity leave from school, and then later on they could arrange for childcare, as they had done with Louise. They could easily manage, he said.

But Rebecca was not so sure. She could not help noticing that other mothers at her daughter's nursery looked at each other with a smile when Lou said proudly that her dad was a cleaner. It would be nice to bring all that to an end, and have Bill working full-time with animals that he loved, instead of ratty old ladies who would find fault with the angel Gabriel if he came down with his duster and polish.

In the end, Bill had said she should decide. He would do whatever she wanted. After all, it was her life that would be changing most, and she would probably need more help from him. Much as she wanted the new baby, she also loved teaching, and would miss it. She had made Bill promise he wouldn't hold it against her if she opted for him leaving New Brooms, and then she made the decision.

Now she looked at her watch. She just had time to whiz over to Farnden shop for milk before Bill came home for tea. Lou was pottering about in the garden, and she scooped her up and put her in the car. "Off we go," she said. "See Josie in the shop?" It was a favourite outing, and in spite of Rebecca's protests, they always came home with a free packet of chocolate buttons clutched in Lou's little hand.

Josie greeted them cheerfully. "Hi, Rebecca! And how's little miss?" As Rebecca rushed round the display unit to deal with a shoplifting Louise, the doorbell jangled and a man walked in. He was a stranger to Rebecca, and she called to Josie to carry on serving, as she was not in too much of a hurry. This was not strictly true, but she was curious. For some reason she didn't like the look of this new customer, and remembered tales of shopkeepers being held up for the contents of the till.

"Can I help you?" Josie said sweetly.

"Doubt it," said the man. He was tall and heavily built, his dark hair slicked back, and his eyes hidden behind thick-lensed, horn-rimmed glasses. "I'm just passing through, and need toothpaste. Forgot to get it in Tresham. It's a special brand. DenFresh, it's called."

Josie looked smug. "Come with me," she said, and led him to a shelf stacked neatly with toothbrushes and pastes of several kinds. She held out a tube to him. "DenFresh," she said. "I use it myself."

"Well done," the man said grudgingly. "How much? Bound to be a damn sight more than Boots, I bet."

"How much in Boots?" Josie asked.

"Two fifty."

"Two forty-five, please," Josie said, and walked to the till. "Now you know we have it, I hope you'll call again when you're passing," she said, and beamed at him. She was looking her best today, nut-brown hair washed and shining, face pink and healthy, and her own teeth white and gleaming.

"I'll do just that," said the man, persuaded at last to smile broadly as he turned to leave. "Make sure you're on duty that day," he added at the door. From behind the biscuits Rebecca muttered, "Yuk!" and made a face at Josie.

"Who was that, then?" she asked, but Josie said she had no idea. She agreed with Rebecca that he was a slimy toad, and then they talked of babies and other things. At last Louise had made her selection of suitable sweets, and they went out to the car. "There's Mrs. M," Rebecca said. "Shall we say hello?" They waited until Lois caught up with them, and Lou greeted her with enthusiasm.

Inevitably the subject of Bill leaving arose, and Lois tried to sound upbeat and cheery. "We've been lucky he's stayed so long," she said. "When's the baby due? I must get Gran to start knitting."

Inside the shop, Lois came straight to the point. "Who was that man who came in?" she said. "I saw him from up the street. He passed me in his car."

"Never seen him before," said Josie, surprised at her mother's vehemence. "Why?"

"He looked just like somebody Bill described to me. The son of that new client, the blind lady in Gordon Street. He was visiting when Bill was there. Nasty customer, he reckoned. Unkind to his mother—shouted at her—that kind of thing. What was he like?"

"Slimy, sniffy, patronising, and finally disgustingly flirty. We can do without the likes of him. Though of course," she added hastily, knowing that her mother was keen on the customer always being right, "I was very nice to him. Sold him some toothpaste. Me and Rebecca decided he was a creep, but unlikely to murder us in our beds."

"Why did you say that?" Lois said sharply.

"What?"

"That about murdering us in our beds."

"No reason, Mum! It's just a thing people say! Nothing for you to get your teeth into."

Lois said that was quite enough about teeth, as she had just made an appointment with the dentist and was dreading it.

The slimy toad, whose name was Alastair, cruised back home in his big car, thinking about his encounter with Josie in the village shop. Nice bit of bum in her jeans. It had looked like a really good village all round. Solid old stone houses, pretty church, plenty of light and space. He had been thinking for some time of moving out of the dreary suburb where he had been born, into the countryside. He would have to stay within reach of all his contacts, of course. Long Farnden might fit the bill. He made a mental note to call in at the estate agents in Waltonby next time he was in the area.

He stopped at traffic lights, and a blonde girl, walking quickly on stilty heels, crossed in front of him. The second fanciable blonde who had come his way today! He licked his lips, and then the lights changed and he moved on. He thought about the first girl. She had been hurrying down Gordon Street. He had got out of his car outside Braeside and whistled. She had glared at him and then gone into the house lived in by the old codger opposite. Him that was always staring out of his window. The girl was obviously his niece or granddaughter or something, and Alastair smiled. Maybe he would see her again and apologise for whistling. He chuckled and accelerated. Soon be home.

Fourteen

A few days later, Dot Nimmo was toiling up Sebastopol Street, on her way home. She had waved to Hazel in the office as she passed. Whew! It was very warm for the time of the year, and Dot reflected that maybe global warming really was on the horizon, if not here already. She was reluctant to believe that anything as legendary as the English weather could change. Not in her time, surely.

It had been a busy day. The best part had been the job for a lonely old lady living in the poshest suburb of Tresham. Alice was very disabled by arthritis, but had an iron determination to stay in her own home, and with the help of Dot, she managed very well. The most important thing that Dot did was to keep her company for a couple of hours twice a week. They had lunch together—an unpaid hour, Dot insisted—and had become firm friends.

Dot sat down at her smart new kitchen table with a cup of

hot tea. She looked around with satisfaction. All new and shining. It had not always been so. Before she worked for New Brooms, she had been a widow for a while, and had let things slide. Her husband, Handel Nimmo—Handy for short—had been drowned under mysterious circumstances. Did he fall or was he pushed? He had been good to her and she missed the old man. Then her precious only son, Haydn, had been killed in a road accident, and her standards had slipped to nil. Her house had become dirty, smelly, and neglected, and she had not cared.

Then Mrs. M had given her a chance to work for her, and gradually Dot had realised how much nicer it was to live in a clean, fresh-smelling house. Typically, she had taken immediate action, turning out the house from top to bottom, new paint everywhere, inside and out, and a complete makeover for the rest. Loads of old furniture and curtains had been taken away by members of the Nimmo family and dealt with. The Nimmos were a close-knit, dodgy-dealing lot, and could always find a way of turning misfortune to a small profit.

Dot's telephone rang. It was Lois, and Dot said, "How're yer doin', Mrs. M?"

"Fine, thanks," Lois said, and apologised for ringing at teatime.

"No problem," Dot replied. "Ring any time. What can I do for you?"

"It's really about Bill," Lois began. "You know a new baby's on the way. Well, he won't mind my telling you that Rebecca and him have decided that he'll have to leave New Brooms and concentrate on his job at the vets', where he can work towards more money. He's sad about leaving, but for the sake of the family he has to do it."

"Blimey, that's bad news!" said Dot, who always came out with the first thing that entered her head.

Lois was grateful that she didn't have to pretend, and said, "Yeah, it is. But life goes on, Dot, and we'll manage. He's going in two weeks' time, and I'd like you to take on the blind lady in Gordon Street. She likes Bill a lot, and he's found useful ways of handling the job. Helps her a lot, according to her."

Dot sniffed. "You can rely on me, Mrs. M. I think I can be just as helpful as Bill."

"Of course you can," Lois assured her. "No need to get huffy! Now, I want you to go along with Bill for these two weeks and see how he does the job. It's quite difficult now and then, and he'll introduce you and show you the ropes. So no more taking offence, please, Dot. I'll be in touch. 'Bye."

Dot grinned. Not many people were a match for Dot, but in Lois Meade she had met her equal. She took her tea into the sitting room and turned on the telly.

Lois had warned Bill to expect Dot to turn up, and sure enough she was there on time, standing outside the gate talking to old Clem from across the way.

"Known him from way back," she said as she followed Bill up the little path to Braeside front door. "Clem's daughter lived next to my sister Evelyn until they moved away. Nice to know his granddaughter pops in to see 'im now an' then, ain't it?"

Bill reflected that there was very little Dot didn't know about Tresham folk. He reckoned she would get to know all Mrs. Blairgowrie's secrets in a couple of hours, as soon as he was out of the way. Mrs. M was no fool.

"Good morning, Mrs. Blairgowrie," he said cheerily. "This is my colleague, Dot Nimmo. I know Mrs. Meade has been in touch and explained."

"I am very upset," the old lady said, sniffing. "Just as you and I had got used to each other, you are taken away from me. Of course," she added, standing aside to allow them to enter, "I quite understand that with an addition to the family you will have to look for a better paid job. But nevertheless, I am upset." With another sniff, she walked behind them towards the sitting room at the back of the house.

The first thing Dot noticed was that the old thing's stick was hanging on the back of a chair. So she had made her way to answer the door without it.

"Here you are, Mrs. B," she said in her best friendly voice. "Here's your stick. I've been told you're blind, so we don't want you falling about all over the place, do we?"

Bill held his breath, and watched Mrs. Blairgowrie's face. Surely Dot had been told not to go crashing in like an old rhinoceros? And nobody said "blind" these days. "Visually impaired," wasn't it? Oh, Lord, the old girl had gone quite puce in the face. Then, to his amazement, she began to chuckle in a deep voice that seemed to come up from her shoes. She coughed, and held out her hand.

"Thanks, Dot," she said, taking the stick. "And yes, you can call me Mrs. B. And I am blind, and grateful for no pussyfooting around the word. We shall get on fine, you and I. Not that I shan't miss my Bill, but I think Mrs. Meade has chosen well."

Bill raised his eyebrows. Mrs. Blairgowrie little knew what she was in for under Dot's management. Still, maybe that was just what she needed. Companionship, as well as efficiency. But he wasn't at all sure that Mrs. B's son would feel the same.

"Dot," he said softly, as soon as they had gone upstairs to start on the bathroom and bedrooms, "a word of warning." Dot nodded conspiratorially. She loved a secret. "Did Mrs. M tell you about her son, Alastair?" Dot shook her head. "Well," continued Bill, "he comes and goes, and he's not a pleasant character. Leastways, not as far as I've seen. Best to keep out of his way. Doesn't like anyone around when he calls to see his mum."

"No problem," Dot said in an elaborate whisper. Her curiosity was immediately aroused, and she looked forward to Alastair Blairgowrie's next visit. Blimey, they certainly went in for tongue-twister names! She went back to shining up the bathroom taps, determined to show the old lady she was just as good, if not better, than precious Bill Stockbridge.

Halfway through the afternoon, Mrs. Blairgowrie appeared, this time with her stick, and said it was time they had a break, and she could certainly do with a cup of tea herself.

Fifteen

Clem watched closely as Bill and Dot emerged from Braeside at the end of the afternoon. How had it gone? Fancy him bumping into Dot Nimmo after all these years! She was a lot younger than him, of course, and she'd been hot stuff when he'd first seen her out with old Handy Nimmo. None of them could understand what she saw in him. After all, she came from a solid, respectable family, and nobody could say that of the Nimmos. Still, she'd stuck to him until he got shoved into the Farnden gravel pits. Accident, they'd said in the papers. Some accident! Nimmos were as crooked as a bent pin, and very good at proving their innocence.

Hadn't there been something about Dot's loopy son getting killed, too? Poor old gel, she hadn't had much luck. Perhaps he could nab her to come in for a cup o' tea sometimes, after she'd finished over the road. A trip down memory lane, that would be! He felt quite excited at the prospect.

Ah, there they were. He peeped around the edge of the curtain, and at once Dot waved and smiled in his direction. Same old Dot! Didn't miss a trick. Well, it would be very interesting to hear what she had to say about the ins and outs at Braeside. He went to check on Satan, and to tell him the latest news.

Some people talked to their bees, kept them up to date with family news. But Clem talked to Satan. He got more than a mindless buzz in return. The bird seemed to know, and always clucked and crooned in reply.

As Clem turned around to go back into the house, he noticed that his skinny neighbour's back window was uncurtained. This was very unusual, and Clem stood stock-still, making no noise. Nothing happened for a few seconds, then a dark shape came to the window, and as an arm was raised to draw the curtain he could see the shape of a woman. Rounded in all the right places, and with a fuzzy-looking hairdo. The curtains snapped shut, and Clem went in. Quite a day! First Dot, and now a woman definitely moving about next door. Maybe he'd hear some talking if he went to the listening place. He'd discovered this at the time of the previous tenant, and it had come in very useful. Inside a cupboard beside the fireplace the wall was very thin, and if he put his ear up close, he could hear every word.

It was all quiet at first, and Clem twiddled his finger in his ear, in case it was blocked with wax. He couldn't remember the last time he washed his ears, and he didn't much care, except that now it might be interfering with his eavesdropping. Then he heard a voice, a man's voice. He recognised it as his skinny neighbour's, and jammed his ear closer to hear the reply. Sure enough, it was a woman, speaking very softly so that he could not distinguish the words. After a few seconds more of the skinny one talking, the woman again replied, and this time her voice was stronger. But what on earth was she saying? It was not English, Clem realised. He had no idea what language it was, but now she was shouting and it sounded to him as if she was crying at the same time. Then a door banged, and all was quiet again.

Clem shut the cupboard door and sat down in his chair. "What's goin' on in there?" he muttered. He had a fleeting notion that the skinny man was running a brothel, and he chuckled. If he'd been a few years younger...He switched on the telly and concentrated on the football match.

When he was in bed, half asleep, Clem thought again about what he had heard and seen. He dismissed the idea of the brothel. There would be clients coming and going and he would have noticed. No, she must be a relation—but a foreigner? Perhaps. Or maybe old Skinny had got a cleaner. He felt drowsy, and as he fell asleep he reminded himself to ask Dot if Skinny was a New Brooms client.

Before he was deeply asleep, Clem was aware of unusual scuffling noises coming from outside. Something had woken him, and he got out of bed to check from the window. Nothing going on outside. The door on Satan's house was still firmly locked. He walked through to the front bedroom and looked down into the street. There was no light directly under his window, but in the shadowy darkness he could see the outline of a large van parked outside next door. Almost immediately, the engine started and it cruised down the street and out of sight. Everything was now quiet, except for a yowling cat at the end house. Clem shrugged. If the bugger next door had been burgled, it was his own stupid fault, he thought. God knows he had plenty of experience in keeping people away! Maybe the foreign cleaner had left the door unlocked. If there was a foreign cleaner. Anyway, nowt to do with him. Clem went back to bed, and fell asleep at once.

Also wakeful, Clem's granddaughter turned over for the tenth time and went through the relaxing programme she had learnt at yoga classes. Once more the spiral of thoughts went through her brain. Staff at the supermarket were being interviewed all over again, one by one, by the police, and she was on the list for tomorrow. She had agreed with her mates in the rest room that this continual questioning was making them feel guilty. They had all taken advantage of special privileges, but few had overstepped the mark, and then in a very minor and unrepeated way.

"O' course," Susie had said, "we don't know about new ones as they come in. But us lot are fed up with it. Can't we do something?"

"What new ones?" asked one of the others.

"Oh, they come in all the time. Mostly stacking shelves. Blokes, mostly."

Susie rolled over once more. This snippet of conversation had gone round and round in her thoughts, and she groaned. What else had they said? Some daft suggestions had been made, like refusing to speak to the police, or getting a solicitor—who could afford that!—and threatening to leave if they weren't left alone. This last suggestion had been firmly sat on. None of them could rely on finding other jobs.

Think of something pleasant, Susie told herself. In the rosy glow of the night light that she had had since childhood, she grinned. She thought of Granddad's new neighbour. Douglas, he'd said his name was. Man of the world, Granddad had said. Moving in on Saturday, probably. She planned to visit Granddad and casually offer help to the nice-looking young man. Just to be neighbourly an' that. He could certainly be very pleasant. I'd better wash my hair tomorrow, she thought, and finally fell asleep, soon dreaming of sandy-haired Douglas Meade in wonderfully erotic situations.

Alastair, driving the cruising van, looked back into the empty interior. It was more of a minibus than van, though there were no windows at the rear. Under the seats he could see something whitish. Damn! He was halfway home after dumping his cargo, and had no intention of returning tonight. He continued driving, and in another half hour drew up outside a row of lock-up garages. Opening an up-and-over door, he drove in and switched off the engine. He climbed into the back and with relief saw the white object was only a crumpled newspaper.

As he walked to the end of the row of garages, he lifted the lid of one of the recycling bins placed there for the block of flats where he lived. "Doing my bit for the environment," he said aloud, and felt virtuous. His spirits rose as he reviewed what had been another successful mission. Lambs to the slaughter, he laughed to himself, and knew that he would sleep soundly tonight.

Sixteen

"Hey, Mum, have you seen Pickering's house is up for sale?" Josie had left the shop in Gran's capable hands for half an hour and had run up to the house with the news. It wasn't just that the Pickerings were moving, and any removal from the village was hot news, but their daughter Floss was one of Lois's best cleaners and might be moving away.

"I know," said Lois, pouring out a coffee for her daughter. "But they're not going far. They've bought that empty house next to the Cullens in Blackberry Gardens. Mrs. Pickering was fed up with the old house, and said she wanted central heating, taps that worked, and not to have to spend money on repairs every couple of weeks."

"That'll be cosy," Josie said. "Floss and Ben living next door to each other."

"Nothing wrong with that," Lois said. "They can set off for the church together."

"No, no. That's not how it's done. Husband-to-be stands trembling at the altar, waiting for his bride. He takes one look back, sees a vision of loveliness approaching up the aisle, and all his nervousness drops away. They will be One, for ever and ever."

"Yes, well, very funny. But I wouldn't know, since my children seem very reluctant to go anywhere near an altar." Lois tried to sound as if it was not really important to her, but secretly she hoped that one day she would be a proud mother of the bride.

"Give us time," Josie answered quickly. "Anyway, it'll be interesting to see who buys Pickering's old house. Seen anyone nosing about?"

"Not yet. Anyway," Lois added sternly, "I don't spend my time gazing out of the window. Too much work to do."

Josie took the hint and stood up to go. "Would you like me to keep you informed?" she said innocently. "Might be useful to get in there first with a New Brooms commercial."

Lois nodded. She knew that Josie was thinking of more than just New Brooms. All information was useful to Lois in her work for old Cowgill, and although at the moment she wasn't specifically ferretin'—as Derek called it—she had a knack of remembering what was useful.

"Thanks, Josie," she said. "By the way, does our notice in the shop need renewing? Could be a bit fly-blown by now."

"I'll get Rob to do it," Josie said. Her partner, Rob, was into computer graphics and would make a good job of it. "Cheerio, then, Mum," she said. "Better go and relieve Gran. She's started advising customers not to buy things she doesn't approve of. Could cost us millions! See you later."

She walked back down the street, and glanced over towards the Pickerings' house, where a For Sale notice had appeared. It would be really nice, she thought, if she could afford to buy it and move out of the flat over the shop. The phrase "living over the shop" was never truer than in Josie's experience. She was always on duty, spending much of her free time in the stockroom or setting out new displays while there were no customers to interrupt.

She walked on, and when she saw old Miss Beasley from Round Ringford being helped out of a car and into the shop, she ran the last few yards. Gran and Ivy Beasley were like sparring boxers in a ring. Sometimes amusing to watch, but they needed a referee.

"Morning, Miss Beasley," she said as they met on the steps. "Lovely morning."

"All right for them as can take time off to gad about the village," Ivy replied sharply. "I suppose you've got time to serve me? Your grandmother's on duty, I suppose, and she doesn't know a loaf from a biscuit."

Josie made a big effort and smiled. "Let me take your arm," she said. "We are both very pleased to see you."

As it was Saturday, Josie shut the shop at four thirty and set off immediately for Tresham. Douglas was moving into Gordon Street, and she had promised to be sisterly and help him sort things out. She parked in the supermarket car park, as always, and walked down to Douglas's house. The street was jammed with his rented van, and angry shoppers were mounting the pavement outside Braeside in order to get by. Tempers had obviously risen during the day, and the air was blue.

"Stupid idiots!" Douglas said when he saw her. "Look at that fool over there, shouting his head off through a closed window. Ah, now the fist. Don't look, Josie. I ignore them. Come on in. I need you to help unload, and then I can park the van somewhere else."

"In the supermarket?" she said. He laughed and nodded. "Come and meet my helper," he added. "Works at the supermarket, but has time off. She's old Clem's granddaughter. And don't laugh, Josie. I think I've got a groupie."

"Blimey," Josie said. "That was quick work. Lead on, Dougie."

Susie blushed scarlet as Josie came in the door. She was dishevelled, dusty, and very happy. Since early morning she had made herself useful, and Douglas had been really nice to her. Now she said nervously, "Shall I make us all a cup of tea?"

Josie took pity on her and said that was a terrific idea. She'd come straight from the shop and a cup of tea would be wonderful. Susie blushed deeper, and disappeared into the kitchen.

"Very pretty," Josie said. "Maybe a bit young for you."

Douglas raised his eyebrows. "Just the right age gap," he said, and handed Josie a pair of work gloves. "Takes five minutes for that kettle to boil," he said, "so we can shift some stuff now."

"Yes, boss," Josie answered meekly, and followed him out to the van.

To Josie, who prided herself on being tough and healthy, the next two hours resulted in total exhaustion. She and Douglas and Susie, who refused to go home, worked solidly until everything was unpacked and in its place. Every so often Clem appeared in his garden to cheer them with good advice and encouragement.

"Yer don't want to carry it that way," he said, more than once. "If I was younger, I'd come and show you. No, grab the other end!" And so the time passed until the van was returned to the hirers, and all three sat slumped in Douglas's sitting room. A knock at the door caused them to look at each other, and Douglas reluctantly got to his feet.

"Hi, kids! We come bearing gifts!" It was Derek, carrying

champagne and glasses—"In case you ain't got the right sort"—with Lois following up with fish and chips from across the way.

Susie began to say something, and then stopped.

"Spit it out, gel," said Derek cheerily.

Susie blushed again, and said, "Would it be all right if Granddad came in? He'll be a good neighbour, Douglas, and he's not a bad old boy."

Clem was fetched, and had news for them. "Did you see that son of hers over in Braeside?" he asked. "He arrived an hour or so ago, and has been at the bedroom window ever since, staring out over 'ere, watchin' what was goin' on. Nosy bugger. 'E got two fingers from me. That sent him packin'." Clem laughed happily, and downed a glass of bubbly in one go. "Not a bad vintage," he said. "I always get Sainsbury's meself."

Seventeen

It was still dark when Douglas awoke. For a moment, he could not remember where he was. The outlines of the door and window were in the wrong place. Then he remembered. It was his first morning—or night?—in Gordon Street. He scrabbled about for his watch and looked at the illuminated dial. Ten past five. Then he heard it. A piercing alarm from just below his window.

So that was the famous cockerel. Well, complainers certainly had a point. Douglas had chosen to sleep at the back of the house to avoid traffic noise, but now he wondered if he would have to choose between two evils. A second succession of cock-a-doodle-doos shattered the peace of the darkness. It wasn't really that old comforting nursery sound at all. More like a soul in agony! Douglas pulled the duvet over his head and tried to get back to sleep. After three more avian alarms, each spaced so that it came just as sleep was returning, there was blissful silence, and Douglas slept soundly until his own clock woke him up at the right time.

After a quick breakfast, he decided to plan his day. Today was Sunday, and tomorrow his first day at the new job. He walked through to his small front room and looked over towards Braeside. There had been no movement yesterday, and he hadn't expected any help from the old blind lady. But this morning, curtains were drawn back and he could see the front door was ajar. To his surprise, he saw a figure emerge, bent and using a stick. Now he could see the figure was a woman, and she walked tentatively down her path towards the gate, tapping with her stick as she went. Should he go and offer help? No. He remembered once offering to escort a man with a white stick across a busy road, and had been told in no uncertain terms that his help was not needed, and moreover was unwelcome.

He continued to watch, ready to dash out, and saw that she was about to cross the road. She did this with firm steps and at speed. Where now? Maybe she was heading for the supermarket. They were all open on Sundays now. But no, she opened his gate and came up to the door. Douglas was there at once, opening up with a smile.

"Come in, come in," he said. "Here, let me help you over the step." The old lady took his outstretched hand and walked daintily into the house.

"Good morning, Douglas," she said. "I do hope you don't mind my calling you by your Christian name, but I am fond of your mother, and have heard so much about you." She wondered to herself whether this wasn't piling it on a bit. Still, Alastair had told her to make friends as soon as possible with that Meade chap. He'd heard rumours about the boss of New Brooms and the police, and wanted to find out just exactly what went on.

"I do hope I'm not too early," Mrs. Blairgowrie said. "It wasn't possible for me to come over and offer help yesterday, but I would like to welcome you to Gordon Street and make sure that you know you have a friend across the way. I could hold a set of keys for you, that sort of thing. As you can see, I am pretty useless at most things, but I can take messages and so forth. Most people in this street are out at work all day, but I am there most of the time, unfortunately." She smiled bravely.

"Of course, thanks very much," Douglas said, patting her arm. It was unexpectedly firm. "But Mr. Fitch next door is usually about, and I believe the man on his other side is a kind of recluse, and always there. Still, apparently he never answers his door, so he wouldn't be much good in an emergency!"

"What kind of emergency?" This was said urgently, and with some alarm.

"Oh, car accident, chimney fire, that sort of thing," Douglas replied, unaware of the guarded look in her eyes.

"Well, with our new, strong young man to help us out there'll be no need for emergency services," she said firmly. "What kind of work do you do, Douglas? You know how rumours fly about, and my son, Alastair, had heard you work with the police, is that right?"

"Good God, no," Douglas said, laughing. "That's Mum's little hobby. I'm in computers, like most people. New job over at InterWorld on the bypass estate. I start tomorrow."

"Fancy your mother having time to work with the police, as well as managing her business," Mrs. Blairgowrie said lightly.

Douglas, who was a friendly, open sort of man, was about to tell all, when he felt a sudden jolt, like someone digging him in the ribs. Why had this old duck come over so early, and why was she asking so many questions? He looked at his watch, and said that his mother did not work with the police, but cleaned their offices for them. At least, the girls did. They'd had the contract for ages, he said.

Mrs. Blairgowrie had seen the time check, and turned to go. "Now just remember, Douglas," she said, "I'm always at home and pleased to see you. Time does go slowly sometimes for me, though Alastair is very good and comes when he can. You must meet him," she said, and then thought maybe that wasn't such a good idea.

"Great," said Douglas, and insisted on shepherding her across the road and back into her house.

Clem had seen it all, the visit to Douglas and the return. "She's nippy on her pins when necessary," he chuckled to himself. "Missed that car by inches."

Lois had asked Gran whether she would like to go over to see Douglas, maybe help with getting him settled. "Me and Derek will be going this morning. Don't want you scrubbing floors nor nothing, but I expect he'd like to see you."

Gran refrained from saying that Lois had never forbidden

her to scrub floors at home, so why not in Gordon Street. But she said only that she would love to go with them. She'd made a beef casserole, and it could simmer in the oven until they got back.

"What? No Sunday roast?" said Derek, coming into the kitchen carrying tools for all eventualities. Gran gave him a withering look, and the three of them squashed into the front seat of the van and were on their way.

They parked in the supermarket car park as usual, and Lois said she just had to dash in to get some gluten-free bread for one of her old ladies. She snaked around the aisles looking for FreeFroms, and finally found them. A man was there, hogging the shelves, moving from side to side so that she could not see what she wanted. He was shortish and skinny, and Lois backed away, wrinkling her nose and thinking he could do with a good scrub. To her dismay, she saw him pile all the wrapped gluten-free loaves into his trolley and move off quickly. "Hey!" she shouted. "Leave one for me!" But he kept going, and the next time she saw him he was checking out a trolley full of cartons of juice, the loaves, and, as far as she could see, the entire contents of the sausage shelves.

As she walked crossly down to Douglas's, she suddenly remembered the floating pork chops. A whole pack of chops, bobbing merrily along in the current of a swollen river. And then the robbery, with quantities of basic supplies stolen. She was still thinking about this when out of the window she saw the smelly man go by, carrying heavy bags that weighed him down. He turned into the house beyond Clem's, and she heard the door slam shut.

"Who's that, then, Douglas?" she said. "Who lives on the other side of Clem?"

"Dunno his name," answered Douglas. "Clem says he's a recluse. Lives alone and is never seen."

"Well, I've just seen him, and he was carrying enough food to feed an army," Lois said, and decided that it was time to put in a call to Cowgill.

Eighteen

After an evening of rubbish on the television, Clem supposed he might as well go to bed, though he didn't really feel tired. The quiz had been mindless junk, with questions a child of five could have answered, and the contestants humiliated for the gratification of viewers. He picked up the Sunday newspaper and riffled restlessly through the pages. Nothing but bad news and naked women. He tossed it onto the floor, and sighed. Then he thought he heard a noise. A woman's voice, coming from next door.

Stationed at his listening post inside the cupboard, he concentrated hard. It was the same voice that he'd heard before, but this time the language was English, broken English that he could hardly understand. One or two words, however, began to give him the gist of what the woman was saying. "When...going...Must...help."

Blimey, thought Clem. He began to wish he'd minded his own business. If something dodgy was going on in there, he wanted nothing to do with it. And if the woman needed help, he was certainly not the one to give it. He shut the cupboard door quickly, put out the lights, and retreated upstairs to bed.

He had been asleep for several hours when he was startled awake by a familiar noise. It was Satan crowing. Surely not dawn yet, Clem muttered to himself. He listened, and knew that it was not a wake-up call. A different sound, more of a cackle. The bird's alarm signal, warning of danger. Clem fumbled for his watch. One o'clock exactly, and confirmed by the distant striking of St. Peter's church clock. Then he remembered he had not shut up Satan. Damn! Perhaps he would be all right with his netting frame against the door. Clem's eyelids drooped, but opened again immediately. Satan had not crowed for nothing. Foxes had been known to get through wire netting. They had teeth like wire cutters. Oh, bugger it.

It was cold and very dark outside, and Clem was glad he'd brought his torch. He secured Satan's door, and turned to go back to bed, but stopped when he saw a light snap on inside his neighbour's house. It was in the kitchen, but he could see nothing behind the curtains except two shapes close together. Then he saw the shadow of a raised fist, and heard a scream.

Without thinking, Clem began to walk towards the man's back door, but he'd gone only a couple of steps when it opened violently and a woman ran out into the yard, screaming, "Help me, help me, please!"

Now Clem could see the man close behind her, and he shouted in a voice he hadn't used for years. "What the bloody hell's going on?"

There was a sudden silence as the woman stopped screaming. The man grabbed her and bundled her into his house. Then he turned back.

"Clear off and leave us alone!" he shouted.

But Clem had spent years dealing with yobs and drunks on the station platform, and it would take more than a weedy little bloke like that to daunt him. Anyway, it was a helpless woman in distress! He had a chivalric impulse and advanced.

"Let me talk to her!" he yelled, pushing the man to one side to get inside the house. It was then that he saw the cosh, lifted high, and he ducked, but too late. The blow to his head was vicious, and his legs buckled. He fell to the ground and was still.

Nineteen

a

Light was creeping round the edge of Douglas's bedroom curtains when he awoke. He surfaced slowly, feeling vaguely uneasy. Something not quite right. He looked at his watch and saw that it was seven thirty, and then he remembered it was his first day at the new job. He flew out of bed and into the shower, and it was not until he was grabbing a quick coffee that he was struck by a disturbing thought. Why had he not been woken by Satan's wicked call? Surely he couldn't be used to it already. After all, it was only his second night in the house.

He grabbed his jacket and was about to the leave, when he stopped. Blast! He should go across and make sure the old man was all right. He unlocked his back door, went across the yard, and knocked, at the same time shouting for Clem. "Hey! Are you okay? Still asleep, you lazy old..." He knew already that this was the kind of language Clem would respond to, and waited. Nothing. Not a sound. He looked through the window, but could see only dirty dishes and an empty room. Better check on Satan. He could at least open him up and give him some daylight.

At first he could see only the bird, lying crookedly on the floor by the wooden lavatory seat. Then he gasped. Protruding from one of the holes where generations of Fitches had sat was a carpet slipper, and inside it a foot.

Douglas tore aside the netting frame and looked more closely. He began to retch, and turned away, collapsing to the ground and burying his head in his hands. After a few seconds he pulled himself to his feet and took another look. It was Clem, of course, cold as charity, and as dead as his beloved Satan by his side.

After he'd made the necessary calls, Douglas finally telephoned his new boss to explain.

"Good heavens," said the departmental manager. "That beats having to attend your grandmother's funeral." Her voice softened, and she added, "Get here when you can, Douglas. Anything we can do, let us know."

Josie was opening the shop when she saw the police car coming slowly towards her. It stopped, and she drew a quick breath of surprise. The tall, immaculate-looking young man approaching was familiar. "Hi, Josie," he said, "remember me?"

"Goodness, of course I do! Hello, Matthew. What brings you here?"

It was Matthew Vickers, plainclothes policeman, nephew of Hunter Cowgill, and potential rival of Josie's Rob. He had spent some weeks with the Tresham police in the past, and had met and admired Josie during the last of Lois's involvements with Cowgill. She had thought him very tasty then, but now he was more so. That smile!

He followed her into the shop and suggested she sit down on her stool behind the counter. The smile had gone now, and he was looking serious. "What's happened?" she said quickly. "Has there been an accident? Mum, Dad...Gran?"

He shook his head. "No, no. None of your family. Well, that's not quite right. Douglas is involved in a pretty nasty happening in Tresham."

She sat rigidly holding on to the counter as he gave her a

brief account of what they had found when summoned by Douglas. The old man, dead and stuffed alongside the bird-seed in his old two-hole lavatory, with the brilliant plumage of his strangled cockerel fading by his side. Matthew rushed towards her as she swayed on her stool. He caught her as she fell, and with his arms tight around her and her head resting on his chest, he said a polite "Good morning" to Rob, who had emerged from the flat above.

The news had been broken to Lois more or less immediately after Cowgill had heard it. She'd picked up the phone as she made a cup of tea for Gran, who was having a rare lie-in.

"Lois," he'd said urgently, "not good news, I'm afraid. Old man next door to your son has been found dead in an outhouse. Douglas found him. The lad is shaken up, but got himself together. Determined to go to work after we've finished with him. I was sure you'd want to know, my dear."

Ignoring the affectionate words, Lois said sharply, "What d'you mean, 'after we've finished with him'?"

"Just the usual questions. No worse than that, Lois. I'm off now to Gordon Street. D'you want to meet me there? I expect Douglas would like a little support."

"He's a fully grown man, and perfectly capable of supporting himself," Lois snapped. But after she'd signed off, she yelled to Derek that she was going straightaway, giving him the details as he rushed downstairs in alarm. "Explain to Mum," she said, as she got into her van. "I'll ring you from Gordon Street."

There were police cars outside Clem's house, and a small crowd had gathered as close as they were allowed. Lois parked at the supermarket and walked swiftly down the street. Cowgill saw her coming and cleared a way for her.

"Where's Douglas?" she said, and without speaking or delaying her in any way, he led her into Douglas's house and shut the door behind them. The curtains had been drawn to shield the little group inside from prying eyes of curious neighbours and passersby.

"Hi, Mum," Douglas said.

A note-taking policeman stood up to give her his seat, and Lois swallowed hard. "What's been going on here, then?" she said. Cowgill stood behind her and put his hand on her shoulder.

She shook it off at once.

Douglas looked at him, and he said, "You fill her in, Douglas. Better coming from you."

"It's poor old Clem," Douglas began, and his voice shook. "Somebody killed him and Satan, and I found them. In that old bog that Satan lived in. Clem was shoved into where he used to keep the bird's food. He's out now. Decently laid out. And his cockerel..." He choked, and Lois reached for his hand.

"Bloody hell," she said, and that was enough. She released his hand and sat quietly while questions and answers droned on. She stopped concentrating after a while, and began to think in a different direction. Who? Why? What had Clem done to deserve such a horrific end?

What did she know about him? Precious little, in fact. Her one interview with him had centred on her tenants' complaint about the cockerel crowing. That might have been one reason why he was disliked, but not enough, surely, to drive someone to such desperate measures.

What secrets might Clem have known? He'd always lived in Gordon Street, and his family before him. They'd seen people come and go, had got to know all about them, gossiped and criticised and taken a liking to some. One or two had become firm friends, like Clem's old neighbour, the one before the recluse.

She interrupted Cowgill midflow. "What about him next door?" she said loudly. "Didn't he see nothing?"

Douglas reflected wryly that his mother's grammar always went out of the window under stress. He waited for Cowgill to reply, but the inspector nodded at him to answer.

"No sign of him, Mum," he said. "Police have tried knocking him up, and then bust their way in. Nobody there. Not a trace. Dirty dishes in the sink, a freezer full of food—including your gluten-free loaves—and a tap left running in the bathroom. Done a runner."

Lois turned to Cowgill. "So you've got him, I expect, by now?" she said tartly. "No, of course you bloody haven't. You've sat here quizzing my Douglas, wasting his time when he's supposed to be starting a new job. Same old questions, not satisfied when he says he doesn't know. For God's sake, Cowgill, get your priorities right!"

The note taker looked across at his chief in alarm. Not known for his tolerance towards women, Cowgill would have her in leg irons, at least. But no. He looked on wonderingly as the inspector grinned.

"Good point, Lois," Cowgill said. "But we have got the bloodhounds out, and they'll be picking up the trail in no time. Meanwhile, Douglas has been very helpful and given us extremely useful information. That'll do for now, Douglas," he added. "We'll need to talk some more, but I know where to find you." He beckoned to the note taker and they walked out, tactfully leaving Lois and her son together.

"He's a good bloke, Mum," Douglas said. "Knows what he's doing. I'm off now. See you later. Take care, and don't worry." He pecked her on the cheek and was gone.

On his bicycle, Lois noted with surprise. Ah, well, nothing like making a good impression on right-minded employers. She walked through to the kitchen and then out into the yard, where several experts were still searching for evidence. Cowgill stepped forward when she was intercepted and her way barred.

"It's all right," he said. "Mrs. Meade can be of help to us. Come with me, Lois dear," he said, and led the way into the recluse's house.

"You can forget the 'dear,'" she said, and then sniffed, wrinkling her nose.

"Ugh, that smell! That's what he smelt like, for sure."

Cowgill stared at her. "How do you know?" he said.

"Because I stood behind him in the supermarket. He grabbed all the gluten-free bread, and took bugger-all notice when I said I wanted a loaf. I saw him again from Doug's front window as he went past with it and into his house. And this is his smell. Yuk."

"Can't smell anything," Cowgill said. "My wife used to say it was lucky I'd got where I am in the force, because a good sense of smell should be part of every policeman's armoury."

Lois looked at his face and felt a pang of sympathy. The woman must have been a real drag. "Don't worry," she said. "You can always take a sniffer dog with you."

He smiled gratefully.

They walked slowly around the house, and Lois's eyes took

in everything. The emptiness of it. Very little furniture, except for the bare essentials. A couple of chairs and a small wooden table. Empty bookshelves, but markings in the dust where books must have been. A small portable radio. "Battery ran out," Cowgill said, as she looked at it. There was no television.

"No phone?" she said, and Cowgill shook his head.

"Either he didn't need one, or he used a mobile," he answered.

"How could he live like this?" she asked. "What did he do with himself all day?"

"Good question," said Cowgill. "Shall we go upstairs?"

Upstairs was much the same, virtually empty. A single bed against the wall, with grubby sheets rumpled all anyhow. A solitary wooden chair had acted as bedside table and bore a single unwashed mug, indelibly stained. The back bedroom had been divided to make a tiny bathroom, where rust stains spread over basin and bath. A tap continued to drip.

"So there's just a box room left," said Cowgill. He opened the door, looking at Lois for her reaction.

"Ye Gods!" she said. "What on earth...?"

"Sleeping bags," said Cowgill. "Dozens of 'em."

The pile reached from floor to ceiling. Lois moved to touch them, to count them.

"Don't touch!" Cowgill warned.

"Must've been expecting visitors," Lois said.

"Exactly," agreed Cowgill. "But who was he expecting? It's hardly bed-and-breakfast accommodation."

"Or," said Lois, "was he mad as a hatter? Nutty as a fruit-cake? And who the hell was he?"

Twenty

Mrs. Blairgowrie saw it all. She sat behind the curtains in her bedroom and watched as the drama unfolded. She saw the police arrive, the pavement cordoned off, the nosy group assembling and then being dispersed. She saw Lois marching down the street and being met by Hunter Cowgill. When Douglas set off on his bicycle, she watched until he rounded the corner at the end of the street. Shapes appeared inside the recluse's house and she identified them as Cowgill and Lois. She saw the ambulance, and knew that the shrouded body was that of Clem.

Poor old Clem! He had been a friendly old man, and she'd been touched and amused at his scheme for helping her out if she was in trouble. She had even looked out a brightly coloured scarf to dangle at her window should it ever be needed. And now he'd gone, with no warning and without a friend standing by.

Finally the street was quiet, and she moved slowly away from the window, remembering to take her stick as she made her way to the telephone.

"Is that you, Alastair? Yes, well, I think it would be a good idea for you to postpone your visit today. But we need to talk soon, so keep in touch. 'Bye. Oh, and wait a minute! The new cleaner woman is coming tomorrow afternoon, so best not to come then either. 'Bye."

As she put down the telephone, she heard a sharp knock at her door. She put on the dark glasses, picked up her stick, and went through to see who was there.

"Good morning. Sorry to trouble you, madam. Inspector Cowgill. May I come in for a few minutes?"

Susie was at work, and when the manager came out and asked very nicely if Susie would come into the office for a moment, she wondered what on earth she had done. Up to now, she hadn't put a foot wrong. In fact, she'd received one or two compliments on how well she had settled in and grasped all the details of the routine. She coloured, as always, and followed Mrs. Higham into the office.

"Sit down, my dear." Susie sat on the edge of her chair and waited nervously. When Mrs. Higham told her gently what had happened, Susie sat rigidly without moving or saying anything. After a few seconds, her boss came over and put her arm around her shoulders. "I expect you'd like to go home, my dear. I'll get one of the girls to come with you. Let me know how you're feeling, won't you?"

Susie came to life. "There's nobody at home," she said. "No point in my going back there." She hesitated, and then said, "I'll just carry on, if you don't mind. The girls are a nice bunch, and if you could just tell them, I'd be happier among friends. I'm not going to collapse in front of the customers or anything. I expect I'll cry later."

Most girls would grab the chance of a day off, thought Mrs. Higham. This one was a brave soul. "If you're sure, Susie. I'll have the girls in one by one, and then there'll be no disruption to upset you. Stay if you like for a while, and I'll get you a coffee." But Susie said she preferred to get on with her work. It would be better that way, would give her something to think about.

"Fine," said Mrs. Higham, "and there is one other thing. The police have been in touch, and will want to talk to you later. They know you used to call in to see your granddad quite often. But they're very tactful and nice, and won't frighten you."

Susie looked at her now, dry-eyed. "I don't frighten easy," she said, and went quietly back to work.

Douglas was not doing quite so well. He had turned up, found his way to the right office, and been welcomed tactfully. The first day, he'd been told, would be spent familiarising himself with colleagues, the geography of the place, and—most important—the ways and wonders of his computer. He sat staring at the screen, his mind back in Gordon Street, seeing not the high-tech surroundings of his new job, but the small back yard of Clem's house, the brick lavatory with its polished wooden seat and Satan on the floor beside it. He tried hard to concentrate on what he was supposed to be doing, but a sudden picture of Clem's slippered foot with its stringy greyish ankle sticking up like a cry for help flashed through his head.

He stood up, and walked quickly towards the door to the toilets. This had fortunately been one of the first landmarks pointed out to him. He had the place to himself, and splashed cold water over his face, taking deep breaths and trying to compose himself. This wouldn't do. The old man was almost a stranger. They'd met only once or twice, and he'd been a nosy old sod. Then Douglas remembered Susie, and wondered if she'd been told. She'd given him her mobile number, and he had wondered if he was doing the right thing to encourage her. Now he checked the number and dialled. He had no idea about company rules on private calls in work time, but he'd make it quick.

"Hello? Is that you, Susie? Douglas Meade here."

"Oh, Douglas, thank goodness it's you. I thought the police ..." She trailed off, embarrassed.

"Have they told you? About your granddad, I mean?"

"Well, yes. I know. It's horrible. It hasn't quite sunk in," she said, and he could hear that she was fighting tears.

"I'll be home about six. Can you drop in, or are you going home? We could, perhaps, well...you know, help each other. I found him, actually."

"I know. Yes, I'll be there at six. Thank you ever so much for ringing. Better go now. 'Bye."

Douglas put his phone back in his pocket, aware that his dizziness had subsided. He walked back to his desk with a lighter step.

"Feeling better, mate?" His colleague looked concerned. Douglas reassured him, and explained that he'd had a bit of bad news this morning, but he'd be fine.

By the time he turned his bicycle into Gordon Street, there was no trace of anything untoward. Cars were crawling nose to tail to the supermarket, and most of the houses presented blank, net-curtained faces to the street. Then he saw Susie, waiting inside his tiny front patch of garden. She was quite still, staring into space. When she saw him, she moved forward and waved, opening the gate to greet him. Her face was pale now, but full of relief at his arrival.

"Hi, Susie," he said, and on an impulse rested his bike against the fence and put his arms around her. He hugged her gently and felt her begin to shake. He managed to unlock the door and shepherd her inside before the storm broke. It was several minutes before she was able to detach herself and reach for a tissue. "Sorry," she said, and sniffed.

"I'm not," Douglas said. "Not at all, really. Except about Clem, o' course. Here, take your jacket off and I'll make us some tea."

Twenty-One

"Hello, Dot. Mrs. M here. Have you heard about Douglas's neighbour in Gordon Street? You have. I thought you probably would have." Uppity voice from Dot in response. "Now, listen, Dot. You're due at Mrs. Blairgowrie this afternoon, and we need to have a chat before you go. I shall be in the office with Hazel later on this morning, so can you pop in? Say about twelve? See you then."

Gran put her head round the door and said, "Have you spoken to Douglas this morning? How is the lad? I was really worried last night when he didn't ring."

"Yeah, I spoke to him first thing. Seems he went out to take his mind off it all. Took that granddaughter, Susie, to the movies."

Gran brightened. "That's nice," she said, and disappeared. Lois was not so sure. The girl was a lot younger than Douglas, and though she wouldn't hear a word against her son, she did know that he'd had a good few girlfriends, and none of them so far had lasted more than a few months. Still, that was how it was with young people these days. She smiled. That sounded like an oldie speaking! Still, she did sometimes feel as if the world was becoming a place where she felt ill at ease, didn't quite belong. She and Derek had more and more conversations about the good old days, when they were youngsters. Things were better then, they agreed.

But of course that was nonsense. Lois stood up and went to the window. She looked down the street and saw houses big and small, and all with an air of prosperity, even smug self-satisfaction. She told herself that she was thinking rubbish. But she remembered Gran telling her that when she was a child, she'd been brought from where they lived on Tresham's Churchill estate to Long Farnden for a picnic. It had been a lovely day, warm and still. They'd sat by the river on a rug, and eaten sandwiches and jam tarts. Gran had been about six, and had wandered off. She'd leaned over the edge of the bank to look at the tiny fish in the shallows. Two seconds later, she had fallen facedown into the water, then surfaced and screamed blue murder. Before her father reached her, a man had appeared, waded in, and pulled her unceremoniously onto the bank. Her dad had thanked the farm worker profusely, and he had said it was nothing. He was hedging upriver and heard her scream. Dad had said he'd buy the man a drink, and the two of them had gone off to the pub laughing.

Where was Health and Safety then? Today she'd be wearing

a life jacket, and the bank would be fenced off. There'd be no fish in the water, anyway, and farmers cut their hedges with monster machines that completed the job in no time. The skill of laying a hedge was all but gone. What was laying a hedge, anyway? Lois realised she had no idea. Sounded like something to do with chickens.

Lois's daydream was interrupted by a car drawing up outside the gate, and a familiar figure coming up the path. It was Hunter Cowgill, and Lois waited until Gran came through to answer the doorbell.

"Oh, it's you, Inspector," Gran said. "I'm not sure, but I think she's out. Shall I tell her to call you?" Lois couldn't believe her ears. The old bag! Still, she no doubt meant it for the best. Lois decided to call her bluff.

"Hi, Mum, I'm back," she said, coming up behind her with a false smile. "Good morning, Inspector. How can I help you?"

Cowgill knew perfectly well that Lois wasn't out. He'd seen her looking out of the window. But he decided to ignore the fib. That was between the two women. He said blandly that he was sorry to disturb them but he needed to ask Mrs. Meade a few questions.

"Come into the office," Lois said, and added, "No, Mum, no coffee. The inspector is not allowed to take bribes."

When the door was shut, Cowgill said, "Really, Lois. You are not very kind to your mother. I'm sure she's only trying to protect you from my fiendish intentions."

"Leave my mother to me, if you don't mind," said Lois. "Now, what d'you want? I've got work to do."

Cowgill explained that he was anxious to find out everything possible about Clem Fitch. "On the face of it," he said, "he was a nice old man, if a bit nosy." He'd had an exemplary career on the railways, and his daughter and family kept in fairly frequent touch with him. He was belligerently independent, not very clean, and extremely fond of his granddaughter, Susie. His family had lived in Gordon Street for generations, and he was usually very suspicious of incomers. But one of the residents from the far end of the terrace had said Clem seemed overfriendly with that blind woman in Braeside right from the beginning.

"Maybe she's rich," said Lois. "I wouldn't put it past him

to have an eye on the main chance. He thought quite a lot of himself, you know."

"He might just have fallen for her, Lois," Cowgill replied. "Cupid strikes at strange moments," he added, a soft look in his eyes.

"Oh, for God's sake, grow up!" Lois frowned, and added that she knew nothing about the blind lady's love life, but doubted if there was much going on. "She was the new girl on the block, and Clem would have felt it was his right to check her out. Anyway, Dot Nimmo's going there this afternoon. My team don't gossip, as you know, but she'll probably have something to tell me later. If I reckon it's useful, I'll pass it on. Was there anything else?"

Cowgill nodded. "Your Josie," he said, "I don't want to go into the shop and spread rumours at these early stages, but could you ask her to keep her ears open? Anything to do with Clem Fitch. She can report to you."

Lois bristled. She had always tried not to involve the family in her ferretin', and Cowgill knew this. He also knew that she sometimes failed. Lois saw the confident look on his face and retaliated. "Too late, Cowgill," she replied. "You've been upstaged. Your handsome nephew has been talking to my Josie already. Broke the news, actually. You could ask him to pursue his enquiries." She stood up and added, "Now, I've got a new client to meet, so I'll see you out."

There was no new client, but Lois had had an idea. She'd remembered offering to find Clem a new home for Satan. Her previous tenants had found the bird disturbing enough to move out. Where had they gone? She remembered their name was Freeman, and that they'd been very stroppy in the end. Definitely worth a trip to the agents to see their records. The Freemans might have something useful to say, apart from how they would have strangled the so-and-so bird if they hadn't moved.

The letting agents were helpful, and immediately found the details Lois wanted. The Freemans had moved to a small house on the east side of Tresham. This sprawl of new housing had grown larger over the years and had become a magnet for trouble, or so it seemed to the decent citizens who'd first moved there. As a result the house prices had stayed low, and the Freemans had managed to afford one in order to make a new start. He had been on sickness benefit for a long time, and she had had serious depression. Now, at last, he'd got a job and she had finally shaken off the miseries.

Lois listened to all this with interest. Her former tenants were not likely to be all that pleased to see her after what they would see as noncooperation over Satan. But at least now she'd have other topics to talk about.

First, to the office to see Hazel, and then to have a talk with Dot. "I'm off now, Mum," she said, passing through the kitchen.

"I'm glad to hear you being a bit more polite to that policeman," Gran said. "A pity you can't extend it to your mother."

"Sorry, Mum," Lois said breezily. "Won't be back for lunch. I'll grab a sandwich with Hazel."

"Much good that will do you," said Gran acidly.

"I'll make sure it's organic," Lois replied, and left quickly before her mother's all-that-organic-nonsense diatribe began.

Hazel was waiting for her, and was her usual efficient self, with lists and notes ready for their weekly conference. She'd had several new enquiries, and went through with Lois the ones that would need a visit from her. Some of them were returning to New Brooms after a break. It was quite usual for women clients to say that after all they could do their housework themselves, and then, as a few weeks of enthusiasm quickly dwindled to boredom, some would say jokingly to Lois, "Come back! All is forgiven."

The two had finished their business, and were having a quick coffee and sandwich, when Dot appeared, spot on time. "Morning both," she said, sitting squarely on the remaining chair and opening her bag. "Don't mind if I join you, d'you?" She pulled out a venerable-looking meat pie and began to munch.

Lois gave up trying to maintain a position of authority and opened the subject of Mrs. Blairgowrie. "She'll probably be in a bit of a dither, Dot," she said. "Just go easy with her. Bill used to say she followed him about, and I know you hate that. But…"

"What d'you mean?" Dot interrupted. "How could she follow him about if she's blind?"

Hazel spoke up. "I had an aunt who was blind," she said.

"She knew her house so well that she could walk around in the pitch dark and never bump into anything."

"Must've saved on the electric," said Dot grumpily.

"I expect Mrs. Blairgowrie is the same," Hazel continued. "Anyway, Bill said she had vestigial sight in one eye, didn't he, Mrs. M?"

Lois confirmed this, but said that she reckoned it was possible Mrs. Blairgowrie saw more than she owned up to. "Still, that's none of our business," she added. "We're just there to do a job to the highest standards."

Dot said it was time she went, and shook the crumbs from her pie into the wastepaper basket. "See what high standards I got," she said with a smirk.

"I don't know why you put up with her," Hazel said, making it sound like a joke, though it wasn't. "I'll go and wash the mugs, Mrs. M."

Lois sighed. "She's right, Dot. Now, before you go, there's one more thing."

"Will I keep me eyes an' ears open in Gordon Street? I knew old Clem, y' know, from way back. He were quite a nice ole boy. Pity, really."

"And whatever you find out, keep it to yourself."

"Except to tell you? You can trust me, Mrs. M." With an expression of deep concern, Dot left the office and disappeared up the street.

Hazel returned, and they continued to talk about the Clem tragedy and to speculate who on earth could have murdered the old man and why. "They say they've had a lead on that theft from the supermarket," Hazel said.

"Who says?" Lois looked up from an account book she was checking.

"I heard it from John, and he heard it in the pub in the village." John was her husband and they farmed at Waltonby. It was well known that if you wanted reliable gossip the Waltonby pub was the place to go.

"Did he say any more?"

"No. I don't think any of them knew the details. Seems odd, though, don't it, that the two crimes should have happened in Gordon Street? But there, it could be anywhere in Tresham. Your Douglas is welcome to it. Wouldn't catch me and John living there."

"Not many farms in Tresham," Lois said lightly. She remarked that any more details John heard in the pub would be welcome. All for the good of New Brooms, she stressed. She didn't want a breath of suspicion to fall on any of her girls.

"Which reminds me, Hazel," she added. "I've got a possible replacement for Bill coming here for interview tomorrow at eleven. He's coming from Fletching."

"He? Well, that could be a good thing. With murder in the air, girls could be put off. We need a bloke for the rougher jobs."

"We've got Dot," replied Lois, and they both laughed.

Twenty-Two

Dot knocked loudly on the door of Braeside, then opened the letter box and shouted, "Yoo-hoo! It's Dot from New Brooms! Don't hurry yerself, dear. I know you can't see, so take your time!"

"Don't worry about me, dear," she said, as Mrs. Blairgowrie opened the door. "You just sit in your chair and listen to your nice book, an' I'll do the rest. Come tea break, I'll make a good cup for both of us. I usually start upstairs, and you can give me a shout if you need any help."

Thank God she'd told Alastair not to come today, Mrs. Blairgowrie thought, tapping her stick as she walked back to the sitting room. She did as she was told and settled in her chair. It was a beautiful afternoon, and she could see blue-tits and a robin feeding from the old bird table. She'd never been remotely interested in birds before, but now found she could pass the time more quickly watching out for new species. She'd asked Alastair to bring her a bird book, and now could identify several different kinds of finch. He'd told her to keep it out of sight, and she had answered that he should mind his business and she would mind hers. As far as people knew, she had some vestigial sight.

Dot set to work with her usual thoroughness. She would have liked to find something Bill had missed, some dusty corner or tidemark on the bath. For some reason Bill had made it clear he didn't approve of her. And the feeling was mutual. She thought he was too good to be true. She wondered who would replace him, and supposed Mrs. M had it all in hand. She picked up a hand mirror from the dressing table in Mrs. Blairgowrie's bedroom, and looked at herself. Not bad, she decided, and then noticed a thumbprint that she knew was not hers. Out of habit, she'd held it by the handle so as not to smear the glass. Mrs. Blairgowrie's thumb, of course, but why would she want to look at herself when she couldn't see? Dot shrugged. Just get on with it, Dot, she said under her breath.

She had finished upstairs, and was about to carry her tools down, when she heard a knock at the door. "Shall I go, dear?" she called out.

"No, I can manage," was the answer, and Dot heard footsteps in the hall. She retreated to the landing and stood silently by the banister rail.

"I thought I told you not to come today." It was the old lady's voice, and a man answered her.

"Need to talk," he said. "Urgently. Go on through and tell the woman to keep clear of us."

"She's upstairs, Alastair," Mrs. Blairgowrie replied, her voice wavery and faint.

Dot heard the man swear, and then he shouted up the stairs, "I'm her son, and we have confidential things to discuss. Please find things to do and don't disturb us. Thanks."

The last word was very much an afterthought, and Dot bridled. She was not used to being spoken to like that. She would report it to Mrs. M, along with several other things about this house. She heard the key turn in the sitting-room door, and crept softly downstairs. He needn't think he could order her about. She went silently into the front parlour and left the door ajar. If the conversation got heated, she guessed she would be able to hear. Now, she would polish everything possible to a high gloss and probably clean the windows as well. That should give him time for his confidential conversation! It would be her tea break soon, anyway, and that was part of her contract. She began with a coffee table and moved on to a brass-edged fireguard. She noted with glee that the brass was tarnished. Black mark, Bill. That would take quite a while to polish up.

It wasn't long before a raised male voice could be heard.

Dot moved swiftly to the open door and listened. Mrs. Blairgowrie's reply was too soft for her to distinguish words, but the next thing was him shouting angrily, "You stupid berk! Can't you be more careful? One stupid mistake could give away the whole thing."

"Shhhh!" It was Mrs. Blairgowrie, and Dot heard no more. She shut the door carefully and got on with her work. Not long afterwards, heavy footsteps went past to the front door, and with a loud slam he was gone. Dot flew to the window and caught a glimpse of a large, dark-haired man in a grey suit. As he shut the gate, he turned and looked at the window. She backed further behind the curtain and heard his car being revved up and driven away with a squeal of tyres.

That small glimpse had been enough.

Twenty-Three

It was towards the end of the afternoon by the time Lois parked outside the Freemans' house. She wanted to be sure that David Freeman was back from work. There was a car in front of the house, and she went to the door and knocked. It was a small, semidetached house on an estate designed to avoid straight rows and similarity, but ending up like a rabbit warren. The Freeman house was redeemed by sunny windows and a very neat garden. Light and airy, unlike Lois's house in Gordon Street. She hoped they were not too resentful about the move.

Mary Freeman saw her coming. The door opened immediately, and Lois was relieved to see her smiling. "Mrs. Meade! What a surprise! Did we leave something behind at Gordon Street? Anyway, now you're here, come on in."

David Freeman was sitting in an armchair with his shoes off, and he did not get up when she came in. He didn't smile. "Oh, it's you," he said. "What can we do for you?"

"Sit down for a minute. Would you like a cup of tea?" Mary Freeman scowled at her husband. "We were so sorry to hear about poor Clem Fitch," she said. "It was a big story in the paper. Poor man."

"Huh, he would have been delighted to have made the front

page," said Freeman. "Awkward old sod."

Mary put her hand to her mouth. Then she said she would go and make the tea. "Tell Mrs. Meade about our lovely garden," she said as she left the room.

Freeman glared at her, and Lois smiled bravely. "I can see it looks very well cared for," she said.

"Best thing about it is there's no bloody cockerel next door," he said.

"Yes, well," Lois began in a soft voice. "I think if you had seen Clem and his bird stuffed in an old lavatory, even you would have been sad. The cockerel was strangled and his head almost pulled off. He'd obviously put up a fight. There were feathers everywhere. Those beautiful feathers, all muddy and torn."

Freeman was quiet for a moment, then said, "And the old man? Had he, well...?"

"Bashed on the head from behind. Must have been a terrible blow. Real butchery. They reckon he died instantly, thank God."

There was a long silence now. Lois could hear crockery being rattled in the kitchen, and prayed for Mary to come in soon. But Freeman had something to say now, and it was obviously an effort.

"I did think, when I saw the story in the paper, that if we'd still been there it probably wouldn't have happened. My wife is a very bad sleeper, and the slightest noise wakes her. Me, too, for a year or so. That bird would have made a terrible noise. We know that from bitter experience, don't we, Mary?"

The tray of tea was set down, and Mary sighed. "I do know one thing," she said. "That wretched recluse from the other side of Clem wouldn't have stirred. Nothing would get him out, except a fire! Yes, Dave, you're right, if we'd still been there we'd have stopped whatever went on. It's a horrible thought, Mrs. Meade."

"The recluse has gone now," Lois said quietly. "Done a bunk. That night, it was. By the time Douglas got there, and the police, there was no sign of him. House left unlocked, and everything looking as if he left in a hurry."

Mary's colour drained. "You mean it was him? Him that killed Clem? But why on earth...?"

Lois was waiting for Freeman to say that perhaps he was

allergic to cockerels, but he didn't.

They drank their tea, and chatted quite amiably now. Lois deliberately changed the subject for a while, and asked about Freeman's new job and how they felt about the area.

Mary made a face. "Well, it's not exactly Nob Hill," she said. "Kids are rough and swear at you at the drop of a hat. You have to double lock everything, and nobody puts garden pots or ornaments out the front. But our neighbours are nice and helpful. We're lucky that way. And the house is, well, you can see. It's new, and light and clean. We like it a lot. And Dave gets out in the garden when it's fine. Would you like to take a look when you've drunk up?"

They walked slowly round the garden, and Lois was knowledgeable and complimentary. Her dad had been a keen gardener, and she herself had taken over the front lawn and flower beds back in Farnden. Derek had encouraged her in an attempt to give her something else to think about other than cleaning and crime. She had discovered it was a great way of seeing what went on in the High Street, and spent many evenings out there.

"You'd do really well in our horticultural show, Mr. Freeman," she said. "O' course, it's just for our village and a five-mile radius, but I bet there's one around here. You'd win firsts in most classes!"

He beamed, as she had intended, and escorted her back to the house as if she were a visiting celebrity about to present the prizes. They begged her to stay a minute or two longer and see the photographs of their visit to Monet's garden in France, and she followed them once more into the sitting room.

They had been talking about an old gardener they knew who lived in his potting shed and talked to nobody, not even on the bus when he made his weekly foray into town. Lois saw her opening. "I suppose," she said casually, "you never saw much of that other man we were talking about, lives the other side of Clem?"

Freeman shook his head. "Only once or twice," he said. "He'd come out to empty rubbish in the bin. Piles of it, there was. God knows what he got up to in there."

"Occasionally I'd see him in the supermarket," Mary chipped in. "Mind you, he never answered if you said hello, and always scuttled off like a frightened rabbit."

"There was one night, d'you remember, Mary, when he was out the front talking to somebody. It was half-dark, and the other bloke was shouting at him. Tall, he was, and heavily built. Throwing his arms about and walking up and down." Freeman gesticulated and paced back and forth.

"Fancy you remembering!" Mary said. "Now it comes back to me. The other bloke crossed the road and got into a car parked outside Braeside. He drove off like a maniac. We thought of going along to make sure the little man was all right, but he'd disappeared and we knew he'd never open the door."

"I don't suppose you remember what kind of car?" Lois said. "Douglas rang me earlier and said he'd seen one parked out there by a big man who went into the blind lady's house. A big black job with darkened windows."

"That's it!" Mary answered. "That's right, isn't it, Dave?" Freeman nodded. Then he looked straight at Lois. "Is that why you've come?" he said. "To ask us questions about Gordon Street?" He didn't seem too angry, and Lois decided to tell the truth.

"Well, partly," she began. "I was also wondering how you were getting on. I felt a bit guilty about not being able to do anything about poor old Satan. But yes, owning a house next door to a murder has worried me. It'll certainly lower the value for a while, until people forget. Luckily my son Douglas is there at the moment, and he's not in the least put off! In fact," she added, "he's taken a fancy to Clem's granddaughter Susie. But I'd like to help the police as much as possible and get the whole thing cleared up. There'll be two houses empty there for a while, and it don't look good for the rest of the terrace."

"Nice girl, that Susie," said Mary. "Better than her mother. That woman never came to see Clem, not the whole time we were there. Why don't you have a chat with Susie? She was there regular, and could well have seen or heard something. Maybe Clem told her about the skinny little man, some things we don't know. Worth a try."

Lois extricated herself from the Freemans with difficulty. It seemed that once they'd made peace they were only too anxious to be friends. "Pop in and see us anytime you're this way," Mary said as Lois got into her car.

"And if we think of anything else to help with your enquiries"—Freeman chortled at the official phrase—"we'll be in touch.

Twenty-Four

Lois arrived at the office in Sebastopol Street at half past ten the next morning, and sat down to read Andrew Young's curriculum vitae. He was twenty-five, unmarried, lived in a flat in Fletching, a village a few miles from Long Farnden, and had been looking after himself for six years. His parents had been killed in a car crash in Australia whilst touring. He had dropped out of university and gone off on a protracted trip around the world in an effort to come to terms with the tragedy.

"Does he say why he wants to be a cleaner?" Hazel asked. She remembered Gary, a nice lad who'd worked for them for a while. But his unsavoury past had caught up with him and he'd left under a cloud.

"No. That's our first question, I suppose." Lois had decided on enlisting Hazel to the interview session. Usually she did it all herself, and preferred to talk to candidates in their own homes, but Derek had been nagging her lately about delegating and this was a tryout.

"It'll probably emerge naturally," Hazel said, knowing by now how Mrs. M worked. "I shall be guided by you. You're the boss," she added reassuringly. Like most of New Brooms' team, she recognised all Mrs. M's faults, but would have stood by her through thick and thin, if necessary. It had been necessary once or twice, and Hazel had no doubt that it would be necessary again. All the cleaners knew they had to keep quiet about Mrs. M's sleuthing, and this minor conspiracy kept them faithful to a job which normally would see a fairly rapid turnover of staff.

"Looks like this is him," Hazel added, standing at the window and peering up the street. "Tall, thin, round-shouldered. Dark hair, lopes along like a farmer."

"How does a farmer walk, Hazel?" asked Lois, laughing.

"Better come and sit down now."

Lois sat behind the desk, and Hazel took a chair over by the window with an empty one not far away. She had been reading a book about interviewing methods, and decided one person behind a desk was enough.

He came in, stumbling over the doormat, looked frantically back and forth from Hazel to Lois, and said, "I'm Andrew Young and I'm so nervous I think I'll go now, before I make it worse."

To Lois's surprise and eventual relief, Hazel burst out laughing, hearty, cheerful guffaws. "Well, that's a new one!" she said. "There's nothing like that in the book!"

"Sit down, Andrew," Lois said, noting that he'd stared open-mouthed at Hazel. "Take no notice of Hazel. She's always had a weird sense of humour. Now," she added, leaning back in her chair and folding her arms in what she hoped was a motherly gesture, "why don't we all have a coffee and relax."

Hazel jumped up at once and made for the kitchen. Lois could hear her chuckling as the kettle was being filled. This would be something to tell Derek, him and his delegating!

After they'd settled, Lois began to ask questions. She thought it best not to start with "Why do you want to be a cleaner?" "Where did you go in your travels?" she said instead, and was amazed at the list of countries, some of which she'd never heard of. How could he have managed, if walking down a familiar street to a job interview sent him into such a tizzy? "I had company," he said, as if he'd read her thoughts. "She was a sort of girlfriend at the time. We're split now, but still friends. Nothing like travel to get to know someone really well," he added. "Oh, and she dumped me, in case you're wondering. Married a high-flying banker. Couldn't blame her, really."

Hazel risked a question. "Better prospects than a house cleaner, would you say?"

He nodded. "I must tell you honestly this wasn't something I'd always wanted to do."

"So why are you here?" Lois said gently. "You'll appreciate that I'm looking for someone who's likely to stay with us for a reasonable time. We've had fly-by-nights now and then, and they're more trouble than they're worth. There's all the paperwork and training. And my clients do like continuity of staff."

Andrew Young looked uncomfortable. "The thing is, Mrs. Meade," he said, and stopped.

"Yes?"

"Well, since my parents died, I sold the family house and looked after myself in a modern flat in Fletching. At first I couldn't think positively at all, but after a while, when I got back from travelling, I began to get out and about, interested in furniture and fabrics and decorating the flat. I wasn't all that good at it, but several friends gave me jobs to do, painting and decorating, and I got better. I really like homemaking. I suppose that's it. And I hate scruffy homes. You'd be surprised at how some people live, Mrs. M."

Lois laughed. "I don't think so, Andrew. We've seen it all in New Brooms."

Gathering confidence, Andrew continued. "And so when I saw your advertisement, I thought it would be the ideal combination. I could do as much cleaning as you wanted me to, and then do the interior décor bit the rest of the time."

Lois said nothing for what seemed like minutes, and Hazel looked at her enquiringly.

"I've had an idea. Something to think about." Lois finally uncrossed her arms and sat up straight. Andrew was looking nervous again, his confidence evaporating in the silence.

"I'm going to ask you a really personal question, Andrew," she said. "How much money have you got? In the bank. Capital, I mean."

Hazel's eyes opened wide. "Um, I wonder if that's…" The book had been very firm about intrusive questioning.

"Ah, well, I'm not too sure," Andrew replied, frowning. "My travels made a bit of a hole in what Mum and Dad left me. But there was quite a lot left from the sale of the house, and Dad was good at investments."

He was beginning to feel irritated by this tactless woman. The girl was fine, but Mrs. Meade was decidedly blunt, bordering on rudeness. He decided that his honesty deserved a straight answer. "What is this idea, and why do you need to know what I'm worth financially? Doesn't seem to have too much to do with my ability to clean other people's houses." He reckoned she was going to turn him down, anyway. She probably thought with money behind him he would come and go as he liked. Well, to hell with her. He stood up.

"I'll not waste any more of your time," he said, but Lois interrupted him.

"Sit down, Andrew," she answered firmly. "Just listen to what I have to say. It'll need a lot more thought, but it might appeal to you."

Hazel thought she knew Mrs. M inside out, but listened with amazement. Lois outlined a plan for extending New Brooms. If Andrew was prepared to put money into it, and, of course, take his cut, they could add interior decorating to the list of services the business would offer. It would all have to be worked out properly, Lois stressed. She had no intention of taking a partner, but profits could be apportioned fairly with not too much difficulty. Her Josie, she said, was good at that sort of thing. They could all put their heads together and come up with a really workable arrangement. "If you're interested, that is," she said, smiling at Andrew's rapid changes of expression. "Think about it, and give me a ring," she added.

Hazel was stunned into silence, but Andrew stood up and extended his hand. "You're on, Mrs. Meade," he said. "My dad always said strike while the iron's hot. I'll be in touch very soon. And thanks," he said, turning to Hazel. "Carry on laughing."

He strode out of the office, and Lois stood next to Hazel at the window, watching him disappear up the street.

"He's walking fast," Lois said.

"And his head's in the air," said Hazel. "See what you've done, Mrs. M? Let's hope it's a good morning's work. Quite a charmer, in his funny way."

Twenty-Five

At breakfast Susie said very little, having slept fitfully. She went to work as usual and was as conscientious as always, but her mind was not fully on the job. She had not yet taken it in. Granddad dead? It didn't seem real. He had always been there. She loved her parents, of course, but at an early age saw their faults. She'd had school friends whose houses were warm and spotless and smelt of polish and lavender, instead of the all-pervading frying sausages. Their folks never missed a parents' evening, and whole families came in force to school plays and concerts. Susie was lucky if either Mum or Dad came, never both. But Granddad was always there. Sometimes in his railway uniform, smart and proud.

The day passed slowly, and when it was finally time for her to leave, she put on her jacket and hurried away down Gordon Street. It was a dismal evening, damp and overcast, and the street was empty for once. Douglas had invited her for a meal at the pizza place in the town centre, but it was too early. Instead of going home, she decided to go along the footpath that led round the back of the terrace and have a quick look at Granddad's back yard. Her heart fluttered as she wondered whether the police had left Clem's tools and other familiar, forlorn things around.

She steeled herself and lifted the latch on his gate, but it was locked. She smiled, remembering the set of keys that Granddad had given her. Fishing them from her bag, she turned the big rusty one in the gate lock and pushed it open. It was like a punch in the stomach, seeing the old lavatory shed with its door firmly shut. Now there was no Satan to peck at the stale bread she used to bring from the supermarket. She walked past quickly, and saw that the back door of the house was also shut, and the windows blank. No smiling Granddad waiting for her at the door. She gulped. Granddad never shut his door except in severe weather, and his grubby curtains were always drawn back unevenly. Everything had soon become grubby after Granny died. But further back in time, when she had been really small, she remembered the warm, comfortable sitting room with a leaping fire that sent flickering reflections in the brass coal scuttle, and twinkled on the gleaming barley-sugar twist candlesticks on the windowsill that had been her grandmother's pride and joy.

The house had been emptied, of course, and for once Mum and Dad had been united. They had stripped the place indecently quickly, removing anything that might fetch a few pounds and consigning the rest to a skip dumped on the pavement outside the front door. It was removed quickly, once they had done with it, being a traffic hazard in such a narrow street. Susie had not been allowed to be part of the clearing operation, but she had been walking down Gordon Street when the lorry came to load up the skip. She caught sight of a biscuit tin, rusty at the edges and with a colourful picture of a coach and horses outside a ridiculously clean and freshly painted village inn. She remembered Granddad laughing at it, asking Granny where was the horse shit and where were the drunken farmers throwing up in the water trough? That's what it was really like, he had told a wide-eyed Susie.

She also remembered what was in it. After all the biscuits had been eaten, Granddad had taken it off to his toolbox and kept it in case it would come in useful. In due course, it had come in very useful. One long-ago day at Tresham station, there had been a VIP visit. Red carpet runners had been put down, and the local florist had arranged flowers at every turn. Granddad had taken a major part in the planning, and had proudly stood to attention as the special train drew in. The sparkling carriage door had opened, and a large, bald, and well-fed–looking man had stepped out, followed by his elegant, smiling wife. Granddad had a special place in his heart for this woman. After all, they shared a name—well, almost.

After a couple of hours, the VIP and his wife, still smiling, returned and prepared to board the train. The trademark cigar was now lit, and the curling blue smoke caused Granddad's eyes to water. At least, that's what he told Susie. Then one of the aides had presented Grandad with a narrow leather box. "Thank you so much for looking after us," the big man said, as he mounted the steps into his train.

Granddad did not open the box until he was back with Granny by the fire. They both looked speechlessly at a handsome commemoration coin, specially minted to mark the visit which celebrated the opening of the rebuilt town hall after its direct hit during the war. A signed message from the VIP was carefully folded into the box. It became one of Clem's proudest possessions, and he had hidden it, cushioned in screwed-up bits of newspaper, certain that his despised son-in-law would sell it when the time came. He had told only Susie about it.

"He was right, was Granddad," Susie had muttered to herself as she grabbed the tin out of the skip just as it began to rise. She fully expected the tin to be empty, but even so, it would remind her of Granddad's finest hour. But it was not empty. Inside, it looked like a tin full of old newspaper, but Susie had slowly emptied it and found the leather box carefully hidden away.

All this flitted through Susie's mind as she inserted a key into the back door and tentatively stepped inside. She hadn't meant to go in, but could not resist one last look in case there might be something else overlooked by Mum and Dad. She reminded herself that the house was hers now, though she still could not quite believe it. Granddad had left it to her in his will. Her parents had not even known he had bought it after years of paying rent! "Evil old sod," Dad had fumed, but Susie had said nothing.

The empty rooms smelled damp now, and there were light patches on the walls where Granny's precious pictures had hung. Susie realised how much work there was to do and knew she had to think about that. She would just check quickly upstairs and then go off to meet Douglas outside the new pizza place in the market square.

Front bedroom, fine. New paint and perhaps get rid of the old fireplace. Tiny box room. She remembered a cupboard in there, where Granny had kept linen. Better just check. She walked in and too late heard a soft step behind her.

Leaving his prey trussed up like a dangerous animal, the intruder crept away, down the narrow stairs and out through the back door, which he locked with Susie's key. He put it quickly in his pocket.

Douglas looked at his watch. Ten minutes late. It was unlike Susie, who was usually a punctual girl, arriving before time. He was getting cold, and stamped his feet. Perhaps he should go inside and find a table. It was early for the usual crowd, but at least he could wait in the warmth. But then, Susie was such a shy one she'd probably run off home without looking in the restaurant.

He looked at his watch again. Eleven minutes late. He would give her until a quarter past, and then go and meet her. He was fairly sure he knew which way she would come. It was possible she'd made a mistake and was waiting for him outside his house. She had seemed cheerful enough, but he knew a brave face concealed real grief at the death of her grandfather.

"Time's up, Susie," he said aloud, and set off in what he hoped would be the right direction.

Twenty-Six

Lois was tired. On Derek's instructions she had taken Jeems for a long walk along the riverbank, across the meadows and back through the woods. It was not a particularly nice day for a walk, but the air was refreshing and she had stepped out at a good pace. It had been a quiet time for thinking, and finally, when she had begun to feel weary, she'd leaned on a gate in time-honoured fashion and stared at the last field she had to cross before rejoining the road. Her boots were heavy with mud and Jeems's white coat would need serious attention. A couple of weeks ago, the little dog had disappeared down a rabbit hole in the woods and not reappeared until long after Lois had given up and gone home, trusting her to find her way back. The mud on her coat had dried to a hard clay, clamping her ears to her head and making a mockery of her fluffy white tail.

But this afternoon's walk had been a good idea. Lois's thoughts had cleared, and she set off again across the field. There were two people she needed to talk to urgently. The skinny recluse, obviously, but that was going to be difficult since he'd done a runner. And, as suggested by the Freemans, Susie Mills. That should be easy, and she would ring Douglas as soon as she was back home. Best to ask him first, and let him arrange to bring her over to tea. Yes, that would be it. Then she could approach the subject of poor old Clem and his neighbour naturally.

She had reached the stile into the road, and lifted up Jeems, who expected a helping hand. Just then, a car went by at speed. Lois caught only a glimpse of the driver, but had a sudden jolt. It couldn't be, could it? If not, it was his twin brother. She felt she would know that skinned rabbity man anywhere. She set off home at a smart jog.

"Don't bring that dog into my kitchen!" Gran said, on seeing the two of them arrive back in the yard. "Put the hosepipe over her. It's the only way when they get in that state! I haven't spent a good half hour on my hands and knees scrubbing this floor to have it covered with muddy dog prints!"

"Okay, okay, keep your hair on, Mother!" Lois refrained

from saying that her mother had not been on her hands and knees for years, and instead she hosed down a shivering Jeems, rubbed her vigorously with an old towel, and then asked permission to come in.

"Don't be silly, Lois," Gran answered. "For goodness' sake take those boots off and put Jeems in her basket by the Rayburn to dry her out. You'll need a cup of tea to warm you up."

Lois, who was glowing with healthy warmth, knew it was no good arguing, and said that she would love a cup and she'd take it to her office to make one or two phone calls. She was about to dial Douglas when her phone rang.

"Hello, Mum?" It was Douglas, and she laughed. "We must be telepathic," she said. "I was just going to call you. Anyway, what did you want?" She realised now that his voice sounded strained.

"You haven't heard or seen anything of Susie Mills, have you?"

"No, not today. But I've been thinking about her. Why d'you want to know?"

"We were supposed to meet, outside that new pizza place in the market square. I gave her plenty of time, then thought she might have got it wrong and was waiting outside my house. So I'm here, and she isn't."

He sounded worried and she told him that girls were notoriously bad time-keepers. She was probably still in the bath. Couldn't he ring her mobile? He'd done that, of course. "She's not answering, Mum. Do you think something has happened to her?"

"P'raps she's stood you up, Dougie," she said gently. "You're lucky if it hasn't happened before."

"Thank you!" he said impatiently, and rang off.

So, not the right time to ask him to bring her round to tea on Sunday. She wondered idly where the girl had got to. There could be a hundred different reasons why she had not turned up to meet Douglas, and she was a little surprised at his obvious concern. After all, he was not your anxious teenager on a first date. It must be more serious than she had thought. Better consult Derek when he came in.

For the moment, she had forgotten her sighting of the recluse, but now recalled her shock. She should do something about it, she knew, but who would believe her? Cowgill, that's who. He believed everything she said, bless him. She called his number.

Douglas waited for another fifteen minutes, then decided he must ring Susie at home. She had asked him always to ring her on her mobile, as her mum and dad were so nosy, her dad especially, and he was quite likely to say she had to be home by half past nine, just to be difficult.

"Hello?" It was Tony, Susie's dad, and when Douglas asked if Susie was there, he asked who wanted to know. Douglas explained as nicely as he could, but Tony began to shout.

"She should be with you! What d'you mean, she hasn't turned up? My Susie is never late. Never bin known!"

Douglas heard Tony wrangling with his wife, and then she came to the phone. "That's Douglas, is it? Well, nice to talk to you. We've heard about you from Susie. But not much! She likes to keep her private life private, if you know what I mean."

More of Tony's loud voice in the background, then his wife was back, asking questions about what time and where they were supposed to have met, and finally suggesting Douglas try the supermarket. Maybe she'd had to work late.

Now Tony had grabbed the phone, and shouted that Douglas should ring them back in half an hour, and if he hadn't found her by then, the police would be told.

Douglas rang off and sighed. Now he could see why Susie wanted to keep her private life private! He checked with the supermarket, but she had left at the usual time. Well, he might as well go back to his house and see if she turned up. He passed the footpath entrance, and turned to go down behind the terrace. He hadn't tried his back gate yet, and he might find her down there, desperately wanting to find him. He knew it was a ridiculous thought, but walked on.

Locked, of course. He remembered then leaving the key hanging on the board by his kitchen door. He looked along the path, and idly tried the latch on Clem's gate. To his surprise, it opened. He walked in, knowing there would prob-ably be nobody there, but looked around just in case Susie had wandered in. There was no sign of her, and he went up to the house and tried the door. This was locked and he looked in the window and shouted, "Susie! Susie! Are you there?"

There was no answer, and he suddenly felt chilly. Shivering, he made his way across the yard to his own house.

Susie had heard him. She had been flooded with relief when she'd realised it was Douglas's voice. She dreaded her captor returning, fearful of what he might do next. She had tried to answer him, but there was a gag across her mouth and she could hardly breathe. Then she'd tried drumming her feet on the floor, but her ankles were tied tight together. She could make no noise at all. When she heard Douglas's footsteps retreating, she wept bitterly.

Darkness fell, and slowly the room was full of shadows, lit only by a solitary lamp halfway up the footpath. Susie was cold, in pain from her bonds, and thirsty. But most of all she was scared, and knew that she must stay awake at all costs.

Twenty-Seven

Douglas set off again, trailing around Tresham, until he realised he was looking in areas where there was absolutely no reason for Susie to go. He had no idea what to do, except to go back home and ring the police. But Susie was an adult, and he knew she found life at home difficult. She could have decided, as Mum had said, to stand him up and go out with someone else, or sleep over at a girlfriend's house. She wouldn't thank him for alerting the police, he was sure of that. So long as he didn't have to talk to her father again, he reckoned it would be up to Tony to act. He was slightly ashamed at ducking out of responsibility for her, but in the end decided to go home and see what happened next.

Gordon Street was quiet, and though Douglas had even resorted to prayer on the way home, Susie was not there. He let himself in through the front door and opened a can of beer, slumping down in an armchair by the electric fire. His concentration was at nil, and not even the sports pages interested him. Eventually he got up and walked backwards and forwards across the room. On the one hand, he could not help imagining the worst, and on the other he knew that a perfectly satisfactory explanation was possible. But on the other hand . . .

He noticed the cupboard door by the fireside was ajar, and he moved to shut it. But as he did so, he heard a sound. He opened the door wide, and put his ear to the wall. Nothing. But he was sure he had heard something. What was it people did to listen through a barrier? A glass held tight against it? Galvanised into action now, he rushed into the kitchen and found a tumbler. Good God! He heard it again, and it sounded like a woman's muffled cry, very faint, so that he could hardly hear it.

His heart racing, he rushed out of his house and into Clem's yard. He put his shoulder to the door and with the strength of a young man in a panic he burst inside, shouting as he went, "Susie! Susie! Where are you?"

And then he found her, bound and gagged, sobbing and shivering. He picked her up as if she were a swaddled newborn babe and made for home.

At last Susie was free, wrapped in a rug, sitting with a mug of hot chocolate in her hands and smiling weakly at Douglas. He had been amazed at the intricate way she had been bound, and had noticed a swelling on the back of her head.

"Susie, you poor darling," he said over and over again. "What hurts most?"

Finally she rubbed the bruise, and said her head throbbed. "He hit me there." She winced and added that she supposed it had been a man. She hadn't heard or seen him coming. Her arms were bound so she could not see her watch and could only guess at the time from when it got dark.

The telephone rang, and Douglas said, "That'll be your dad. Shall I talk to him?"

Susie shook her head, and made to get up.

"Stay there!" Douglas ordered. "I'll do it."

She shook her head. "No, bring me the phone and I'll set him straight," she said.

"He was going to send for the police," Douglas warned, and added that she was very welcome to stay the night. He would make her quite safe from marauders, including himself. They stared at each other, and the telephone continued to ring. Douglas finally picked it up and brought it to her.

"Hello? Yes, Dad, it's me. And for goodness' sake, calm down." Susie held the phone away from her ear, and Douglas could hear the loud ranting clearly. She frowned, took a deep breath, and said into the phone, "Listen, Dad, I'm quite safe. Just got held up. I'm fine, and staying here with a girlfriend. Yes, in Douglas's house. That'll be three of us. Safety in numbers! I'll see you tomorrow after work. 'Bye. Love to Mum. And Dad, I'm a big girl now."

Twenty-Eight

Next morning, Douglas got up early and made breakfast. He took a tray into the small back bedroom where he had settled Susie, who was wearing a pair of his pyjamas, into a narrow single bed.

She smiled at him. "Cool! Breakfast in bed!" She was feeling much better, she assured him, and patted the bed for him to sit down. "What's the time?" she asked.

He said it was quite early, but he had to get to work, and he supposed she might want to, too. But there was something serious he had to say to her. She nodded, and he began.

"We have to tell the police, Susie. I'll come with you, and we can ask for the cop Mum knows."

She interrupted him at once. "No, Douglas! No, no, no! I'm scared enough as it is. If I tell the police, that man will know it. Them kind always know, and then he'll be after me. I can't face all of that. Please don't make me, Douglas. I'm fine now, but I might not be, next time."

Douglas sighed. "Well, I'm not sure. That man is a violent criminal, whoever he is, and we'd be breaking the law not reporting him." He hesitated. "Look," he said, "will you agree to me telling my mother? She's had loads of experience with this sort of thing, and does have contact with her inspector friend. I know she'll be sympathetic and advise us what to do. Otherwise, I think I shall have to insist." He trailed off, looking pleadingly at her.

Eventually she replied, "Couldn't we just tell her you saw a man next door to your house, going in and out? I can make a pretty good guess at the time. I'd just left work and had come down Gordon Street. Could we do that, just at first, anyway? Oh, and by the way, Granddad left me his house in his will. Did I tell you that? That's why I was there."

Douglas shook his head, amazed. She spoke as if this was an unimportant afterthought, when it could be a vital piece of information. But now he wouldn't make too much of it. At least she'd agreed that he could tell Lois some of it. First things first.

"That's a very small bed, Goldilocks," he said with a grin, leaning over and kissing the top of her head. "Next time, we'll try Father Bear's bed, shall we?"

"You're joking!" she said. "Go away, you big idiot. I'm going to finish this and then get up." She realised now that she felt completely at ease with him. Must have been the bash on the head.

Lois was having a coffee after lunch in her office when Douglas rang. "Oh, hi, Douglas. Did she turn up?" She could tell from his voice that there'd been a happy ending.

He said that Susie had, and had given him a satisfactory explanation. "They always do," Lois said philosophically.

Douglas was anxious to get Lois into serious listening mode, and said quickly, "But that's not the only reason I rang. Listen, Mum, I saw that recluse bloke yesterday. Soon after I got home. He looked very furtive and ran across Clem's yard and disappeared. I watched for quite a time, but he didn't come back again."

Lois was instantly serious. "What d'you mean, you watched for quite a time? How long? Did you go and knock at the door? You know he's wanted by the police. Have you reported it?"

Douglas said nothing for a few seconds, then muttered, "Um, no. Thought it was better to tell you."

"Douglas Meade," Lois said firmly. "You are not telling me the truth. Not the whole truth, anyway. You'd better come round this evening and make a bit more sense of it. And bring Susie, if you like."

"Yes, Mum," Douglas said, and rang off.

Lois frowned and stared at the phone. Should she ring Cowgill straightaway? Douglas's story tied in with her sighting of the man driving towards Tresham. She decided reluctantly that she wouldn't. One day wasn't going to make much difference. Oh, yes, it was, her conscience told her, but she ignored it. After all, Douglas was her son.

She looked at her watch. She had to go into Tresham to

see Hazel, and wondered if a call at Braeside might be a good idea. She hadn't yet checked to see if Mrs. Blairgowrie was happy with Dot. Maybe the old lady had seen comings and goings out of her bedroom window.

Mrs. Blairgowrie had a visitor, and it was not Lois. The old lady sat in her chair facing the window where she watched birds. Opposite her, hidden by the curtain from outside view, though there was nobody in the garden, sat the skinny man. His face was pale and haggard, and he looked thinner than ever. "Oh, God," he said, "what am I going to do?"

The old lady's reaction was strange. She laughed. "We'll think of something," she said. "But what were you doing in the old man's house anyway? And why on earth did you wallop the girl, you fool? You could have hidden until she'd gone, couldn't you? Or gone back next door—you still have a key, don't you? Mind you, if I were you I'd be a hundred miles away by now."

"I had a job to do. One of them little books packages, as Al calls them, had been delivered that morning. I couldn't leave it in my house. Police would be in there as soon as they discovered I'd done a moonlight flit. I couldn't take it there and then, because the woman was yelling and screaming and I had to get her out of the way. So after that, and when I'd arranged Clem's resting place, I fetched the pack and hid it inside the box room in the old man's house. Reckoned nobody would turn out his things for a week or two. I meant to come back for it as soon as I'd sorted the black woman."

"Not sorted her like you sorted Clem, I hope!"

"No, no. She's safe with Al. But she'd been trouble and it was getting light, too late for me to go back for the package. Clem could have been found by then. And anyway, I reckoned I'd have a chance to get it before his family emptied his house."

"Sounds a very stupid plan. You've excelled yourself!"

"After that I couldn't screw up courage to go back. Cops around like flies. All of that. You know I get these panic attacks... Then Clem's daughter cleared his house much sooner than I expected. I was desperate. Thought they'd be sure to have found the package. I was terrified what Al would say, and knew I had to go back and check."

"And had they found it?"

"No. Blimey, what a relief! Still there where I'd put it, in a space behind a drawer. I was just reaching for it when I heard the girl. I shut the drawer with the pack still hidden. I was trapped then, so I made myself scarce as I heard her coming upstairs. She was opening every door in the house. What I did was impulse, Babs. She went into the box room, and I panicked. Put her out of action, not thinking what would happen to her. I took the package and spent the night sleeping rough. Well, not sleeping, just trying to think what to do next. I reckon it's all up with me."

"Don't be ridiculous. Did she see you when you hit her?"

"No, I'm sure she didn't. Went down an' out at once."

"Then how would she know it was you? You got nothing to worry about, as far as I can see. Which is not very far, of course." She laughed again, and added, "Where are you going now?"

"Well, I don't fancy another night with the down-an'-outs. I thought I might lie up with you for a few days until Al tells us what's happening. He needs what I've got for him, so he'll be around."

In the Sebastopol office, Hazel greeted Lois with a big smile. "That Andrew's been in again," she said. "Asked anxiously if you'd made up your mind yet. Said he'd been thinking over your suggestion and still thought it was a great idea."

"Did he mention money?" Lois said sharply.

Hazel nodded. "Yep," she said. "Said he'd been counting his pennies and had a good bit to put into the business if a watertight arrangement could be made."

"Get him on the phone, could you? I'll speak to him now. No point in delaying. I mentioned it to Derek."

"What did he say?"

"What he always says," Lois said, smiling.

"'You make the decisions, me duck,'" said Hazel, in a very good imitation of Derek Meade. She looked up Andrew Young's number and dialled. "Hello, Andrew? I have Mrs. Meade for you." She got up and signalled Lois to come and sit at the desk. "Boss talk," she said, and disappeared to put on the kettle for coffee.

After she had arranged for a time when Andrew, Josie, and she could get together, Lois told him to turn up at next

Monday's team meeting, when he could meet the rest of the staff. "In the meantime," she said, "I need references. Do that pronto, can you? Sooner we get going, the better."

"Decisive, very," said Hazel, when Lois put down the phone. "What did he say about refs?"

"Said he had them all ready and waiting. Looks like we might be in luck there, Hazel. Now, I must get going. I shall call on Mrs. Blairgowrie on my way. Have you had any feedback from Dot?"

Hazel shook her head. "Nope. But then, you know our Dot. A law unto herself, unless she gets herself into a pickle. I expect she's been all right. She's good with old ladies."

Lois said she was sure she would find out. For a blind lady, Mrs. Blairgowrie seemed very observant.

When she had gone, Hazel thought about that last remark. It was the way Mrs. M said it, with just a touch of acid in her voice.

Twenty-Nine

"Sod it! Who's that, Babs?" The skinny man heard the knock at the door and shot to his feet, looking around wildly for a hiding place.

"Don't panic! And don't call me Babs. Just go quietly out of the back door and you'll see an old washhouse on the right. Go in there and hide behind the pile of rubbish. I'll call you when it's safe."

He vanished, moving quietly as always. There's nothing to him, thought Mrs. Blairgowrie as she put on her dark glasses and took up her stick. She knew what her son would say. A puff of wind would blow him away. But he wouldn't mean a puff of wind.

She looked through the spy hole on the front door, and saw Mrs. Meade. She liked this woman, and opened the door.

"Hello, Mrs. Blairgowrie, how are you? It's Mrs. Meade. I'm just making a routine call to see how you are getting on with Dot Nimmo." Lois noticed for the first time that the old lady's fingers were nicotine stained. Not exactly lavender and old lace.

"Come in, my dear, come in. I'm glad to have company. I've been alone all day, so it's nice to see you."

They sat down, and Lois offered to make Mrs. Blairgowrie a cup of coffee, but she declined, saying it was not long since she'd lunched. She answered Lois's questions positively, said she was more than satisfied with Dot, who certainly brightened up the house while she was here. "Once you get used to her, Mrs. Meade, she's a ray of sunshine in this gloomy old house."

Lois remembered Dot's report about the man who'd come in and shouted at the old thing. And before that, a similar account from Bill. No wonder the poor woman was pleased to have a ray of sunshine in her life. A gloomy life, of necessity. She looked out of the window at the sunlit garden. "A pity you can't see the birds," she said. "It's obviously the best birds' caff in town! Do you manage to fill up the feeders by yourself?"

Mrs. Blairgowrie assured her that she could do most things by touching and feeling with her stick. "So long as nobody moves anything without my knowing," she said, "I manage very well."

Lois made a mental note to remind Dot to replace everything exactly where she found it, and took her leave. As she got into her car, she glanced across at the terrace. Nothing moved. She noticed a vase of flowers on Douglas's windowsill, and knew that it was the last thing he would think of. A woman's touch, as sure as eggs is eggs. She remembered that he and possibly Susie were coming over to Farnden later on, and sighed. How was she going to put it to Cowgill? She would certainly have to tell him anything important, whatever the young ones said.

And another thing. She had noticed two dirty mugs on a side table in Mrs. Blairgowrie's sitting room. So she had had recent company. Cowgill would no doubt be interested in that, too.

The disagreement between Susie and Douglas on the way over to Long Farnden had turned into a full-scale row by the time they stopped outside the Meades' house. Lois saw them from the window, and walked quickly to the door. She was glad Susie had come, too, even though they looked grim. She watched them get out of the car and come up the drive, Susie lagging behind.

"Hi, you two. Come along in. Go in the sitting room, Douglas, and I'll get Gran to make us some coffee." She offered food, but they said they had eaten. Then she remembered that Gran had gone to see Mrs. Pickering, cleaner Floss's mother. The two had become good friends, and now that the Pickerings were moving house, Gran spent a good deal of time there helping with sorting and packing.

Lois left the doors open while she made coffee, and could hear no sounds of friendly chatting. She guessed what had caused the argument. There was something they had not told her, and they disagreed about whether they should now. She put some biscuits and mugs on a tray and went back to join them.

"So how are you now, Susie?" she said, and they both looked alarmed. Lois was puzzled. What had she said? She knew that the girl had been very upset at the death of her grandfather. "It must have been such a shock for you," she continued.

"How did you know, Mum?" Douglas said, frowning at Susie.

"Well, of course I knew! What are you talking about? Poor old Clem. Naturally Susie was upset."

Their faces cleared, but it was too late. Lois pounced. "So you'd better tell me what else has happened to Susie, hadn't you? No good keeping things to yourself. There's been a serious crime, and it has to be sorted out. Clem was murdered, don't forget."

This was too much for Susie, and she burst into racking sobs. Words came tumbling out, and Lois had difficulty following. Something to do with being bashed on the head, tied up, and very frightened, and Douglas coming along just in time. Douglas had his arm around her and Lois silently handed her a box of tissues.

"Take your time, Susie," Douglas said. "Mum's a very good listener. She'll tell us what to do."

Touched as she was by this demonstration of confidence from her son, Lois was very worried. It was important that she should get this story straight, and complete. She settled back in her chair and smiled at them both. "Well, I'm glad to see you two have made it up, whatever it was," she said. "Now, when you're ready, let's begin at the beginning. Seems

Douglas came into the story late, so why don't you start, Susie? Nobody'll interrupt us. Gran's down at Pickering's and Derek's gone to the pub. It's about when you went missing, isn't it? Let's start there."

Douglas now took Susie's shaking hands in his, and she made a stuttering start. Gradually they both relaxed, and the whole sorry tale emerged, including the reason why Susie had been scared to explain what happened.

"Don't worry, me duck," Lois said. "I'll have a chat with my friend Cowgill. I'm afraid I must do that. But he's a good old cop, though I don't tell him so, and he'll be very discreet. They're used to all of that, anyway. Nobody'd ever report anything unless they trusted the police." She crossed her fingers behind her back. There were times when she wouldn't trust a policeman as far as her front door. "But you have to admit the bloke who trussed you up was more than likely the skinny man who did a bunk," she continued. "God knows why he came back, or what he was doing in Clem's house. The sooner the police find him, the better. Looks like he's into something seriously dodgy, and not on his own, that's for sure."

Douglas nodded. "Then are we going to give Mum the okay to do what's best?" he asked Susie.

She thought for a moment, then said, "Yep, I suppose so. But I'm scared, Mrs. Meade."

"It won't matter whether I tell Cowgill or not; your attacker could still come after you when he realises you got away. He was probably coming back for you later. He wouldn't want another dead body on his hands."

"D'you think it was him killed Clem, then?" Douglas asked.

Lois said she thought they had probably speculated enough now, and they should talk about something else. She asked Susie if her family was putting Clem's house on the market, and was impressed when she was told he'd left it to his granddaughter. She knew exactly what Gran would say, and smiled. Wonderful, she would enthuse, her eyes sparkling, so they can knock through when they get married and have a good-sized house!

"What's funny, Mum?"

"Nothing really," Lois said, thinking rapidly. "I just love the idea of Douglas carrying you away on his white charger. That's my boy, Douglas," she added. She could see from his face that he didn't believe her, but Susie smiled.

"He's my brave knight, Mrs. Meade," she said, and gave him a peck on the cheek.

"Who's had a brave night?" Derek said, coming into the room. "Bin to a horror movie, you two?"

Lois decided that it would be impossible to explain, and asked about the darts match. On hearing of the local triumph, she suggested they all have a beer to celebrate.

Thirty

Monday at noon, and the New Brooms team were gathering in Lois's office in Farnden for the weekly meeting. So far, Sheila, Bridie, Floss, and Dot Nimmo had arrived, also Andrew Young, the new recruit. They were waiting for Hazel, who would be coming from Tresham, having shut the Sebastopol office for a couple of hours. Evelyn Nimmo, Dot's sister, who had covered for her when she had been in hospital, was also there. She was supposed to have finished when Dot returned, but had now asked if she could help out on a part-time basis. She missed the interest of meeting new people and being part of a team, she said. She, like Dot, was a widow. The sisters had married two Nimmo brothers and had remained close, treading the rocky paths of Tresham's underworld together. Life had been full of action and anxiety, and Lois never knew when they would trip up.

"Sorry I'm late, Mrs. M," Hazel puffed, as she came into the office. "Traffic snarl as usual. Hi, everybody. Hi, Andrew."

Lois assured her she hadn't missed anything. "You know Andrew already, so we can make a start. Nice to see Evelyn back, by the way. She can't keep away, you see."

They all laughed, and in a pleasant atmosphere the meeting got going. After the routine of schedules and assigning cleaners to new clients, Lois said she had something to say. "As most of you know, our Douglas has moved into the Gordon Street house, and the one next door to him has become vacant."

"Where that old man was murdered?" Floss said.

"Mr. Fitch, yes," said Lois. "It now belongs to his grand-daughter Susie. She'll want to rent it out, but she's young and hasn't had experience in being a landlady. The thing is, the whole house needs a thorough cleanup and redecoration. Now this is where Andrew comes in. He's an expert on interior décor—right, Andrew?—and so I've offered New Brooms' complete services. Advice on decorating an' that, and the work involved, an' then the rest of us can do a major cleanup session, and maybe a regular cleaning check once all the work is done. I've put together a package, and I reckon it'll be accepted. Does that sound all right to the rest of you? What's that you said, Hazel?" She had seen Hazel whisper something to Floss.

Hazel flushed. "Sorry, Mrs. M. Just remarking how you'd got all the jargon. A regular high-flyer, our boss."

"Quick thinking, Hazel," Lois said, and frowned. "Right, then," she said. "Andrew, would you stay behind for a few minutes, and the rest can go and get on with what really matters. Item number one: customer satisfaction. 'Bye, girls. Stay in touch."

"Did you hear what Hazel actually said?" Lois asked Andrew when they were alone. He shook his head. Lois smiled, and revealed that Hazel had said, not quietly enough, "Douglas fancies the girl, so it'll be a doddle."

"Ah," said Andrew, realising in time that this was an important test of his suitability. "Then she's obviously forgotten item number two on your list. We don't gossip?"

"Good lad," said Lois. "You'll do."

Cowgill had decided it was time for him and Lois to meet. Telephone conversations were too vulnerable. Lois had a habit of cutting off the call just when it was vital to keep going. Vital from whose point of view? he asked himself. If he was honest, the vital bit was hearing the sound of Lois's voice. Listening to her sharp retorts and critical remarks was the food of love to him. Let other people swoon at Mozart and Beethoven, he could live on a high for a couple of days after hearing Lois tell him he was a silly old fool.

"I am also an important policeman," he said aloud, and his assistant, coming in with a pile of papers, raised her eyebrows. "Of course you are, sir," she said. She was new, and extremely respectful. He cleared his throat and looked around to the corners of the room, as if surprised that the person he had been addressing had gone. After he'd dealt with the papers, he called Lois.

"Hello. I'm just going out," she said.

"What's on your agenda today?" he replied conversationally.

"Usual—hard work and looking after my family," she answered sharply. "What d'you want? I told you the latest earlier on."

"I have been thinking that we should meet and discuss the whole picture on the Gordon Street case. As usual, my dear, you have given us some very useful information, and I would really like to use your agile mind to attempt some evaluation of what we know so far. Time to see it as a cohesive whole."

"Come again?" said Lois. He'd done it this time. "Swallowed a dictionary, have you?"

"Lois Meade," he said, his voice warm, "you know perfectly well what I mean."

"You mean you want to see me, waste my time, and dredge out anything else I might know. Right?"

"Wrong," said Cowgill. "Now, Lois, this is the policeman talking. Not the silly old fool. We do have a lot of pieces of information which need putting together. You are the common denominator... sorry, you have a finger in every pie in this case. You knew Clem, your son lives next door, he's fallen for Clem's granddaughter, you and Douglas have both seen the skinny man, as you call him. Susie might very well have been tied up and abandoned by him. There's more. Your Dot Nimmo cleans in Braeside opposite, which certainly has some connection with all this. Josie has spoken to Mrs. Blairgowrie's son, et cetera et cetera. Enough?"

There was a pause, and then Lois said, "I suppose it might be useful to chew it over. When and where? I'm sick of pleading a bladder weakness so's I can go to the supermarket loo and meet you in the staff room. They'll think I'm a right old slapper, with infections to match."

"Don't be ridiculous, Lois! Still," he said hastily, "I see your point. You won't come down to the station?"

"Of course not. Even you must see that it's dangerous. There's enough villains know already that I'm hand in glove with the cops. Leastways, they think I am."

"I've just had an idea," Cowgill said.

"Must be a lovely new experience for you," Lois said. She

heard him chuckle, and smiled herself. She wondered if he was one of them that liked a bit of rough and tumble.

"Concentrate, Lois," he answered. "You know my nephew Matthew. Well, he's hoping to join us here in Tresham on a permanent basis shortly. He likes the countryside round here, he says, and has just bought himself a bachelor pad. More of a crumbling cottage, actually, and he intends to do it up himself. At the moment, it's empty and remote enough. Nobody will witness a plainclothes cop and a lovely girl going there."

"You mean Matthew and his girlfriend," Lois said, deliberately obtuse.

"No, no. You and me, Lois. Would that do?"

"Sounds all right. Where is it?"

"Between Waltonby and Fletching. Stands back from the road, and the drive is all potholes. Sorry about that. It's got a huge muck heap beside it, so you can't mistake it. You can smell it from miles away."

"Better than the Ritz, then. Can't wait, Hunter. When?"

He said the sooner the better, and they arranged to meet next morning. "I'll bring a flask of coffee," Lois said. "Then we can have a lovely picnic by the muck heap. 'Bye."

Thirty-One

"It's tipping it down," Gran said, looking out of the kitchen window. "You're surely not going out in this, Lois?"

Lois smiled at her mother. Mothers never stop being mothers. She still heard herself telling Josie to wrap up warm in cold weather. And Douglas had frowned furiously at her the other night when she told him in front of Susie that he needed a haircut.

"I've got a new anorak, an umbrella, and a watertight van, Mum. I think I'll be okay." She looked at the kitchen clock. Time to go and meet Cowgill. She was not looking forward to the muddy track with potholes, but supposed she should give it a try.

He was waiting for her. "Put your van under that lean-to behind the cottage," he said. "Pity it's white," he added. "Very visible."

"I'll get it resprayed," Lois said between gritted teeth. She parked it and got out, stepping straight into a deep puddle. "Bloody hell!" she said.

"Good job you're sensibly wearing wellies," Cowgill said blandly. "Come on in. I've opened up."

Wallpaper hung off the walls in strips, and there were wide gaps between the floorboards. A startled mouse scooted off as their creaking footsteps approached. Cowgill had brought two folding chairs with slatted seats, and indicated one to Lois.

"Not exactly your latest design in chairs," she said, sitting down with a sigh. "Next time, if there is a next time, I'll bring cushions." She delved in her bag and brought out a thermos of coffee. "No sugar," she said, handing him a steaming mug. "It's bad for you. Especially bad for elderly people. By the way," she added, "when are you retiring? Can't be that far away. Is young Matthew hoping to step into your shoes?"

"I'm supposed to ask the questions," he said coolly. "Now, Lois, I've jotted down what we know in chronological order, as far as I know it. Shall I read it out to you?"

"If you want," Lois replied. "Though you may be surprised to learn I can read and write."

"Please, Lois," he said. "Could we just get on? Now, first, Clem Fitch and his cockerel."

She was forced to admit to herself that he was very efficient. He took her through all that had happened since she'd first bought her Gordon Street house, and as they went along she could see a connecting thread emerging. Skinny Man's house was at the centre of a web. Everything that had happened could be linked to it. Even the supermarket thefts seemed to tie in with Clem's sightings of Skinny Man dumping dozens of empty juice packets, and Lois seeing him loading up his trolley with gluten-free bread.

There was a silence between them, and Cowgill said, "Go on, then, Lois, say something."

She shifted her position on the uncomfortable chair, and said, "Right. Now then, what we want to know is, first, where and who is Skinny Man, and why does he need so much food? Not difficult, that one. Every so often, he has mouths to feed. Expensive mouths to feed. That theft was a big mistake, I reckon. Leads right back to him, don't it? So get him first.

Second, where and who is Mrs. Blairgowrie's son? And is he? Her son, I mean. Third, what are they up to? And fourth, fifth, and sixth, is the ladylike Mrs. Blairgowrie blind, or what?"

"You think she isn't? What makes you think she isn't?"

Lois told him exactly what she thought, and said that Dot Nimmo had noticed odd things as well. "Quite difficult to keep up pretending you're blind with your eyes open," Lois said. "I tried it for half an hour in the house. Research, Hunter. Not as green as I'm cabbage-looking, see. Gran was in on it, and said I was useless. Anybody would know in two minutes, she said."

They went on discussing various points, until Lois looked out of the window and said that the rain had stopped. She had some shopping to do in Tresham, and must go. This was a lie, as Cowgill knew perfectly well. He would have put money on Lois going straight to Gordon Street to snoop around. She had the perfect excuse now that Douglas was living there. But he got to his feet and thanked her for coming and for the coffee. He folded the chairs and carried them out to his car, then locked up the house.

"You go first," he said. "I'll follow after a while. I can sit and think. Very useful session, Lois. Thanks. Take care," he added, and really meant it.

Lois looked down at her van, now half-covered in dirty splashes. "Can I claim car-wash expenses?" she said, and was off down the track, spraying mud in every direction, before he could reply.

Cowgill would have won his bet. Lois drove into Gordon Street and parked outside Douglas's house. She had noticed with surprise that Josie's car was also outside, and wondered what was up. Josie almost never left the shop unless Rob was there to take over, and Lois was sure she saw him on his way to work this morning. Gran had been fine, but lately Josie had noticed that her arithmetic was not so good. Sometimes the cash did not balance at the end of the day. She did not say anything to Gran, for fear of hurting her feelings, but no longer left her in charge for any length of time.

Josie answered the door, and laughed. "Come in, Mum," she said, "and don't look so alarmed. Douglas gave me keys. He's not here. I shouldn't be here either," she continued, "but Susie called me and said she'd not been able to get hold of

Douglas. She sounded scared and upset, so I said I'd nip over and see if I could find him. I had to go to the wholesalers anyway, so I've left Gran in charge for once. I'm going back now."

She glanced out of the window and froze. "Hey, look," she said. "See that man getting out of a car opposite? That's the one I told you about. Him that came into the shop that day and chatted me up. Slimy character, I thought. Look, now he's going up to that house."

Lois caught sight of a big man with dark hair and a well-cut suit disappearing into Braeside. "Ah," she said. "That's her son, I think. You know Dot is working there now? She reported that a big man had been shouting at the blind lady, and had upset her. None of our business, of course, but Dot was worried."

"Ah, well, all sons are not as nice as our Douglas—hey, Mum! Where are you going?"

Lois was out of the front door and crossing the road in seconds. She knocked at the Braeside door and waited. There was no reply, so she knocked again. After a few seconds, the door opened a fraction and Mrs. Blairgowrie looked out, her face pale and anxious. "Who is it?" she said.

"Mrs. Meade," Lois said firmly. "Dot Nimmo has reported that she left behind her watch. Took it off to do some scrubbing in your bathroom, she said. I wonder if you'd let me have a look? I shan't take a couple of minutes. Thanks." Lois pushed the door quite hard to open it, and Mrs. Blairgowrie moved back, muttering that she supposed it would be all right.

All doors into the ground-floor rooms were closed, and Lois went quickly up to the bathroom and looked out into the garden. She thought it was empty, until a movement directly under the window caught her eye. A small line of outbuildings led from the back door, and she saw the same rear view of the man she had seen a couple of minutes ago. This time he went into an outhouse and shut the door carefully behind him. Why on earth should he do that? She slipped off her own watch and went downstairs.

"Found it," she said with a smile, showing her watch to Mrs. Blairgowrie, who was still standing in the hall. "By the way, I thought I saw someone in your garden. Is there a back way? Perhaps you should keep it locked."

Mrs. Blairgowrie shook her head, but Lois was already at the sitting-room door. She opened it and went in. Mrs. Blairgowrie followed. "I think you must be mistaken," she said. "There is no back entrance. Makes it safer against burglars, fortunately. We've even got broken glass on the top of the wall. I didn't put it there, of course. I couldn't bear it if children came over to get a ball or something, and hurt themselves. No, it was there when we came, and I haven't yet had it taken away. You may have seen my son, Alastair. He's around somewhere, and probably went to use the outside loo. I'll be fine now, thank you."

Lois took a deep breath, remembering in a flash Susie's tale of being bound hand and foot. Still, Josie knew where she was, and would raise the alarm. "I'd like to meet him," she said, and sat down in an armchair. Mrs. Blairgowrie remained standing, and Lois thought maybe she had been impolite, so stood up again. They had a short, halting conversation and then the door opened.

"Have you got rid of—" He stopped, glaring at Mrs. Blairgowrie. Then his expression changed to a polite smile, and he extended his hand. "Mrs. Meade, isn't it? Pleased to meet you. Your cleaner's been doing a great job, hasn't she, Mother?"

How does he know who I am? thought Lois. Aloud, she said, "Clever of you to recognise me."

A flash of irritation crossed his face, and was gone. "Mother keeps me up to date on local news," he said, and looked at the old lady, who frowned meaningfully at him.

"She's pretty good, considering how little she can see, don't you think?" he added hastily. "But the neighbours are kind, and tell her what's going on."

"Like the murder of Mr. Fitch," Lois said calmly. "That was horrible, wasn't it? Are they anywhere near catching the man who did it? You must be worried about your mother living here alone."

Mrs. Blairgowrie answered for him. "I'm fine," she said. "So many locks and bolts at night that no one could get in. Alastair has made sure of that."

He shrugged, ignoring her. "I really have no idea about the investigation, Mrs. Meade," he said. "As you know, I live quite a long way from Tresham. But I am sure the police are following up a number of lines. We can trust them to do a good job, don't you agree?"

Mrs. Blairgowrie was overcome by a sudden fit of coughing, and excused herself to fetch a glass of water. Alastair moved nearer to Lois, and she stiffened. But he merely leaned close to her and hissed, "Do not alarm my mother, Mrs. Meade. And if you take my advice, you will leave everything to the police. Very unsafe to do otherwise. This could be a very dangerous operation."

Lois did not flinch. "Operation?" she said. "What operation?"

Mrs. Blairgowrie came back into the room, no longer choking, and said, "We mustn't keep you, Mrs. Meade, and Alastair and I have business to discuss."

"I'll see you out," Alastair said, leading the way. As they reached the front door, he repeated in a whisper, "Very unsafe. Don't meddle, Mrs. Meade."

Thirty-Two

"What was all that about?" Josie said.

Lois sat down heavily in one of Douglas's new chairs. "Make us a coffee, Josie, there's a good girl," she said.

Josie realised that her mother was shaking with anger, and went swiftly into the kitchen.

"I'm perfectly okay," Lois called after her. "Just livid. That gross character actually threatened me! Told me to mind my own business, more or less."

Josie answered her gently. "Why did you scoot across there, Mum?" she said.

"To check on whether Mrs. Blairgowrie was satisfied with Dot, of course. And to meet her son. He shouts at her, Dot said."

"Well, that's none of your business, is it," Josie said. "New Brooms just cleans. It's not a branch of Social Services."

Douglas had appeared, and heard Josie's last remark. "Nor the Secret Service, Mum," he said, and added, "What is all this? Why are you two here anyway?"

Josie explained about Susie's anxiety, and Lois was glad to

change the subject. "At least you weren't gagged and bound in the attic, Douglas," she said. "Better give the girl a call."

After Lois had left, saying she had another client to see on her way home, Josie stayed on with Douglas for a while. "Mum was really shaking," she said. "D'you think she's getting into something dangerous? Old Clem was murdered by somebody very nasty indeed, and whoever it was, he won't stop at anything to throw the police off the scent. Should we warn Dad?"

Douglas thought for a few minutes. "We can do," he answered, "or we could help. See if we can uncover something new to get the whole thing sorted out quickly. You know what Mum's like. She takes no notice of warnings, even from Dad."

"What? You mean join the New Brooms Detective Agency? No, thanks, not me. I've got a business to run. And you ought to stay clear, too. New job, new house, new girlfriend. You don't want to muck it all up, do you?"

Douglas shook his head slowly. "But she is our mum," he said.

Josie sighed. "Oh, all right," she said. "But what can we do?"

"You're well placed to listen and ask innocent questions in the shop," Douglas said. "And I can ferret around up and down the street. Somebody must know something. What did Mum say about the Braeside lot?"

"Nothing much. Just that the old lady's son had threatened her to keep her nose out of their business. And something to do with Dot Nimmo. She's cleaning over there now."

"Right," said Douglas. "Let's give it a week, and then meet up and report. Now," he added with a sudden pang of conscience, "I'll ring Susie. Poor kid's nervous since that awful business with Clem."

He had a somewhat soppy conversation with Susie, and then brother and sister left the house together.

It was midafternoon when Lois parked her van and went thankfully into Gran's warm kitchen.

"WI tonight," was Gran's greeting. "Why don't you come? Do you good to get out a bit. It's an interesting speaker, a woman from Tresham Museum, talking about what they've got there, and maybe arranging a visit."

Lois frowned. Would Gran never give up her campaign on behalf of Women's Institute recruitment? "I didn't know there was a museum in Tresham," she said.

"Nor did I," said Gran, "and I lived there for forty years. Should be good, anyway. Why don't you come, just for once, just to please me."

Lois was too weary to argue, and to Gran's surprise and delight said she would think about it. When Derek came home, he added weight to Gran's suggestion. "Take your mind off things," he said encouragingly.

"What things?" Lois answered grumpily.

"Oh, just things," Derek said airily. "Let's have tea, Gran," he added. "Chocolate cake, if my eyes don't deceive me. Cheer up, gel," he added to Lois, "and give us a kiss."

Lois kept her mother in suspense until seven o'clock, and then said, "I'll come, Mum. Just this once. Funny to think there's a museum in Tresham and none of us knew of it."

"Tell the woman I got some old farming bits and pieces if she's interested," Derek said, seeing them off at the door. "Enjoy yerself, me duck," he added, and Lois scowled at him.

WI members were bustling about the village hall when they walked in. Several of the women stopped setting out chairs and welcomed Lois. "Nice to see you, dear," they said. Lois nodded and managed a smile. "Can I help?" she said, and endeared herself to them for life by offering to carry a heavy trestle table from the shed outside into the hall.

The speaker was a chubby woman in her sixties, pleasant-faced with a ready smile and a friendly voice. She arrived carrying a large cardboard box and carefully unwrapped several strange-looking articles and placed them on the trestle table.

A loud voice from the row of members commented, "My mother had one of those! I remember it very well."

"Trust old Ivy Beasley to one-up the speaker," Gran whispered to Lois. Lois had had some dealings in the past with Miss Beasley from Round Ringford, and turned to look at her. Same old hatchet face, iron-grey hair, and accusing expression. "Evening, Miss Beasley," she mouthed across the others.

"Pity they don't put her in the museum," muttered Mrs. Pickering, Floss's mother, sitting the other side of Lois.

"My name is Audrey Lambert," the speaker began, and in no time the audience was hooked. She described the setting up of the museum a number of years ago, when an old farm-house—Brightwell Farm—was bequeathed for the purpose by a rich and lately deceased farmer. Like most small market towns, Tresham had grown into a widespread urban commu-nity, and this philanthropic ex-farmer and county worthy had felt strongly that the old town and its way of life should be remembered. He had endowed the project with a suitably large sum of money, and in the years since it began, a unique collec-tion of old domestic and agricultural artefacts from all aspects of life had been established. Mrs. Lambert had set out a row of heavy pottery spiral moulds for jelly and blancmange, a board with bells to summon the servants, and an enamel meas-uring jug belonging to a milkman who called with his horse and cart laden with churns of fresh milk.

"I've still got one of those jugs," Ivy Beasley said chal-lengingly.

Mrs. Lambert was used to the likes of Ivy. "How lovely," she said. "Perhaps you would like to donate it to the museum?" Ivy's mouth shut like a rat trap.

The time went quickly, and members were still asking ques-tions when two committee ladies came in with tea and cakes. Mrs. Pickering popped up and said she was sure Mrs. Lambert would be exhausted very soon, and perhaps it was time to thank her very much for such an interesting evening. Enthusiastic applause greeted this, and she was led to a rickety card table to share tea and homemade cakes with the presi-dent and secretary.

Gran and Lois sat with Mrs. Pickering and chatted about village matters. Then Lois said, "Have you got a buyer for your house, Mrs. Pickering?" Floss had told her that several people were interested.

"Look's like we've had a reliable offer," Mrs. Pickering answered. "So many of these people are just curious, or else they've got houses to sell and are in a chain stretching back miles. But this man seems to have ready cash. No house or flat to sell, he says. Man on his own, apparently."

"What's his name?" Lois asked.

"Smith, believe it or not!" Mrs. Pickering laughed, and then people began to clear plates and cups and the speaker was seen off with another round of applause. Gran said they needn't stay to help wash up. "Mostly the committee do that," she said, judging correctly that Lois was keen to get home.

Thirty-Three

Mrs. Blairgowrie set the breakfast table for two, and went into the hall. "Get up now, if you want any breakfast," she yelled. She saw the post flop through the letter box and onto the doormat in the hall. Modifying her voice, she called, "Thank you, dear," to the plump, red-haired postlady, who always knocked lightly on the door to tell Mrs. Blairgowrie her post had arrived.

"Oh, my, a vision of loveliness," she said, turning back to the stairs where a slender woman was descending. She wore sensible shoes, a calf-length grey skirt, and a pale cream jersey, topped off with a single string of pearls. Her hair was neatly crimped into queenly waves.

"Those are real pearls," Mrs. Blairgowrie added, "so just be very careful with them. And I want them back. They were my mother's."

The thin woman nodded. "It's very kind of you to lend them to me," she said, in a high, genteel voice. "How do I look, Babs? Good enough to join the club?"

"Like every other respectable old dame in the supermarket queue," answered Mrs. Blairgowrie. "Come and eat your porridge, Pat. Best that Scotland can produce, though I says it as shouldn't."

"Scottish!" laughed Pat. "That's a joke, for a start." But she ate the porridge hungrily.

"So where are you going next?" Mrs. Blairgowrie slid bacon and egg onto a plate and put it in front of Pat. "You can't stay here, obviously," she said.

"Thanks for nothing," the woman replied. "But don't bother your little head, Babs. I've thought of the perfect place for someone wishing to be inconspicuous."

"Where?"

"You're the last person I'd tell," Pat said. "I know very well that dear Mummy can't keep anything secret from her darling son. So no, I'm not telling you. Maybe you'll find out someday, when you need a place yourself."

Pat got up and walked over to the bookshelves behind Mrs. Blairgowrie's chair. "Ah, I see you've still got one of mine," she said. "Hang on to it. It'll be worth a few bob one day," she added, and disappeared upstairs.

"They're exchanging contracts in two weeks," Floss said to Miss Ivy Beasley. The young girl and the old dragon got on surprisingly well. Lois had not been too sure that Floss would have the strength to stand up to Ivy, and quite expected her to come back in tears after her first session of cleaning for Miss Beasley. But Floss had a soft heart and a clever head, and summed up her crabby old client in no time.

"She's not been used to depending on people," she had reported to Lois. People in Ringford had told Floss that Ivy was more or less boss of the village in the old days. She had looked after her mother until she died, and then carried on living in the same house, keeping it chilly and immaculate and planting her vegetable garden in disciplined rows in the spring. "Must be hard for her to accept help now," Floss said. "I treat her with great respect, and make her feel important. Seems to work. I like going there."

Lois breathed a sigh of relief. Not many people would willingly put themselves at Ivy Beasley's mercy. She had only two real friends: Ellen Biggs at the Lodge, and Doris Ashbourne in the old folks' bungalows in Macmillan Gardens. With typical ironic wit, villagers knew them as "the Three Graces," and all of them were getting on in years.

Now Floss had made the usual cup of tea for Ivy and, under instruction, perched on the edge of a kitchen chair, stroking Ivy's cat and munching a biscuit. "Let's hope it all goes through," she added.

Miss Beasley had been very interested in the sale of the house. Years ago, she told Floss, the house had belonged to a rich aunt of hers. "A widow woman," she said acidly. "And then this gold-digging man came along," she continued, "and the silly woman went off with him. Married him, what's more. She didn't last long, needless to say, and he got all her money."

"I expect he married again," Floss said. "They usually move on to the next lonely rich widow."

Ivy was silent for a minute, sipping her hot tea. Then she said in an unusually quiet voice, "It happened to me once. But I had more sense," she added sadly. "I discovered what he was up to just in time." This was not strictly true, as Ivy had been left at the altar by her unscrupulous lodger. She had weathered the blow, of course, and reverted to the old sour Ivy in due course. Now she looked at Floss, who smiled back sympathetically, but knew better than to quiz Ivy.

After a deep sigh, Ivy was back to normal. "Who's buying it, then?" she asked. "That couple you told me about?"

"No," answered Floss, "they backed out. It's a man on his own. Mr. John Smith, he says his name is. He's got cash, and wants to move in as soon as poss."

"John Smith? Sounds suspicious to me," said Ivy. "Better tell your parents to get everything signed and sealed before they hand over."

Floss assured her the solicitor would take care of everything. "And Dad's no fool," she added. "Not many people get past him."

After she had left, Ivy sat motionless in her chair. The cat mewed for milk, but she ignored it. "John Smith," she muttered to herself. It was almost too corny not to be true, but she had a dim memory of somebody else who had called himself that, and had turned out to be rotten through and through. Maybe if she had a little bit of shut-eye, it would come back to her.

Long Farnden was agog, as was usual when a newcomer was due to appear. Josie was fed up with endless questions as to who was coming to the Pickerings' house, and were they likely to be an asset to the village, or like that stuck-up lot in the Dower House?

"It's a man on his own, a Mr. Smith. And that's all I know," she said, parrotlike, and making it clear she didn't want to discuss it further with the brassy-looking woman in front of her. Daisy was a relative newcomer herself, and a hopeless gossip.

"Oh, come on, dear," she said. "You hear all the dirt. You know you can tell me in confidence. I'd never breathe a word."

Josie shook her head firmly. "I really don't know anything more," she said, and then remembered her promise to Douglas. "But I expect you do," she added and managed a smile.

"Ah, well now," Daisy said, folding her arms comfortably. "I did catch a glimpse of him, and knew at once I'd seen him before. If I'm not mistaken, he used to work at the Job Centre in town. Manager, he was, but left. Under a cloud, I heard. Mind you, I could've got the wrong man. That's why I asked you, dear. Village shops are usually a clearinghouse for all the local news."

"How interesting," said Josie, politely. "If you do get another look at him, let me know, won't you; then I can do my job properly."

Josie's voice was cool, but Daisy was not fooled. "I'll keep my eyes open, then," she said.

With no customers in sight, Josie went into the stockroom to do some checking. After only a couple of minutes, the doorbell jangled, and when she returned to the shop she saw Matthew Vickers, policeman and nephew of Cowgill, standing by the notice board where she put up cards for people offering services in the village.

"Morning, Josieo." He greeted her cheerfully. "I'm off duty at the moment, so you can relax. My only question this morning is, do you know any good builders?"

"Might do," Josie said. "And, by the way, you can ask me any questions you like. I've nothing to hide."

Matthew was so taken aback by echoes of Lois Meade that he laughed aloud. "Thanks very much," he said. "I'll remember that. Now, how about good builders?"

Josie walked round the counter and stood in front of the board. He moved closer to her, and she took a step away. He took another, and remained close. "I've looked at these," he said, "and this lot look quite possible. Coleport Brothers. Nothing too big and nothing too small, they claim. Do you know anything about them?"

Josie nodded. "Father and son. It's an old family business. They did several jobs for Mum and Dad when they moved to Farnden. Dad's done some electrical work for them on building jobs. He likes them. Says they start a job when they say they will, and carry on until it's finished."

"That's rare, these days," he said, putting his hand on her shoulder to peer past her at the other end of the board. The hand was warm and firm, and she did not move.

"Do you want Dad to put a word in for you? What's it for, anyway? You must have builders in your home area."

Matthew smiled straight into her eyes, and said, "Oh, yeah, but I've bought this cottage over Waltonby way. Between

Waltonby and Fletching. It's not been lived in for years, and is very dilapidated. It'll need a lot of careful work on it. I've got the plans, and by the time it's finished I hope to spend a lot of time there."

"How? It'd be very early retirement."

He laughed again. "Too right," he said. "That's in the dim and distant future. No, I'm hoping to get transferred to Tresham. I love it round here, and my uncle could do with some companionship since Auntie died. It'll be a kind of weekend and holiday place for a while."

The door opened, and Gran arrived, breathless. Her glance took in her granddaughter standing by the notice board with a good-looking bloke, whose arm was round her shoulder.

"Ahem!" she said loudly. Josie turned round, smiling. "Heard you come in, Gran. You okay this morning? This is Matthew Vickers, and he's a policeman. You remember him. He wants some advice on builders."

Gran ruffled her feathers like an old hen, and said, "You could do worse than the Coleports. I went to school with the old man. Mind you, he's a good bit older than me. He and his son Arnie do a good job."

Matthew picked up a box of expensive Belgian chocolates and handed money to Josie. "Have to keep the girlfriend sweet," he said, grinning. Gran relaxed. That was all right, then. He was already spoken for. Perhaps he was just one of those touchy-feely people who can't keep their hands to themselves.

After Gran had gone, Josie tried not to think about Matthew Vickers. Work was the thing. Always something to do in a shop. She hadn't checked the display of flowers outside yet, and filled a watering can. She removed a bunch of wilting roses to relegate them to her own sitting room, and tucked behind them she found a box of Belgian chocolates. For Josie had been scribbled on the white and gold cover.

"Oh, no," she groaned. What would Rob say? She couldn't keep them, could she? She decided to hide them and eat them in delicious secrecy.

Thirty-Four

As Gran returned home, the telephone was ringing and she rushed to answer it.

"Mrs. Weedon? This is Gladys Pickering here. Just to say we shall be moving on the twenty-fourth. I wanted to thank you for all your help, and to ask you very nicely if you could possibly spare time to give us a hand on moving day?"

Gran said that of course she could, and would be only too pleased. "You're only going round the corner," she said. "We might get Lois to help if she's not too busy."

Mrs. Pickering protested that she wouldn't dream of asking. "She's Floss's boss, don't forget," she added. " 'Bye, then, and thanks a lot. Oh, and by the way, that Mrs. Lambert has fixed a visit for the WI to go to the museum. Members were really keen, apparently. It's after our move, on Tuesday. Maybe Mrs. Meade might like to go, too? We need the numbers for a guided tour. Could you ask her?"

Gran said she'd certainly mention it, but her daughter was not usually keen on group outings, and in any case was extremely busy. But she would love to go, she said. She was like most elderly people, she guessed, who enjoyed looking back at the past. "It's more interesting than the future, dear, as you'll find out one day," she said, and after Mrs. Pickering had made the usual reassuring noises, she said goodbye.

To her great surprise, Lois seemed quite keen. "When did you say, Mum? Oh, yes, that would be fine—in the afternoon? It'd be a really nice idea. Do you think Josie would like to go? Maybe not. Anyway, there'd be nobody to look after the shop."

"Rob might be able to take time off," Gran answered. "Seems a law unto himself, that lad. Anyway, I'll ask her when I go down the street."

In Gordon Street, Douglas, Susie, and Andrew Young were having a meeting. Douglas was not strictly supposed to be there, but he had been in town on business, and said he could spare ten minutes to give Susie confidence. As it happened, she didn't need it. Andrew was extremely charming, and seemed to know his stuff. The two of them chattered away about wallpapers, paint colours, where to get cheap curtains. "Letting agents always like an unfurnished residence to have curtains," Andrew said. "It makes a better impression."

"Letting agents?" said Susie. "I hadn't thought of using agents. Can't you do it for me? For a fee, of course," she added hastily.

Andrew was not sure about this, and said he would have to ask Mrs. M. But in principle, he said, he would be happy to do that for her.

Douglas listened in amazement. This was a new Susie, keen and sure of herself. Maybe that's what untold riches did for you. He'd noticed a change in his parents, sure, but they had won the lottery and been very sensible about it. They were mature, family people. But here was his childlike girlfriend, Susie, always needing his advice and protection, rapidly metamorphosing into a landlady figure with a mind of her own. What's more, this Andrew bloke was twinkling away at her while she blossomed before his eyes.

"Right, Susie," Douglas said, standing up and looking at his watch. "I must be getting back, unless you need me for anything else? You can always ring me on my mobile if necessary," he added kindly. He expected the two of them to pack up papers and follow him out, but they didn't. Susie blew him a kiss, and Andrew leapt to his feet with a manly handshake, but then they sat down again and scarcely seemed to notice his departure.

Jealous thoughts were quickly banished from his mind as he emerged into the street. From Braeside opposite a timid-looking figure walked down the path and opened the gate. It was not Mrs. Blairgowrie, but a woman of about the same age, neat and trim, carrying a shopping bag and wearing horn-rimmed spectacles. She walked with rapid steps up the road towards the supermarket.

Mrs. Blairgowrie's sister? Nothing like her, Douglas decided. Probably a friend doing her shopping. He was sure he had not seen her before, but there was something worryingly familiar about the way she carried her head, bent down and looking at the pavement, as if not sure where her feet were taking her. As he watched, she disappeared round the corner. Not going to the supermarket, then. Douglas Meade, he addressed himself sternly, you'll be spying behind lace curtains next!

Pat had seen Douglas. Her lowered gaze was a habit designed to deceive, and she had noticed him clearly from the corner of her eye. As far as she could tell, he had shown no sign of recognition. Good. She hurried on, finally entering the tourist office in a small side street. Tresham did not boast many reasons for tourists to linger awhile, but they did their best. An old marketplace building took pride of place, and had been carefully preserved, with its arched, pillared space where stallholders had cried their wares for centuries and a beautiful timbered upper storey.

"You could take in the museum, too, dear. Are you staying in Tresham long?" The friendly girl behind the counter handed her a bunch of leaflets.

"Thank you," Pat replied, ignoring the question. "Now, that looks very interesting. How do I get there on public transport? I have no car."

Armed with maps and bus timetables, she left the office and set out purposefully for the bus station.

In Long Farnden, Gran was also walking purposefully, but she was heading for the shop and a chat with Josie. Luckily there were no other customers, and she opened the subject of the museum straightaway. "Why, Josie," she began, "is your mother suddenly interested in a WI outing to a museum in Tresham? She has announced her intention of coming along, and I am worried."

"Why worried?" Josie laughed. "I'd like to go myself. Can I come? Or is it just the blue-rinse brigade? As for Mum, there's no telling with her. You ought to know that by now."

"Well, I reckon she's up to something. Anyway, you can certainly come. But I'm going, so who'll look after the shop?"

"Rob," Josie said confidently. "He's not been very nice to me lately, so he can earn a few Brownie points. When is it?"

The doorbell jangled, and a large, dark-haired man, wearing the latest in what Gran called sunglasses and Josie knew as shades, walked in. Josie's smile waned, and Gran stood aside from the counter.

"Good morning," the man said, looking directly at Josie and ignoring Gran. "I thought I'd come and introduce myself. I'm soon moving into the house over the road. John Smith," he added, extending his hand. He held on a little too long, and she pulled her hand free. "I hope you'll be happy there," she said politely. "It is a very nice house."

Gran, snitched at being ignored, stepped forward. "And I'm Mrs. Weedon, Josie's grandmother. I shall be helping the Pickerings move out, so you'll probably see me around. Where are you living now?" she asked. "Do you know this area?"

John Smith looked at her from a great height and frowned. "Yes," he said, and turned back to Josie. He bought a newspaper and a packet of cigarettes, handed her the money, and with another oily smile he left the shop.

"Charming!" said Gran. "Looks like he's not going to be much of an asset to the village."

"He's been in before," Josie said. "Can you hold the fort, Gran, for a couple of minutes? I need to wash my hands."

John Smith drove on into Tresham and parked in Gordon Street. He looked up and down the street, and particularly across at Douglas's house, then got swiftly out of his car and approached the front door of Braeside.

"Why didn't you ring? Gives me an awful start when you just come bursting in without warning," Mrs. Blairgowrie said.

"There's eyes everywhere in this street," he said. "Just our luck to choose a street full of gossips. And one of 'em's mother is a snout. Still, once I've moved into Farnden, I can keep an eye on her. Where's our Pat?"

"Gone," said Mrs. Blairgowrie. "Went not long ago. Didn't take much, except old clothes and some grocery supplies. And my pearls, which I mean to get back."

"Looked good?"

"Pretty good, I'd say. Could be quite fanciable, at a pinch."

John Smith threw back his large head and roared with laughter. "That'll be the day," he spluttered.

Thirty-Five

Derek could shed no light on Lois's sudden enthusiasm for the past, but he was pleased. Apart from work and snooping, when Derek had suggested she should look after the front garden, she had spent a lot of time there, but now it was bullied into shape, there was little to do. Weeds hardly dared to show their heads. Perhaps history would be a challenge, and an inexhaustible one. There was no end to what could be unearthed about Long Farnden, let alone Tresham and further afield. Lois had always liked talking to old people in the village, listening to their memories. She said it made her feel part of the place. It took years, she said, to dig yourself into a village. He did not agree with her that their house did not really belong to them. It belonged to all those people who had once owned it, she had said, and to those to come.

"How d'you work that out, me duck?" he had asked her.

"Stands to reason," Lois replied. "We can't take any of this with us when we die. Nothing, not even our dearest possessions. So it can't be ours forever."

"But we can pass it on to our children," objected Derek. "Then it'll be theirs."

"Exactly," Lois had said, ending the conversation.

Now they sat at the supper table talking about the WI outing. "Josie's coming," Gran said enthusiastically. "Looks like there'll be quite a decent crowd."

"Are men allowed?" Derek said, and without a pause Gran said of course they were and she would put him on the list.

Lois changed the subject. "We got a postcard from Jamie today," she said. "I just picked it up from behind the door curtain. He's having a great time, he says. Usual couple of lines, but he seems to be travelling around."

"Where from this time?" Gran said.

"Thailand," Lois said. "Here, have a look." She handed over the card, and Derek leaned across to share it with Gran.

Jamie was the youngest Meade, and had become an up-and-coming young musician of some repute. Gran remembered when his first piano had been smuggled into the house on Christmas Eve, and how his face had lit up when he saw it the next morning. He'd come a long way since then, and was now on a round-the-world concert trip. Derek had never felt he was on the same wavelength as his young son, but loved him dearly and followed his career with pride.

"Right, now then," Gran said, feeling that the silence needed filling before they all began to be sad missing Jamie and to wonder when he was coming home. "I'll just get on to Mrs. Pickering and give her the extra numbers."

Next morning, Andrew Young sat in his clean and tidy flat, drawing up plans and details for Susie's house in Gordon Street. He couldn't believe his luck. Fancy applying for a job as a cleaner, his friends had laughed. "Got your frilly apron, Andy?" they had teased. But here he was, doing exactly what he'd wanted to do, given a more or less free hand with interior décor, and working for a sharp woman who was no fool and seemed to welcome the addition to her business.

Well, one good turn deserves another, and he was determined to do a good job for her. He'd enjoyed the cleaning sessions he had done so far, and discovered that there was more to New Brooms than dusters and spray polish. With some of the clients it seemed to be mostly a social call. Old ladies with nobody to talk to. One was a horsey woman up at the Hall, a martinet Justice of the Peace who was accustomed to servants, and herself such a fascinating relic of past days that listening to her was better than the telly.

The telephone at his elbow rang, and he lifted the receiver. "Hello? Who's that?" he said, but all he could hear was heavy breathing. He was about to end the call, remembering with a smile that a high-class hooker had had this flat before him. Then a deep voice spoke.

"Just a little warning, Andy boy. Keep yer nose out of number six, else you might 'ave to do wiv' out it. An' prob'ly the use of yer 'ands as well. That'd put paid to your fancy decorations!"

"Who's that?" Andrew said loudly. But the man had gone. Andrew immediately dialled 1471, but the irritating voice said that the caller had withheld their number. He sighed. One of the jokers from the pub, no doubt. But it wasn't quite their style. And why number six? He thought back to Gordon Street, and Susie's house—his first commission—was number seven. Douglas Meade was eight, and six was empty, wasn't it? He'd heard a rumour about a suspected killer who'd done a runner from there, but he had no idea who owned it.

He returned to his work, and said aloud firmly, "I have absolutely no need to concern myself with any of it. A practical joke, for sure. Idiots. Pity they haven't got anything better to do."

But later on, as he drove down Gordon Street on his way to the supermarket, he looked at the terrace and shivered.

Ridiculous! He concentrated on parking, hoping that Susie would be on duty.

She was behind the bread counter, which smelt wonderfully of new baking and jam doughnuts. Her blonde hair was mostly concealed by a regulation white cap, but her crisp white overall could not conceal her nigh-on perfect shape. She grinned at him. "Hi, Andrew. What can I do for you?"

He rose to the challenge. "Quite a lot, actually," he said, "but for now, a wholemeal loaf and two apple turnovers, please."

She put them deftly into bags and handed them to him. "How're you doing this morning?" she said. "Working hard on my project?"

She was aware of her colleagues pricking up their ears, and saw through their eyes a rival to Douglas. What nonsense! This was a business matter, and when he asked casually if she knew whether number six next door to her house was occupied or for sale, she shook her head. "I don't think so," she said. "I haven't seen anyone round there. It's all locked up now. Could be the police don't want anyone there at the moment. Not 'til they catch that ratty little bloke."

A queue was forming behind Andrew, and he moved away, saying he'd be in touch when the details were finalised.

"Blimey, Susie," her fellow assistant said, "you haven't wasted much time. What does that nice Douglas think?"

Susie blushed, and said there was nothing in it. He was just someone helping her with smartening up her grandfather's old house.

"They cost, y' know, these interior décor blokes," her friend said.

"I know. But Granddad left me a bit to go with the house, and it'll be an investment, Douglas says. I can ask for much more rent if it's in a decent condition."

Andrew filled his trolley and made his way to the checkout, where he almost collided with Lois and an elderly lady he now knew as Gran.

"Morning, Andrew," Lois said. "Looks like you're feeding the five thousand."

"It'll last me for at least a couple of weeks," he replied, smiling sweetly at Gran.

"Introduce me, Lois," Gran butted in. She knew exactly

who he was, but did not intend to be left out. Lois was not deceived. She had talked enough about Andrew, discussing with Derek the new plan and whether she should employ him. If Gran had not picked up on their conversations, it would be the first time ever.

"Andrew, new recruit, meet my mum," she said.

He stood to one side to allow them to go first through the checkout, and they waited for him to follow. "I'll come and help you pack the car," he said. Lois replied that she was perfectly capable of doing it herself, and at exactly the same moment Gran said in a firm voice that it was extremely kind of him, and it would be a great help.

It took only a few minutes to fill the back of Lois's van, and Andrew turned to go. "All going well with Susie's décor?" Lois asked, and he hesitated. He hadn't meant to tell anyone about the threatening call, but now he found himself spilling it all out to Lois. Gran was full of sympathy, but Lois suddenly snapped to attention.

"Why didn't you call back?" she said sharply.

"I did, but there was no return number. I tried several times."

"Are you sure it was a disguised voice?"

"Yep. Like somebody acting. By the end of the message, where he said 'fancy decorations,' the voice was much lighter, and quite posh."

"And he was definitely warning you off spying on number six?"

Andrew nodded, rather wishing he'd never mentioned it.

"Right. Now, if it happens again, I want you to let me know straightaway," said Lois firmly. "I'll be able to help."

He thanked her and walked off to his car. So it wasn't just a joke. He knew from Hazel in the office about Lois's hobby of sleuthing, and from her reaction just now he began to wonder if he was a victim of something more sinister.

Lois and Gran drove home in silence. Eventually Gran, who abhorred a conversational opportunity wasted, said, "A penny for 'em, Lois."

"Not for sale," Lois grunted, and turned into the drive with squealing tyres. "Can you manage, Mum?" she said. "Got to make an urgent call." Without waiting for a reply she disappeared into the house, and Gran heard her study door shut with a bang.

"Hello? Is that you?" Lois drummed her fingers on her desk. "You took long enough to answer."

"Busy, Lois," Cowgill said. "A policeman's lot is not a happy one." He waved his assistant away towards the door, and settled back in his chair.

"Well, just listen carefully. Maybe I can make your lot a bit happier."

"Anything you say makes me happy," Cowgill said softly.

"Oh, for God's sake! This is serious." Lois gave him a succinct account of what Andrew had told her, and Cowgill sat up straight in his chair.

"Why number six, and why Andrew Young, and why would somebody be so anxious about an empty house?" he asked in a now professional voice.

"If I knew the answers to that, I wouldn't be calling you," Lois snapped. "At least, not yet. Still, if you think about what I've just told you, your brilliant detecting mind may put two and two together and come up with the fact that Andrew is doing a job for Susie Mills, who inherited old Clem's house next door to number six. He'll be in and out with paint and stuff through the back yard, and will get a good view of what goes on in number six from there. And, by the way, have you got that skinny bloke yet?"

"We're following up several leads," Cowgill said mechanically.

"So you've got no idea where he is," Lois replied flatly.

"Well, I might have. But I'm not telling you yet until I'm sure. I don't want PC Plod trampin' in there in hobnail boots."

Cowgill sighed. "If I didn't love you, Lois, I'd be tempted to end our relationship right now. But as I can't live without you, it doesn't matter."

"I hope to God you're joking, Cowgill! And just don't forget I want Andrew Young protected from any more threatening calls. I know you can arrange it. I'll be in touch. Probably."

Cowgill listened sadly to the dialling tone for a second or two, then went to the door and yelled down the corridor at the top of his voice for his assistant.

Thirty-Six

Pat adjusted her diamanté-edged glasses and entered the museum reception hall. She had found a bus which took her directly to the large old farmhouse on the outskirts of Tresham. The house was now part of a thriving museum with new extensions and sizeable tearooms. Excellent, she said to herself, and looked around. The reception area was purpose-built, a large airy space that incorporated a shop selling souvenirs and toys. This morning it was crowded with a school party of ten-year-olds, all wearing uniforms of grey and scarlet. How smart they looked, thought Pat. She approved of uniforms of all sorts, and the more colour in them, the better. She heartily disapproved of the teenagers hanging about town, clad in deepest black from head to foot. No wonder they saw the world through such disillusioned eyes!

"Senior citizen ticket, please," she said, patting her neat grey hair. The tall, harassed-looking man behind the counter handed her a ticket and pointed in the direction she should take.

"It's quite easy from there, dear," he said. "Signed all the way to the tearooms. I know you ladies like a cup of tea and a homemade cake after your tour. I'll be taking a party around in a few minutes, if you'd like to join us?"

Pat shook her head. "If it's allowed," she said, with a pleading smile, "I would really love to saunter round on my own. I know there will be nostalgic moments where I shall want to linger."

"Of course you can, dear," the man said kindly. "Take your time. There's a lot to see!"

Better and better, Pat said to herself, and walked unhurriedly through the double doors into the start of the museum. She found herself in a high-ceilinged room which had clearly been the parlour of the old farmhouse. It was furnished just as it had been in Victorian times, and she clasped her hands together in delight. Cluttered and rather dark, with heavy rusty brown curtains, the room was stuffed with furniture, grandly upholstered in faded red velvet, a solid pianola built to last, with piles of perforated rolls to make it work, glass-fronted display cabinets with many-coloured vases and figurines, a table with its bulbous carved legs made decent by a chenille cloth edged with bobbles, and a solitaire board with beautiful glass marbles, just like the one Pat's grandmother used to have.

A motherly woman stood by the door, answering questions from visitors as they wandered round. Pat approached her and asked about the pianola. "Try it, dear," the woman said. She went with her and showed her how it worked, and Pat pedalled away with gusto. A small burst of applause from the steward greeted her as she stood up beaming with pride.

"Are you a member of staff?" she asked the nice woman.

"In a way," she answered. "We're all volunteers here. The museum couldn't exist without volunteers! But we all love it, you know. We meet so many interesting people, and even the children are mostly well-behaved."

"Do you have to have special qualifications?" Pat asked casually.

"Goodness, no. We just have to be trustworthy, of course, and reliable. You get an interview with the manager, and he decides. You probably saw him. He's on reception this morning. Takes his turn with the rest of us. A very nice man."

Pat thanked her, and moved on into an old-fashioned schoolroom. Everything there delighted her. It was all as her grandmother had described. Scarred wooden desks with tip-up seats, with a slate and slate pencil to each one. A tall black iron stove, cold now but once dangerously hot, by the teacher's high desk. There was even a pan of water on top to keep the atmosphere sweet.

On Pat went, through a cold, dark street of tiny shops, including a post office with sheets of impossibly cheap stamps, a haberdasher's emporium full of lace and frills, a chemist's, with yellowing packets of long-forgotten remedies for every ailment. Then she lingered by the shoe mender, a waxwork figure surrounded by every size of shoe shapes and neat piles of nails and hammers. How comfortable those shoes must have been, each made for an individual foot!

At last she came to the tearooms, and sat down feeling pleasantly exhausted. She looked at the menu, and saw that they catered for snack lunches as well. After hot tea and home-made shortbread, she made her way back to reception and saw that the manager had just finished escorting the children on their lightning-speed tour, and was now selling them souvenirs of their visit. She wandered round the shop, and finally, after all the children had gone, she took a packet of notecards to the desk.

"Did you enjoy your visit, dear?" the manager said, slipping the pack into a Tresham Museum paper bag.

"Very much, thank you," Pat replied. "In fact, I was so taken with it all that I wondered if you have any vacancies for volunteers? I'm recently widowed, and find I have far too much time on my hands."

The manager beamed. "Forgive me if I just manacle you to the desk so you can't get away!" he said, laughing heartily. "My dear, we always need volunteers. Now, why don't we fix a mutually convenient time for us to have a talk, and I'll be able to fit you into our rota in no time at all."

"I'm free all day, if that's any help."

"Ah, well, not today. I have one tour after another to deal with today. How about tomorrow? Shall we say eleven o'clock tomorrow morning?"

Pat nodded, and almost stuck out her hand to shake hands on it, but remembered in time and smiled gratefully instead. As she walked to the bus stop, she looked back at the handsome old house with its treasures of the past. "Splendid," she said aloud, and was pleased to see a bus rounding the corner and heading back into the town centre.

Thirty-Seven

Moving day came not a moment too soon for Mrs. Pickering, who was in that strange instinctive in-between world of being without a nest. All was ready, packed and crowded together in convenient heaps for the removals men. Floss's father had proposed hiring a van and doing it themselves in stages. "It's only just over the road and round the corner," he tried to persuade his reluctant wife.

"I don't trust you and Floss and Ben to take care of my treasures," she'd said, near to tears. Moving house was bad enough, in spite of it having been at her instigation, but the thought of backstrain, breakages, and lost tempers was too much to bear. "I shall hire those nice people who moved us here," she said. "And if it's the money that's worrying you, I am quite happy to dip into my savings."

"Don't be ridiculous," her husband had replied. "Of course we'll have the removals men if that will make you happy."

Gran had come down early, saying that they need not worry about refreshments during the day. It was all arranged, and Lois would bring down soup and sandwiches at lunchtime. "Now," Gran said comfortingly, "a good strong cup of tea will put us all on the primrose path." Not one to be worried about a muddled metaphor, Gran set to work cheerfully with kettle, mugs, milk, and a packet of Rich Tea biscuits.

The men arrived, and it seemed that by coffee time, not much had been moved. Mrs. Pickering noticed that Gran spent some time chatting to one or the other. She knew the family of one of the Tresham lads, and the bored young man listened politely to tales of his old grandfather's roving eye.

"Mrs. Weedon," said Mrs. Pickering, putting a kindly hand on Gran's shoulder, "I wonder if you could do us a great favour? I quite forgot to get batteries for our big torch, and I am sure we shall need it this evening to peer into things. Could you possibly get one of those big square ones from Josie? She can put it on my account."

Gran thought privately that surely there would be electricity in the Blackberry Gardens house, but didn't comment. You had to humour people who were moving house, especially the women. "Of course I can," she said. "Leave it to me, dear. Anything else you've forgotten?"

Mrs. Pickering shook her head. "Can't think of anything at the moment," she said, so Gran quickly rinsed mugs and set off for the shop. As she went out of the gate, a big car drove past very slowly, and a thickset man wearing horn-rimmed glasses looked across at the house.

"That's him!" Gran said. "That's the man who's moving in. John Smith, he calls himself."

"Morning, Mrs. Weedon. Talking to God?" It was the vicar, Mr. Rollinson, passing by like Dracula in his flowing black cloak. Gran assured him that she was indeed praying for fine weather. The Pickerings were moving house, and she was sure they'd appreciate a blessing from himself. This was mischievous, as she knew perfectly well the Pickerings were never seen in church, and she had heard more than once Mr. Pickering hold forth on the evils of organised religion.

The vicar's face lit up for a second, and then he remembered past conversations with Pickering, and with a cheery wave and a promise to visit once they were in the new house, he swooped on his way.

Gran remembered her mission and headed for the shop. Outside she saw the big black car. John Smith could be pouncing on Josie again. She quickened her step in case her beloved granddaughter should need rescuing, but once in the shop she could see several customers and Smith awaiting his turn. He turned round to see who had come in, and looked away without interest.

"Good morning, Mr. Smith," Gran said in a firm voice. "Here to see how the move is going?"

He was forced to take notice, and said irritably, "Not really, just passing through. I shall be over later, of course."

"Much stuff to move in?" Gran said, not in the least daunted.

"The usual," he replied shortly. "I've left them to it. The fewer the distractions, the quicker they get on with it," he added. He had noticed Gran emerging from his new house and said to himself that here was one to be firmly discouraged. He turned his back on her, hoping that would shut her up. It did not, of course.

"No good being ready before the Pickerings are out," she said. "I reckon it'll be around four o'clock before they've finished there."

"Ye Gods, they've only got two hundred yards to go!" said John Smith, losing his patience.

"Ah, yes," Gran replied calmly, "well, I could be wrong. Now, it's your turn, Mr. Smith. Josie's ready."

The big man looked around, as if wondering which one was Mr. Smith, and then stepped forward to the counter. "Aspirins," he said curtly. "A large packet."

Josie frowned. A "please" wouldn't come amiss, she thought. "Headache, Mr. Smith?" she said coolly. "Moving house is a strain, isn't it. I am sure Gran here will give you a hand after the Pickerings have gone, if that would help?"

Gran glared at Josie, but she needn't have worried. John Smith scowled and said that he needed no help, and didn't believe in it. "I'm quite capable of putting my things in the right places," he said. "And I am very particular about my privacy. I hope you'll let that be known in the village, my dear," he added, his voice resuming its oily tone.

Josie bridled. "You'll hear no gossip in this shop, Mr. Smith," she said. "Is there anything else I can get you?"

At one o'clock exactly, Lois drew up next to the removals van. She took out a tray of hot soup and piles of sandwiches previously prepared by Gran and carried them in. She was amazed to see an almost empty house. "My goodness," she said, "they've really got a move on. Soon be finished?"

Gran looked smug. "I've been able to help quite a bit," she said. "Directing operations, an' that."

"I bet you have," Lois said under her breath, and added, "Hello, Mrs. Pickering. Bearing up well?"

"Mrs. Weedon's been a great help," she said, crossing her fingers behind her back. "And now look at this lovely spread. There's enough here for an army!"

"Enough for the chaps, too," Gran said and disappeared to invite them to lunch. Three grinning men returned with her and accepted steaming soup gratefully. Mrs. Pickering exchanged glances with Lois and shrugged. At least they'd had a clear run at it while Gran was at the shop. Then she'd met an old friend in the street on the way back and on returning found the battery was the wrong size, and so had gone back to the shop with the big torch. All this had taken up a useful amount of time.

Finally everything was cleared, and the Blackberry Gardens house now full of tea chests, sealed boxes, furniture heaped in the middle of rooms, and naked beds needing to be made up before dark. It was not until the sun disappeared behind heavy clouds that they discovered all the lightbulbs had been taken by the previous occupants. At this point, Mr. Pickering raged and his wife burst into tears. By this time Gran had gone home, but practical Floss looked at her watch and said the shop was still open, and she'd be only a few minutes before being back with new bulbs.

"Some people take their roses with them," Josie said to Floss comfortingly. "It happened to Mum and Dad, and Dad went after them, told them it was illegal, and brought the roses back with him. Trust Dad!"

She found a large box and put in bulbs of various wattages. "If anything else is missing," she said, "just give me a ring. Doesn't matter if the shop is closed. We'll be upstairs in the flat, and you can come in round the back way. Best of luck!"

As Floss walked back towards Blackberry Gardens, thanking God for a village shop, she passed by her old house. Outside was a scruffy-looking white van, not all that large, with two hooded persons of unknown age or sex heaving out pieces of furniture and scuttling up the path and into the house. Floss slowed down. She could see just inside the front door, where the new owner was directing operations. Curtains left by the Pickerings had been drawn across, and as she stared, the front door was shut with a bang.

Well, sod them, she said to herself. If that's what they want. Still, if they thought their lives could be kept secret from Farnden, they would be wrong. We have ways of finding out.

"Here you are, Mum!" she called out as she entered her own house. Mrs. Pickering had pulled herself together, and asked Floss if she'd seen how the new people were getting on in what she still thought of as her house.

"Nearly finished, I should think," Floss said. "There was just a small van with a few sticks of furniture. Maybe Mr. Smith means to buy new, but from what I could see he'll have to start from scratch. And as I was about to give him a cheery wave from the gate, he shut the door in my face!"

Thirty-Eight

Andrew Young had agreed to meet Susie at her Gordon Street house after she finished work at the supermarket. She was on a late shift until eight o'clock, and hurried out to find Andrew waiting for her outside the house. She let him in with her key and put on lights. "Do you think it would be a good idea for me to get a key cut for you?" she said. "Then you could come and go as you like. After all, once you start, I won't always be around."

"Good idea," he said. He showed her his revised drawings, and they walked round the house, checking everything care-fully. "This is my first real assignment," he confided, "so I mean it to be perfect for you." He was standing close to her and smiled. She did her best to flutter her eyelashes, and said she was sure it would be wonderful. She'd probably want to live in it herself, she said.

Douglas, arriving home after working late at the office, saw the lights blazing next door and knew it would be Susie. And, he supposed, that decorator bloke. Better go and check, he decided, and went out to knock at Susie's back door. He could see over the open yards into Skinny Man's empty house, and was surprised to see a faint glimmer of light behind the drawn curtains. Someone was in there. Surely not Skinny Man? If he had any sense, he'd be a hundred miles away by now. Should he go over and peer through the crack between the curtains? Remember what happened to Clem, he warned himself. Still, the danger should be gone now, together with whatever had been so secret in that house that Clem had died because of it.

He crept silently forward until he was up to the window. He could see very little, but then a shadow crossed, and he saw a woman carrying a candle, head bent. She seemed to be looking for something, but not finding it. Then she looked across at the window, and immediately the candle was snuffed out.

Douglas ran. After all, women could carry guns, knives, weapons of mass destruction! His thoughts were out of control, and he dodged back and into Susie's yard. He banged on the door, and was so relieved to see Andrew that he grasped his hand and shook it heartily. Andrew, surprised, smiled and said how nice to see him.

"It's Douglas," he called back into the house. "Susie asked me to answer the door, in case it was someone scary."

"Absolutely right," Douglas said. "Better lock this door behind me. You never know in Gordon Street!"

He made a poor attempt at a laugh, and Andrew said, "Has something happened, Doug? You look like you've seen a ghost."

Susie had come into the kitchen now, and gave Douglas a hug. "What's up, sweetie?" she said.

Douglas tossed up whether to alarm her by telling, or to keep quiet about what he'd seen. He decided on the latter. "I'm fine," he said. "I just came over to see if we should all go to the pub and have a snack when you've finished?" Safety in numbers, he said to himself.

When they trooped out of the front door, Andrew said calmly, "By the way, Susie, when I was waiting for you out here, I saw a woman go into the empty house. Maybe you'll have new neighbours soon."

"What sort of woman?" chorused Douglas and Susie.

"The usual sort—arms and legs, boobs, nice hair. Wearing an all-enveloping raincoat."

"Did she speak to you?" Douglas tried to make it sound casual.

Andrew shook his head. "Nope. Looked to neither right nor left. Why are you both so bothered? There's bound to be people in and out of an empty house. It surely won't stand empty for long. Rented or for sale, Tresham's quite a desirable place to live."

"Yeah, well, don't forget Susie's granddad. Nobody could forget that in a hurry. Come on, then, let's head for the bright lights of Tresham."

Mrs. Blairgowrie watched them from behind her bedroom curtains, and continued to wait, her gaze fixed on the front of the house opposite. After a while her wait was rewarded. The front door opened and a figure emerged.

"There she is," muttered Mrs. Blairgowrie. "And she's carrying a bag. So she's found his wretched novels. Good." She closed the gap in the curtains and went downstairs. She noted the time, and then sat down to watch her favourite telly quiz show.

Next morning, Mrs. Blairgowrie answered her front door-bell, dark glasses in place and stick held firmly, and found Dot Nimmo standing on her doorstep.

"Mrs. Nimmo? Surely you are not due to clean until this afternoon? I've heard nothing from Mrs. Meade."

"No, dear," said Dot, "I didn't think it necessary to worry Mrs. Meade. I've just called to see if it would be convenient to come in now, as I've got to go on an errand of mercy this afternoon." She did not say what the errand of mercy was, and indeed there was none. Dot had had a hunch on getting out of bed this morning, and she wanted to try it out when she thought she might have Braeside to herself.

"Well, I suppose it is all right," Mrs. Blairgowrie said reluctantly. "Come on in. It is this morning that my son usually calls, so perhaps you could get downstairs finished before he arrives?"

Dot gleefully agreed. Just what she was hoping for. She went into the front room and gave the oddly assorted furniture an extra polish. Then she began surreptitiously to open all the drawers and cupboards. There was a heavy old sideboard, but it contained nothing but glasses and a stained chamber pot. Blimey, that's been there a few years, Dot said to herself. That's where the men used to pee when the ladies went off to powder their noses and the men passed round the port. Dot wrinkled her nose and shut the door firmly.

It was the same with a small oak bureau. Nothing but a few old books and some dreadful pottery souvenirs of holidays in seaside resorts. Dot found these puzzling, not being places she expected the ladylike Mrs. Blairgowrie to take her summer breaks.

"Ready for your coffee, dear?" Dot walked through to the kitchen and put on the kettle. "I expect you have coffee in the mornings?"

Mrs. Blairgowrie was sitting in her armchair, listening to the radio. She looked sightlessly in Dot's direction and nodded. "That would be very kind. Thank you," she said sweetly. "Sometimes I feel very old."

"Cheer up!" Dot said. "At least you're still pretty nimble on your pins. Still getting out to the supermarket? Isn't this your shopping morning?"

"Yes, it is. I don't try on my own, just when Alastair is with me. Too much trolley traffic! Oh, and a spoonful of brown sugar in the coffee, please."

"If it's all right with you," Dot said, "I'll carry on without a break this morning. The sooner I get to see my sister, the better." The smoothest liar in town, she thought. Handy would be proud of me.

She had been upstairs in the bathroom for only a couple of minutes when she heard the doorbell. She nipped swiftly down the stairs and along the hall to the door. She opened it with a flourish, and saw the looming shape of Mrs. Blairgowrie's son standing on the step.

"Good morning!" she trilled. "Madam is expecting you." She found it difficult not to chuckle at herself, but kept up the servant bit, showing him into the sitting room and offering to make fresh coffee.

"No, no, thank you," Mrs. Blairgowrie said. "We shall be going out straightaway, and have coffee when we get back."

Dot retired upstairs, listening carefully so that she knew when they left the house. After a short while, she heard the front door shut and went to the window, where she could see them walking slowly up the street towards the supermarket. Now for some quick action.

Next to Mrs. Blairgowrie's bed she dusted the little purdonium which had once contained coal. She hesitated for a moment, feeling a stab of apprehension. Inside, the cupboard was metal-lined, and a faint odour of damp coal escaped. But there was something else. A small heap of shiny magazines slid forward, and Dot picked one off the pile. She smiled in triumph, and settled down to have a good read.

Five minutes passed, and Dot sat on the edge of the bed, chuckling at the magazines. She did not hear the soft steps on the stairs and jumped out of her skin when a man's voice said, "Well, well. Enjoying Mother's magazines? Wasting time and money, more like." His tone was hard and he walked towards her. She jumped up and retreated to the other side of the bed, but he followed her and caught her by the arm. "I presume you did not expect us back so soon. Mother suspected you were up to something when you turned up so early. Seems she was right."

"Let go of me!" Dot shouted, and kicked him hard on the shin. Alastair gasped with pain, but still kept hold of her. She bit his hand, but he did not release her. Instead, he recovered his breath and laughed. "I'm used to dealing with wayward women," he said. "In fact, I could get turned on by you, little Dot," he added, and pushed her backwards onto the bed.

"That's enough!" It was Mrs. Blairgowrie standing in the doorway, looking at Alastair and then at Dot reproachfully. "I see you've found my fun mags," she continued. "And I suppose you have put two and two together? She's a smart one, is Dot Nimmo," she added to Alastair. "What shall we do with her?"

"Perhaps we should reward her for being so smart?" Alastair still held on to Dot, and she aimed another kick at him. "Now, now. Naughty girl," he laughed, and then turned back to Mrs. Blairgowrie. "A few days' holiday, in a nice private spot?

Good food, pleasant company, all mod cons. How does that sound, Dottie?"

"Not bloody likely!" yelled Dot.

"I'm afraid you have no alternative," Mrs. Blairgowrie said sadly. "I had so hoped I could trust you. But there it is. Don't worry, we'll think of something to tell Mrs. Meade, and Alastair will make sure you are well looked after."

At this, Alastair roared with laughter and they hustled Dot downstairs without ceremony.

Thirty-Nine

Dot, her ankles and wrists tied together tightly, sat fuming in the back seat of Alastair's car. She knew it was no good trying to make anguished faces through the darkened windows at people passing by. She had absolutely no idea where they would take her, but she hoped it would be far enough for her to make a plan. First she had to loosen, but not undo, the knots restricting her. This was one of the first things that Handy had taught her after they were married. "Never know, me duck, where you might end up in my line of business!" He was a good teacher, old Handy, and Dot often thought that if he hadn't been a small-time crook, he'd have made a great scout leader. A sudden picture flashed into her mind of Handy dressed up in scout uniform, and she had to turn a bubble of laughter into a cough.

"Not far to go now, Dottie dear," said Alastair in his slimy voice. "Nearly there. There'll be one or two friends for you to talk to, and you'll be quite comfortable until we decide what to do with you." Dottie said nothing. The cologne-smelling handkerchief that bound her mouth prevented every-thing but a groan, and she wouldn't gratify him by that.

By the time the car began to slow down, Dot had loosened all the knots except the gag and blindfold, but this would soon be done when her hands were free. She had no idea where they were, except that they had at the last minute driven at a crawl over a bumpy surface. There was no sound of other traffic, and all she could hear was the distant yelling of chil-dren at play. In the country, then. Somewhere near a school?

Or playing fields?

She concentrated on timing now, and when Alastair took out his mobile phone and said shortly, "We're here," she realised that he was alone, overweight, a smoker, and flabby. How would he get her out of the car?

"Don't try anything silly, Dottie," he said. "I shall be back for you in seconds."

Dot couldn't believe her luck. She gave him ten seconds, during which she heard a gate click open and shut, then used the final Handy trick to free her hands, followed by a quick release of the rest. As she got out, she saw they were indeed on the car park of a playing field, parked behind a fence that bounded the back gardens of a row of houses. Each had an exit into the field, and to her horror she saw the gate in front of the car begin to open. But she was wiry and quick, and was across the gravel and out into the lane before she could see Alastair and a black woman, heavily pregnant, emerge. They lumbered after her, but she was twice as fast, and on emerging into the main road, she knew immediately where she was. Long Farnden, and a hundred yards down from Mrs. M's house.

On the pavement, she turned towards it, but then changed her mind and dashed across the road and into the shop, where Josie was standing behind the counter. She looked at her in surprise and said, "Mrs. Nimmo! You're in a hurry today. What can I do for you?"

The normality of Josie's kind voice brought a tear of relief to Dot's eye, but she suppressed it firmly and said a dog had been chasing her and she was ridiculously scared of dogs. It was an enormous Alsatian, she began, and then qualified it to a black Labrador, thinking they were two a penny in the country, whereas an Alsatian could be easily identified. She wanted no checking up on her story.

"Can I sit down for a minute or two?" she said, and Josie answered that of course she could, and it was a pity people didn't control their dogs. There were always complaints in the newsletter about dog doings all over the path where the kids came out of school.

"And those idiots on horses," Dot agreed, "with loose dogs they can't possibly control. You should hear Mrs. M on the subject," she added.

"I have." Josie grinned. "Now, I'm going to make you a cup of tea and you can mind the shop for me."

"No!" said Dot, much alarmed. "N-no, dear. I'm perfectly all right. A chat with you does wonders." The last thing she wanted was to be left alone in the shop for Alastair to come after her in an abducting mood. "I see folk have moved into the Pickerings' old house?" she said.

Josie frowned. "Yeah, a Mr. John Smith. Mum says he's sinister. He's been in here several times, and I wish I could ban him from the shop. Horrible slimy character, and very pleased with himself."

Not just now, he's not, Dot said to herself. He must be furious. Now, how to get home, and how to persuade Josie not to tell Mrs. M she'd been in the village? She wanted to sort out her thoughts, but chiefly at the moment she was not keen on admitting to Mrs. M that she had adjusted her rota without asking.

Deceit was Dot's speciality. "Josie, dear," she said, "can I ask a favour? Would you mind not telling your mum you've seen me? I'm moonlighting, I suppose you'd call it. A secret between ourselves?"

Josie laughed and nodded. "Cross my heart and hope to die," she said dramatically. Then she looked at the clock. "I can hear the Tresham bus coming, always on time. You could set your watch by it. Oh, are you off? 'Bye, then, Mrs. Nimmo. Take care." As she watched her run across the road without looking, she wondered why Dot was taking the bus. Surely she must have a car in order to work for Mum? Maybe it had broken down. She prepared for an onslaught of bus passengers who would rush in to buy what they'd forgotten in the supermarket. Dot's strange visit went completely from her mind.

Alastair, seething behind the curtains of his front window, turned to the woman by his side and said, "Sod it all! There she goes, hopping on the bus like she'd just been visiting a sick relative." He turned away and gave the woman a shove. "Get me a drink. And pronto. Then go to your room. I need to think."

When the call came, Lois was dozing in an armchair, digesting one of Gran's three-decker sandwich lunches. "Hello? Who's that?" She struggled awake as Derek thrust the telephone into her hand.

"Oh, Mrs. Meade, I'm really worried about Dot." It was Evelyn Nimmo. "She was supposed to be here for lunch before she went to work in Gordon Street, but she didn't turn up. I've tried and tried to ring her, but no reply. It's not like her, Mrs. M."

Lois agreed that Dot was a good timekeeper, and said that she would be at Braeside this afternoon, but should be free at five at the latest. "In spite of appearances," she said, laughing, "Dot is usually a reliable member of my team."

Evelyn did not laugh in return. She asked if Lois had any idea where Dot might have been, and Lois realised she was very anxious. "Shall I call Mrs. Blairgowrie? See if Dot has turned up there?"

After Evelyn had rung off, Lois got up with a sigh and went into her study. She dialled Mrs. Blairgowrie's number, and when the old lady answered, apologised for bothering her and asked her about Dot. "She has come to you this afternoon, hasn't she?" Lois asked.

"Oh, yes, Mrs. Meade. Always very punctual. We've had a nice chat over a cup of tea." She did not offer to bring Dot to the telephone.

Lois hesitated, then said, "Would you mind asking her to give her sister a ring as soon as she leaves you? That is very kind. Thank you."

In Braeside's warm and cosy sitting room, Mrs. Blairgowrie relaxed in her chair. Well, that had all seemed to go well. It was irritating that Alastair had insisted on taking Dot away before she had finished her work upstairs, but she supposed she would manage.

Forty

"Off to another day of honest toil," Derek said, "but I'll fix that tap in the bathroom first. Thanks for breakfast, Gran. Great as usual," he said, giving her a peck on the cheek.

Gran remarked that not everybody remembered to say thank you for the food she worked so hard at preparing. She was looking in Lois's direction, but unfortunately her daughter was reading the local paper. She was fascinated by a feature on the Tresham police force, and was irritated to see it was largely complimentary. A photograph of Detective Chief Inspector Cowgill dominated the page, and underneath was a quote: "We pride ourselves on our clear-up rate here in Tresham." And in the body of the article he was reported as having said that they were very close to an arrest in the case of Clem Fitch and his cockerel.

"Huh! That's news to me," Lois said, and handed the paper to Gran as she heard the telephone ringing. Probably Evelyn Nimmo apologising for panicking. But it was Cowgill, and he said he had to see her at once. He would be over in twenty minutes. And yes, of course it was official business.

"Can't it wait?" Lois said. "I've got to see a potential client at ten thirty."

"No. Cancel it," he said shortly, and cut off the call.

Twenty minutes later, he knocked at the door. Gran was there at once to let him in, and showed him into the sitting room. Lois followed close behind. "What's this about?" she said crossly.

"Sit down, Lois," he said. "What I have to say is not good news."

"The kids! There's been an accident?"

"No, no. Nothing like that. No, it is to do with Douglas, but not an accident. I'm afraid new evidence has come to light on Clem Fitch's murder that means we have to bring him in for questioning."

"What?!" Lois was aghast.

Cowgill repeated what he had said, and added, "I am really sorry, Lois, but in the light of what has emerged I have no alternative. We shall, of course, be very discreet and get the whole thing out of the way as quickly as possible."

"You mean you think it's rubbish? What new evidence, anyway?"

"It is not rubbish, Lois," he said as kindly as was possible in the circumstances. "And you know I cannot give you details. I have to take it seriously. But I can assure you that I shall—"

"Forget the crap!" Lois snapped. "Wait here a minute. I'll get my coat on."

"Where d'you think you're going?" Derek said. He had

joined them and taken Lois's hand, and now restrained her from rushing from the room. He turned to Cowgill. "When will you take him to the station?"

"He'll be there by now," Cowgill said, still staring sadly at Lois. "And of course you can both come along and see him, if you wish. Though he may not want that," he added.

"Is he in a cell?" Lois said, choking with anger.

Cowgill did not answer, but walked to the front door and stood on the step waiting for them to decide.

"Get going," Lois said roughly. "We know the way to the police station by now. Just leave us alone."

Cowgill felt real pain as he walked to his car and knew that Lois would never forgive him and there was nothing he could do about it.

Douglas sat by himself in an interview room, which was brightly lit with no windows to the outside world. He had been at home when the police came, fortunately. He had been given the day off by his boss, who had been aware that Douglas was staying in the office late every day, working many hours of unpaid overtime. "I know you're a new broom," he said, "but this is ridiculous. Take tomorrow off in lieu."

Douglas had laughed, and said it was his mother who was a New Broom, and by the way, was his boss happy with the cleaning arrangements for the office? He could strongly recommend the New Brooms team, he said.

So there he had been, still in his pyjamas, when Cowgill had knocked on the door and said would he kindly come down to the station as soon as possible, as he needed to ask him some questions. Douglas had asked why Cowgill couldn't come in and ask there and then, but it had been carefully explained to him, as if to a nitwit, that there were rules which had to be followed.

Now he sat, with nothing to read or do. In his hurry, he had left his mobile and watch on his bedside table, and he awaited the next move with considerable impatience. The door opened, and at the sight of his mother, consumed with anger and anxiety, lurking behind a policeman, he suddenly laughed out loud. It was a ridiculous farce.

"Mum! What the hell are you doing here? This is not the condemned cell, you know! And I'm long past needing parents with me," he added, seeing his father following behind.

"Whatever it is this lot have in mind for me," he added. It must all be a mistake, he considered, and he pitied Cowgill when Lois turned on him. But for now, he could see, she was holding her fire, waiting to see what happened next.

Back home in her office, supplied with hot, strong tea by a worried Gran, Lois took from her bag a folded sheet of paper. Cowgill had slipped it to her surreptitiously when they left the station. "Strictly confidential, if you don't want me sacked," he had whispered. Now she unfolded it and read it slowly. It was a brief outline of new evidence gathered in the case of Clem Fitch, found dead upside down in an old lavatory in Gordon Street.

Apparently new facts had been volunteered by an unnamed witness, said to have been visiting a house in Catchpole Street, which joined Gordon Street at a right angle, giving occupants in both streets a sideways view of each other's back yards. The witness had stated that on the night of the murder, he or she had had a clear view from an upstairs window of all the yards belonging to Douglas, Clem, and the unknown tenant the other side of Clem. The witness had seen Douglas emerge from his house, have an argument with Clem, who was shutting up his cockerel, and hit him so violently that he fell to the ground. The witness was apparently riveted to the spot, and continued to watch as Clem was stuffed into the lavatory. Douglas then rushed hastily back to his own yard and disappeared. The witness had seen nobody from the house of Clem's other neighbour.

There was a note at the foot of the page, stating that this was evidence delivered by an unseen and anonymous messenger in an envelope left on the reception desk of the police station.

Lois dialled Cowgill's personal number, and he answered immediately.

"No time to waste," Lois said at once. "Have you tracked down this arsehole witness?"

Cowgill winced. He knew from long experience that Lois's swearing was a sure sign that she was under pressure. "No, we've had no luck there. We have interviewed every single tenant or owner in Catchpole Street, but all are certain they had no visitors that night, nor were they themselves aware of anything unusual going on."

"Well, they would say that, wouldn't they," Lois snapped. "None of that lot would want to help the cops. What d'you expect?" She didn't give him time to answer, and continued furiously, "And so, on this stinking piece of paper, written by an unknown, vanished liar, you have arrested my son and probably ruined his career for life!"

Cowgill sighed. "I haven't arrested him, Lois. He is just helping us with our enquiries at present. You will be happy to know that he will be back home by now."

"On bail?" asked Lois.

"No, no. We have merely asked him to let us know if he is going out of town, with details of where we can get in touch."

"And as a result of him having helped you with your enquiries, have you decided your extremely dodgy new evidence is rubbish?"

"Well, actually, no, we can't do that at present. Douglas repeated that he was at home alone that evening, went to bed early after working hard at getting things to rights, and slept soundly until the morning. He woke late, curious why the cock hadn't crowed, and went to see. That's when he found Clem, he said. This ties in exactly with his first statement."

"But no alibi, then," Lois said flatly.

"Afraid not, Lois. But we have more work to do on that, and I shall of course let you know immediately if we can rule out Douglas completely."

"I should bloody well hope so!" swore Lois, totally unrepentant. "If not, you can kiss goodbye to my help." She cut off the conversation, leaving Cowgill sitting with bent head and stooping shoulders. Suddenly he sat upright, rang for his assistant, and picked up his pen. "I'll find the solution to this one by the end of next week, if it's the last thing I do," he muttered to himself, and added, "and please God it's not Douglas Meade."

Forty-One

Monday morning, and the Meade family was depressed. Lois had had to tell Gran about Douglas in case it should get around by other means, and then Gran had made her own decision to tell Josie in the shop, and then Jamie. Lois had been furious at first, but then realised that Gran was probably right, and it was better coming from her than outside the family.

"You'll be having the meeting as usual, Lois?" Gran asked at breakfast.

"Why not?" Lois said sharply. "We're not in mourning, are we?"

Gran bit back an equally sharp retort, and said she would make sure there was enough milk for coffee. She had to go down to the shop this morning, and would get a paper.

Lois did not ask her why. She was too nervous to buy the local herself, but hoped desperately that Cowgill had kept his word. Discreet, he had said. But he was not the only one at Tresham police station, and good stories leaked out. Cowgill himself had often thought it was no coincidence that the commissioner was a big pal of the editor of the local rag. Reciprocally, of course, the information gleaned by local reporters could on occasion be very useful to the police.

On her way to visit a new client in Waltonby, Lois turned all this over in her mind. There was nothing more she could do . . . But surely, this couldn't be true. There was always something. Maybe she should cancel her outing with the WI to the museum tomorrow and concentrate on ferretin'. But no, Gran would be so disappointed, and maybe she might hear something from the old tabs that could be useful. It was surprising how much they knew from the gossip network.

Dot Nimmo had started this morning at the new client, and Lois expected to hear from her what had happened in the mix-up with Evelyn. It was really a private matter for the two sisters, but Lois liked to know what was going on. She pulled up outside the new house on an estate in Waltonby, and knocked at the front door. Dot answered, and smiled broadly. "Morning, Mrs. M," she said. "The missus is gone shopping, but come in. She was expecting you and dashed out for coffee. She's one of those dashers, if you know what I mean."

Lois followed Dot into the neat, entirely beige sitting room. How did people do it? Not a mark on the carpet, no smudges on the arms of the chairs, no books propped open with reading glasses, or prints on the wall faded from being too much in the sun. Perfection. Still, that's partly what Dot was here for, and she asked her straightaway what had happened with poor Evelyn.

Dot had had time to think out a sensible course of action, and had decided for the moment to lie. She had no desire to send Mrs. M steaming off into the dangerous clutches of Alastair/John Smith, and no Nimmo had ever given useful information to the police. She would bide her time, and in the meanwhile somehow get Slimy John and his so-called mother in her power so that she could go back there and find out more. Then she would alert Mrs. M.

"Oh, it was just a misunderstanding," she answered casually. "Evie thought I was meeting her that day, and I knew it was the next. All sorted out now, and I apologised, though I'm certain it was her fault."

"Right. Well, I'm glad it turned out all right. Now, where's that missus of yours?"

"There," said Dot, pointing through the front window. "Just coming in. She's nice, doesn't give orders, and seems satisfied with my work."

"Yes, well, we'll see. Make yourself scarce, Dot, while I talk to her. I'll see you later at the meeting."

All seemed to be going well, and as usual the new client had fallen for Dot's apparently straightforward and plain-speaking approach. "You certainly know where you are with Dot!"

"Good. Well, let me know if you're unhappy about anything. Anything at all." Lois left, feeling that here was another household in good hands.

All the others had arrived when Dot puffed in ten minutes late. "Sorry, Mrs. M," she said breathlessly. "Big jam on the bypass. Lorry jackknifed, right across the dual carriageway. Why they didn't set up a diversion beats me. And o' course, once you're on the bypass you're stuck until—"

"Yes, well, sit down, Dot. We must get on with the meeting." Lois was aware that she sounded impatient and irritable, but Douglas was at the back of her mind all the time. Douglas, her dear, helpful, accommodating elder son, her firstborn, suspected of an awful murder! It was a waking nightmare.

"Mrs. M?" Sheila Stratford, the oldest member of the team, was looking at her enquiringly. She had asked a question, and Lois had not responded. "What do you think? Shall I take

Andrew with me to the estate agents? I could do with strong arms to help move the filing cabinets. Haven't cleaned behind there for weeks."

"Months," said Dot.

Lois ignored Dot, and said yes, of course, that would be a good idea. She would leave them to liaise. From this point, she decided she must concentrate. She had a business to run, and the team was like a second family. They relied on her, and she would never let them down.

"Thanks, Sheila," Andrew said politely. "I need to get the hang of things. Oh, and by the way, Mrs. M, do you want me to report on the interior décor side of the business at these meetings?"

Lois nodded. "Yes, I do. You will find the girls have very good ideas on most things. Floss will be needing your help soon, anyway, when she finds a house. When's the big day again, Floss?"

"October thirtieth," Floss said with a smile. "In some ways I can't wait, and in others, when Mum goes on and on about her plans, I'd like to creep away with Ben and get the whole thing done speedily at the Register Office."

"Cold feet," said Lois kindly. "On my wedding morning I came out in a bright red rash, and told Gran I couldn't go through with it. You can imagine what she said!"

"Who's taking my name in vain?" said Gran, coming in with the coffee.

"Never mind, Mum. Just put the tray down there, and we'll help ourselves. We've more to do. All behind like the cow's tail this morning. Now, Andrew, update us."

Andrew cleared his throat and gave them a clear and brief description of where he'd got to with Susie and her house in Gordon Street. He wondered if he should mention seeing a woman going into number six, but decided against it. It was nothing to do with New Brooms.

As if reading his thoughts, Lois said, "No more threatening phone calls, I hope, Andrew?"

He shook his head, wondering why she had mentioned it at the meeting. In the next few minutes he discovered the reason. Everyone in the team had had experience of nasty phone calls, heavy breathing, disgusting suggestions, and so on. Mrs. M listened carefully.

"What was it about, Andrew?" Hazel said. "We get the usuals at the office sometimes, probably because there was once a knocking shop over the road. All tastes catered for there. What was the voice like?"

Andrew described what he was certain was a disguised voice, but none of them recognised it from his attempt at imitation.

"Sounds like it was meant just for you. A one-off, probably," said Hazel. "Better watch your step, lad. What did he say?"

Andrew hesitated, and looked at Mrs. M. She nodded, and he gave them the facts.

"Number six?" Dot said. "Nobody living there. They'll have trouble selling that after what happened to poor ole Clem. Bad-luck house, like Braeside over the road."

This resulted in a lively conversation about the long-ago murder case, and Lois had to bring the meeting to a firm close. "Get back to work, you lot," she said. "We have houses to clean and clients to cheer up. I'll be in touch, as usual."

Dot hung back after the others had gone. "Heard anything from Mrs. Blairgowrie?" she said to Lois.

"No. Why? Is something wrong?"

"Not so far as I know. Just wondered if they'd been on to you about anything."

"No, nothing." Lois frowned and looked closely at Dot. "Are you keeping something from me? Something I should know? If so, for God's sake speak up, Dot. It could be very important." Douglas had come back into her thoughts with a vengeance. Dot had so many contacts with the underworld in Tresham, she might well have heard something that would help.

"Would I do that?" Dot said with not a single stab of conscience. "If I find out anything that will help Douglas, I'll let you know at once."

Lois felt cold. "How do you know about Douglas?" she said, beginning to shake.

Dot approached and took her hand. "Haven't you seen the paper today?" she said. Lois shook her head mutely. "Well, don't you worry, dear. I reckon they'll print any old trash just to sell the rag. Don't you worry," she repeated, "we'll get it all sorted out."

Forty-Two

"I can see they've told you," Gran said, as Lois came slowly into the kitchen after the meeting. "I was going to show you the paper after they'd gone. It's only a small paragraph on the inside pages, but there's a photograph."

Lois took the paper from her in silence. She read the bare facts. Murdered Man's Neighbour Under Suspicion. Under this headline, the report stated that Douglas Meade, next-door neighbour of murder victim Clem Fitch, popular resident of Gordon Street, had been questioned again in connection with the case. Douglas Meade, it continued, was the son of the well-known proprietor of New Brooms, Mrs. Lois Meade.

Lois turned on her heel and marched back to her study with heavy footsteps. Gran sighed. She knew exactly what Lois would do next.

"Inspector Cowgill please," Lois said to his assistant, having had no reply from his personal number.

"Not here, I'm afraid, Mrs. Meade."

"Where the hell is he, then?"

"On his way to see you. Should be there shortly. Anything else I can help you with?"

But Lois had rung off. She went to the window to look up the street, but it was empty. She stood there for several minutes, fuming and making no attempt to control her anger. She wished she had a gun.

Then his car came in sight, and her heart began to thump. She went out of the front door, down the drive, and into the street. As he got out of the car, she looked venomously at him. "Well?" she said.

He shook his head and walked round to stand next to her on the pavement. "I need to explain, Lois," he said.

"You certainly do!" she said. "You promised me you'd be discreet." She waved the newspaper at him. "Is this what you call discreet? Don't ever speak to me again. And don't expect my help. I wouldn't trust you now as far as I could throw you."

"That is not very far, fortunately," he said. He walked back around the car and looked over at her. "I can only say I have no idea how the paper got the story and am investigating the leak. I am extremely sorry, Lois. I shall do my best to make amends."

"Amends!" she shrieked. "How can you put that right? The entire population of Tresham reads this rag! Get out of my sight!" She ran back into the house and slammed the door. Cowgill drove off slowly. She was in tears, he told himself sadly, and it's my fault.

That evening there was a family conference. Jamie was the only one missing, but as they sat down round the big kitchen table, he telephoned and said would Mum please let him know what they discussed and would they be sure to let him know if there was anything he could do.

Strangely, Douglas was the only one who seemed relatively unconcerned. "I don't think we should take this too seriously," he said, kicking off the meeting. "The police have questioned just about everybody in the street. They hauled me in again because some joker had left an anonymous message saying they'd seen me from a bedroom window in the next street beating up old Clem. Mum's chum Cowgill said he was not so much interested in me as in who would want to incriminate me, and why."

Lois began to deny hotly that Cowgill was her chum, but Derek shushed her, and said she could have her say later.

"It's obvious," Josie said from her seat next to Douglas. "If you want to cover up your crime, you incriminate someone else. Douglas is an easy target. They should be looking for the reason why Clem was killed. What did he know, or, more likely, what had he seen?"

"I agree," said Lois. "Douglas has no enemies. I'm sure he's never even hurt anybody's feelings. He's just convenient, living next door with no alibi. No, I reckon those dimwits should be concentrating on Braeside across the road. There's definitely something funny going on there. That son of Mrs. Blairgowrie—Alastair, he calls himself—is either the twin brother or the same man as John Smith, the new owner of the Pickering house."

"What's he got to do with it?" Derek said.

"Everything, I reckon," Gran said. "I've never seen such a suspicious-looking customer in my life. A lot of coming and going at that house, too. I reckon he's Mr. Big."

"Too much television, Gran," said Douglas, laughing.

"I spoke some more to him two or three days ago," Josie said quietly. They all turned and looked at her. "I asked him about his family. Just chatting, you know. Got to get on with all my customers, whether I like them or not. He was pleasant for once. Said his mother lived in Tresham, that she'd been married twice, and he was the son of her first marriage to Alastair Smith. She named him after his father, but he preferred his second name, John."

"He told you all that?" said an astonished Lois. "Why on earth should he?"

"Why on earth shouldn't he, Mum?" Douglas smiled at her and said perhaps she'd forgotten that her daughter was a very attractive girl, and most men would rabbit on in order to spend a little more time with her.

"Huh!" said Lois and preferred to think otherwise. It was too glib a story, probably invented to explain the difference in names.

"Anyway," said Derek, taking charge, "we're here to discuss Douglas and what we can do to help deal with the inevitable gossip that'll surround him. Could even affect your job, lad," he added.

"I got sent for in the office this afternoon," Douglas said. "The boss was very understanding, but you're right, Dad, they won't want me around if it goes any further. He made that quite clear. But I'm all right for the moment. We just have to get this whole thing cleared up as soon as possible. All of us together should be able to get to the bottom of it. Or just Mum by herself."

He looked at her with such trust and confidence that Lois felt weak with anguish. Sleuthing was all very well, a bit of a game when it was someone else's family involved. But when it was your own son... She got up and went to the sink to hide her emotion. "I'll make some coffee," she said. "It'll keep us alert. We need a plan of action."

Gordon Street was quiet. A stray cat escaped death by inches as a large car turned the corner and made no attempt to avoid it. The car pulled up outside Braeside, and Alastair John Smith walked up to his mother's front door and disappeared inside.

Half an hour went by, with only a couple of girls giggling

their way along to the supermarket. Then a middle-aged woman, thin and blonde, walked quickly up to Braeside front door and knocked. The front curtains twitched, and she knocked again. This time the door opened and she went in.

"Dot sodding Nimmo!" gasped Mrs. Blairgowrie. "What are you doing here?"

Alastair appeared behind her. "Get her, Babs," he said. "Get her back here in the sitting room."

"If you dare touch me," Dot said calmly, "I shall make sure everything I know about you and your little enterprise is reported directly to the police. I have left all the details with my sister with instructions to take the envelope to the police station if I am not back at her house by nine o'clock."

Mrs. Blairgowrie backed away from her, and Alastair stared, unsure what to do next.

"I 'ave a number of things to say to you," Dot continued, "so I'll come into the sitting room of my own free will." She walked past them and they followed meekly. "And leave the door open," she added. "I'm a bit claustrowhatsit."

Exactly a quarter of an hour later, the door of Braeside opened once more, and Dot Nimmo walked out, head held high.

Forty-Three

The day of the outing dawned grey and wet. Gran woke early and looked at the sky. "Rain before seven, fine before eleven," she said.

Lois came down to breakfast looking a lot more cheerful, and said it didn't matter anyway. Most of the museum was under cover. Derek said he would be better employed mending that leak in the shed, but Gran and Lois turned on him and said he'd promised to come to swell the numbers of the group. And anyway, there was the section of old farm machinery and he was interested in that, wasn't he? He capitulated and said he'd better be off to finish that job in Fletching so he could be back in time for the procession of cars to the museum.

"We could've filled a minibus," Gran said, when they were all assembled outside the church. "Still, at least it means we can leave when we want to."

Lois was subdued, but had decided that the outing would be a good opportunity for her to switch off and think. The family plan had turned out to be not much more than keeping eyes and ears open, and reporting back to Lois anything that might help. But she had been grateful for their support, and was confident that between them they would crack it. "Without Cowgill?" Derek had said, looking straight at her. She had not answered.

It was usually a twenty-minute drive, but the convoy had to go slowly because of the elderly Mini driven by Miss Hewitt and Miss Allen. The two ladies maintained that thirty miles an hour was fast enough for anyone. Derek noticed with chagrin that several cars passed them at speed on the dual carriageway, one containing a grinning mate of his from the pub. Finally they reached the modern entrance to the museum and parked in the spacious area labelled Groups.

"Well, I don't know I'm sure," said Ivy Beasley from Round Ringford WI. She stood looking around her. "You'd not think this was in the middle of Tresham, would you, Doris?" Doris was her good friend and companion, and had endless patience when in the firing line.

The large old red-brick farmhouse stood four-square among venerable pine trees, and in the surrounding park sheep grazed lazily in the sun. As Gran had predicted, soon after eleven o'clock the rain had stopped and the sky cleared. The assorted arrivals gathered together in a body and entered the museum reception area. The pleasant tall man greeted them, and said he was to be their guide. Miss Allen and Miss Hewitt disappeared behind the tempting shelves of the shop. "Come along now, ladies," the guide called. "Plenty of time to shop before you leave us."

They began in a small building dedicated to the origin of telephones. "Huh," said Ivy Beasley, "how fascinating."

"Oh, come on, Ivy," Doris said, "you get one end of this and I'll get the other." She handed Ivy an empty tin connected by string to another, and spoke in a whisper something that she was sure Ivy would not hear.

"Doris Ashbourne!" said Ivy, whose hearing was conveniently erratic. "That's quite enough of that!"

The party spent so long trying out mini-exchanges and telephones they could remember from their childhood that they had to be moved on by the guide. Entering the grand front door of the farmhouse, they turned out of a tiled hall into the best parlour, furnished entirely in the Victorian style. Gran was thrilled. "Oh, look, Lois!" she said. "A pianola! Just like we used to have at my auntie's."

A room steward stepped forward and said, "Would you like to play it, dear?"

Gran beamed. "Just remind me how," she said, and the woman showed her the pierced rolls of paper and the pedals that worked the mechanism. As a result, the tune could be speeded up or slowed down to a dirge, and Gran played "Hindustani" with considerable emotion. Lois stood watching, but chiefly her eyes were on the steward. Why was she so familiar? There was something about her guarded smile, the way she stood, waiting for Gran to finish. When the music ended at top speed, Gran modestly acknowledged a few claps, and joined the others.

"Lois! Come over here, me duck. Look at this sparrow hawk, poor thing." Derek was standing by a stuffed bird under a glass dome. It was moth-eaten and its fine feathers had faded. But its murderous beak and glassy stare made Lois shiver. "Ugh," she said, "I reckon they were a bloodthirsty lot, the Victorians."

"Nothing changes, Mrs. Meade," said the steward, coming up behind them. Lois was startled. How did this woman know her name? And why did her remark sound like a threat?

"On we go, ladies!" said the tall man, and Derek muttered to Lois that he wished the guide had noticed there were one or two men in the party. Lois glanced back once more at the steward, and was sure she had seen that face before. But not with pretty grey hair and pearls.

It had been an inspired visit. Many of the WI members could remember the old domestic exhibits, and the small street of shops intrigued them. The ladies did not linger in the large barn full of threshing machines, red paint faded to a gentle pink; friendly small tractors; and chicken houses, still with a faint odour of warm droppings. But Derek was in his element, and Lois waited for him rather than join the stampede to the tearooms. Then she caught sight once more of the woman steward crossing the yard outside. "Derek!" she said. "Who is that woman? I'm sure I've seen her before." But she had disappeared into the house, and that was the last Lois saw of her before sitting down to a welcome cup of tea with home-made gingerbread.

It was not the last Pat saw of Lois. The party did not know that she was following them discreetly out of sight, and noted with dismay that Lois Meade was accompanied by her mother and husband, and that none of them looked particularly troubled. Why not? All of 'em should be biting their nails in anxiety about Douglas. Pat was worried. She would have to report back to Alastair. Perhaps it would be better to phone Babs to convey the message. Meantime, Lois should have got the message in the parlour. It was meant to be a subtle warning, and it had gone home, judging from the look on her face.

Pat watched them with a sinking heart from the hatch in the kitchen, laughing and enjoying tea with the others. How to explain that to Alastair?

The group returned to Farnden in convoy, still at a steady thirty, and dispersed tired but happy.

Back in the museum, Pat prepared to leave, and said goodbye to the chief.

"Pleasant people, that lot," the tall man said. "Nice to have some intelligent questions. There's a lot to be said for retirement! Which reminds me," he added, "our long-serving care-taker has announced the date she wishes to leave, and it is alarmingly close. I wondered if you would like to think of taking her place? It would not, of course, include cleaning. As you know, we have a team of volunteers for that. But you could live rent free in the flat, and have the run of the gardens and so on. It is a responsible job, and requires a special kind of person. Could you give it some thought?"

Pat beamed. All thoughts of Alastair vanished. "No need for thought! I accept right now. And I can move in as soon as you like. I've been living with my sister, as you know, and she is not as good company as my dear late husband, to put it mildly." It was immensely cheering to think of getting out of that awful crumbling safe house. This would be the perfect hiding place.

The tall man put out his hand. "My dear, you have saved the day. We shall discuss all the details in the morning, and I shall sleep soundly tonight. Thank you so much."

Gran set the table for supper, having had a full postmortem of the visit with Mrs. Pickering. "Went off well, we think," she said to Derek, who agreed, with reservations.

"Just don't try and rope me in on any trips to knitting exhibitions and stuff like that," he said. He looked across at Lois, who was staring blankly out of the window. "You're very quiet, me duck," he said. "Everything all right?"

Lois turned and said she was trying to remember something. "It'll come to me," she said, and gave him a hug.

Forty-Four

In Gordon Street, Douglas, Susie, and Josie were having a council of war. They sat on the floor in Susie's house, having inspected the progress of Andrew's interior décor and pronounced it promising. Even Douglas, who did not trust Andrew with Susie one inch, had to admit that so far it was an amazing transformation.

"Right," he said, taking the lead, "have we anything to report? Susie?" He had insisted that they include Susie, since she had been an innocent victim, and was as anxious as any of them to find the man who had bound and gagged her.

Susie shook her head. "I haven't heard anything at work. The theft seems to have been put on the back burner. I heard they'd decided it was gypos passing through the town."

"Rubbish!" Josie said angrily. "Those poor souls get blamed for everything. They're not all bad. A good excuse for the cops to wrap it up."

"Never mind that now. We should concentrate on the whereabouts of the skinny man and also, as Mum said, keep a special eye on Braeside over the road. I've seen nothing much myself. How about you, Susie, when you've been coming and going?"

Susie hesitated. She was not confident in reporting what she had seen, in case Josie dismissed it scathingly, like she had the gypsies. "Um, well, I did see a woman going in there early on, before you two arrived. It wasn't Mrs. Blairgowrie. You could see she wasn't blind, the way she walked quickly up to the door. Sort of old, but active. Grey hair, neatly dressed."

"Who let her in?" Douglas took her hand. He could see she was nervous.

"It was a man. A big man. He shut the door quickly, and o' course we've not been looking out since, so I don't know if either of them came out again."

Josie said, "The man, the big man. Did you notice anything else about him?" She realised that she'd been sharp with the girl and softened her tone. Susie was very young, poor kid. Years younger than Douglas.

"Well, he'd gone in pretty quickly, but I think he had glasses. Those big, horn-rimmed sort. And a dark suit. That's all, really."

"Well done, Susie," said Douglas, giving her a peck on the cheek. "Looks like we have to identify the second woman. We'll tell Mum. She has ways of finding out! Perhaps we'd better station ourselves at the window, out of sight, and see if anyone emerges."

Inside Braeside, all was silent. The three were sitting in a semicircle round the dining table looking at exhibit A.

"I can't do it," Pat said. "You can do what you like to me, but I can't do that. I never have and I'm not going to start now."

"Oh, I think we can change your mind, don't you?" Alastair John Smith smiled at Mrs. Blairgowrie conspiratorially, and Pat quaked.

"Can't you find somebody else? I'll not breathe a word. You know you can trust me."

"Ah, now that's just what we don't know, isn't it. You've made a mess of things once or twice already. I haven't forgotten the pork chops mysteriously floating down the river."

"I told you. They said it was a bloody dog. Nothing to do with me."

"So you said. But you're beginning to look like a liability. I can't have liabilities on my hands."

"I still can't do it," Pat said miserably.

Mrs. Blairgowrie laughed then. "You'll manage, Pat," she said. "A steady hand and plenty of patience is all you need. I can give you a few tips, if you like."

"There is one thing you've managed to get right," said Alastair. "You've found a really good hiding place, right under the noses of the good folk of Tresham. Now's the time to redeem yourself. You're extremely unlikely to be recognised, especially in the pearls and cashmere. Quite the lady about town. Now, I'd better be getting back to Farnden. I want to keep a close eye on the lovely Mrs. Meade this evening. There's a jumble sale in the village hall, and I mean to go. She's bound to be there. And I might pick up a few bargains on the side."

"Why are you watching her?" Pat said.

"Orders from above. Now, I must be off. You'd better be going, too, Pat. And don't forget that," he added, pointing to the black bag on the table. "Leave about ten minutes after I've gone." He left without a word of goodbye, and slammed the front door behind him.

With all the old clothes, books, bric-a-brac, vinyl records, cassettes, CDs, and magazines sorted on their proper tables, all was quiet and relaxed in the village hall.

Helpers were watching the clock. They would open the doors on the dot of six thirty to the bunch of people waiting outside. There had been some anxiety that most of the likely customers would have been on the WI outing, and would be too tired to come along. But there among others were Ivy Beasley and Doris, Mrs. Pickering, and Gran and her friend, the cook from the pub, all fresh as a daisy and prepared for the fray.

Mrs. Smith from Waltonby, no relation of John, had been drawn in as a committee member after the tragic death of her son in a fall from a horse. She stared out of the window and said, "Blimey! Quite a few waiting, and there's a man in a suit. Shall I open up?" She went to the double doors and with a dramatic gesture much appreciated by the crowd, she stood aside and waved them in.

Alastair was embarrassed, felt out of place, but was determined. He made for the bookstall, and picked up book after book, leafing through them with one eye on the door. He pricked up his ears when he heard someone say, "Isn't Lois coming, Mrs. Weedon?" Gran answered that she was, but would be late as she had some paperwork to catch up on. Alastair moved on to the bric-a-brac. Maybe he'd take home something cheap and colourful for his woman. She was easily pleased.

His patience was rewarded after half an hour, when Lois

came in with apologies for being late. She joined Gran at the household linen stall, and then caught sight of him. She stared, and he came towards her. "Good evening, Mrs. Meade," he said. "You probably don't remember me. I'm Mrs. Blairgowrie's son. We met at Braeside."

"Oh, I do remember," Lois said. "And now you're living in Farnden. Have you settled in? Can I recommend the services of New Brooms? We do a very good cleanup job after people have moved house. Thoroughly freshened up from top to bottom."

It had been an impulse to offer him the team's services. It could be very useful having one of the girls in there, ears and eyes open. It could also be very dangerous, and she was almost relieved when he shook his head, saying he managed quite well, thank you.

He in his turn had been taken aback by Lois's suggestion. He had meant to say something to remind her that he was now very much around the village and would be keeping an eye on her. If possible, a coded threat had been his intention.

He was rescued by an unexpected intervention from Derek. "Lois! Can you come home, quick as you can!" She turned in alarm and in seconds followed him out of the hall and disappeared.

Gran was looking anxious, and Alastair moved closer to her. "Not bad news, I hope, Mrs. Weedon," he said in a concerned voice.

"Who are you?" asked Gran, knowing perfectly well who he was.

"Smith, John Smith. We met in your granddaughter's shop. I've moved into—"

"Yes, yes," Gran said. "I remember now. I have to go right away. I'm helping on teas." She went swiftly round into the kitchen and began washing up cups and saucers with vigour. Huh! she said to herself. He needn't think he can ignore me one day and be best friends the next, just when he wants to know something. Nosy blighter!

Lois broke into a trot outside the village hall, and Derek caught her by the arm. "Hey, he's not going to run away. Whoa!" he said.

"I'm not a horse!" Lois said breathlessly. She slowed down to a walk, and smiled at Derek. "Trust him not to let us know he was coming," she added. "And nobody there to greet him!"

"I was," said Derek. "Anyway, there he is, look. Coming to meet us."

Lois once more broke into a run, and then she was hugging her younger son, and saying over and over, "Jamie, Jamie.."

Later in the evening, Derek and Gran tactfully left Jamie with his mother in the sitting room while they went off to make coffee. "So what's the latest on Douglas?" Jamie asked.

Lois shrugged. "Nothing much new. I've got an idea or two what's behind it all, but they're only guesses really. We're all ferretin', as your father says, to see if anything comes up. The only thing they've got on Douglas is an anonymous letter left at the police station incriminating him. Somebody was supposed to have seen him do in old Clem Fitch. Watching from a bedroom window. Police enquiries have turned up exactly nowt."

"What about your friend Cowgill? Are you still in touch with him?"

"Well," said Lois, "so far he's been useless and untrustworthy. Like all cops. Relies on other people for his information, and doesn't keep his promises."

"Ah, I see," Jamie said with the ghost of a smile. "Right, so can I join the New Brooms investigating team? I've got a couple of weeks free. Sorry I didn't let you know, but it was a last-minute concert cancellation. Earthquake stops play."

"You're joking!" Derek said, coming in with the tray.

Jamie shook his head. "No, quite serious," he said. "One of the hazards of being a globe-trotting piano player."

"Jamie wants to help clear up this Douglas thing," Lois said.

"More the merrier," said Gran. "I still reckon that John Smith, so-called, is deep in it, but Lois won't listen to me."

"Of course I listen," Lois said. "You may well be right, but it'd do no good frightening off the rotten lot who're involved before we can get them safely behind bars. They're good at moonlight flits, as we know."

"Too right," Derek said, and turned to Jamie. "That bugger who lived the other side of Clem Fitch did a bunk overnight and seems to have vanished from the earth."

"Mm." Lois looked thoughtful. "He's probably still round

here somewhere," she added, "and I mean to find him. And soon."

They all stared at her. "She knows something," Gran said acidly, "and you bet she's not going to tell us."

Forty-Five

"Dot? Mrs. M here. Could you come over this morning later on? After you've finished at Braeside."

Dot did not much want a face-to-face talk with Mrs. M at the moment. She had a lot to sort out in her mind. "Anything I can help you with over the phone?" she said. "Schedule's a bit tight today."

"You'll manage," Lois said. "I'll expect you about twelve thirty. 'Bye."

She had sat up late last night, chatting with Jamie and generally discussing family business. Douglas had telephoned to speak to his brother, and then had asked for a word with Lois. He had told her what Susie had seen, watching out of her window, and added that they'd all monitored the place after that, and had seen first the man leave, and then, ten minutes later, the grey-haired woman. He was pleased that Mum was so interested in this woman, and promised to see what he could find out. Other neighbours in the terrace might know a bit more than he did.

Now she needed to quiz Dot. Dot was being very evasive, a sure sign that she had something to hide. Maybe she had forgotten that her job description had included being ready to help out on any matter where Mrs. M needed information. This applied to Dot only, not the rest of the team, and had arisen because of her connection with Tresham's underworld. Dot had been happy to oblige and had been very useful now and then. She fancied herself as being assistant sleuth. Lois would remind her of that.

Alastair John Smith saw Dot arrive. If he'd known how to gnash his teeth he would have gnashed them. That wretched woman had got them over a barrel. He thought back to the day when she had escaped them in the playing field. It struck him that she had not actually been inside his house, and would not therefore have seen any clues to what she called his "little enterprise." So what had she got on them? Abduction, for a start. That would be enough to put the police on their trail, but it would be her word against his, and with a name like Nimmo she would have problems convincing them. What else had she discovered on her cleaning days at Braeside? That was the problem. He had no idea how much she knew. That was why he could not make any moves against her now. What else was she up to? It had all been going so well...He sighed, and turned away from the window. Then he had a brilliant idea. Why hadn't he thought of it before? If you can't beat 'em, get 'em to join you.

"Come in, Dot," said Lois, answering the door. "We'll have a chat in the office. It shouldn't take long. Depends on you, really."

"What d'you mean, Mrs. M? Are you givin' me m' cards?"

"Of course not. I just want to know what's going on at Braeside. I don't think you've been quite straight with me, and you've been with us long enough to know I won't have that."

Dot did not answer for a few seconds. She was thinking hard, as she had been doing since Mrs. M had telephoned this morning. Now she had a straight choice. Either she told Mrs. M everything, or she lied. She decided reluctantly to take the first course of action.

"You're right," she said. "I've been keepin' things back an' though it was for your own good, I know you're going to be annoyed. Might even give me m' cards after all," she added sadly.

Lois said nothing, and waited.

"First of all, and worst of all, I changed my rota that day without permission. It was the day Evie called looking for me. I went to Braeside in the morning instead of the afternoon. I knew that Alastair would be coming to see his mother, and I wanted to eavesdrop, to get some clues. I knew you was interested, and thought I could give you some help."

"Never mind about the rota," Lois said. "Just tell me all of it, from the beginning."

But at that moment, there was a heavy rapping at the front door, and Dot got up to look out of the window. She withdrew rapidly. "It's 'im!" she whispered.

Gran answered the door as usual, and told Alastair John Smith to wait, while she found out whether Mrs. Meade was at home. She shut the door in his face and turned to Lois. "Are you in, or not?"

Lois nodded. "But hang on a minute. Dot, you wait in the kitchen with Mum. Keep the door shut, and don't come out until I tell you." She saw Dot safely out of sight and then opened the door. "I'm very busy. What do you want?"

Alastair smiled broadly at Lois, and edged his way in. Lois grudgingly opened her office door and ushered him in. Without being asked, he sat down in the chair by the desk. She remained standing. "What can I do for you, Mr. Smith?" she said.

"It's more a case of what I can do for you," he said. "I know you have a cleaning business and I wondered whether you have trouble getting staff? Not every woman wants to clean other women's houses, do they?" Lois did not answer, and he laughed again, and continued confidently. "Now, if that's the case, I might be able to help you. I could supply you with good, hard-working labour."

"What exactly do you mean?" Lois asked.

"What I said, dear," he said, gaining confidence. "The likes of us in small businesses should help each other, that's what I believe. Goodness knows it's difficult earning a crust these days. Supermarkets have all but destroyed the small businessman."

Lois took a long, speculative look at him. "Well, that may be so. But supermarkets don't offer cleaning services, so far as I know. No, I'm doing very nicely on my own, Mr. Smith. My team are loyal and content with their jobs."

"Even Dot Nimmo?" he said nastily, smiles all gone. "Those Nimmos are not all that trustworthy, you know, Mrs. Meade." He was angry that she'd turned him down, without even a friendly discussion. Perhaps he'd chosen a bad day. And where was that Nimmo woman? He'd thought she'd be here in the office. He could've killed two birds with one stone, in a manner of speaking. He had planned on showing her how he would be in close association with her boss, and see how she reacted to that. She wouldn't find it easy to get another job. He would see to that.

"If that's all, Mr. Smith, I have a very busy day, and must get on. I'll show you out."

He got up clumsily, while she stood holding the door open. "Perhaps we can talk again," he said in a last-ditch attempt, "when you're not so busy."

"Perhaps," said Lois, and closed the front door behind him. She went through to the kitchen and was annoyed to hear from Gran that Dot had gone off across the field. "What does she think she's up to?" Lois said irritably.

"I'm back," said a voice. "Just needed a breath of fresh air."

"Come on, then," Lois said, and back in the office she prompted Dot to continue where they had left off.

"Nothing much more to tell," said Dot. "I didn't hear anything of interest, just the usual shouting match between the two of them. The rest you know, about me and Evelyn an' that."

Lois stared at her. "Are you sure that's all?" she said. "Everything you were keeping to yourself?"

Lie, Dottie, she said to herself. She had changed her mind. It was too dangerous for Mrs. M to know just yet. "You know me, Mrs. M," she said with a chuckle, "the only completely truthful and reliable Nimmo you're likely to meet. 'Cept Evelyn, o' course. But then, neither of us sisters are real Nimmos, are we? Shall I be on me way now?"

"Before you go, have you seen a friend of Mrs. Blairgowrie visiting Braeside while you've been there? Middle-aged, grey hair, cashmere and pearls. You know the sort."

Dot shook her head. "Probably a friend of the old duck, helping with shoppin' and goin' to the hairdresser's. That sort of thing. Some do-gooder, most likely. Better be off now, Mrs. M, else I'll be late for our new client. Can't have that, can we?"

As she made for the door, she turned back and said, "Why d'you want to know about that cashmere woman? You on to something?"

"Mind your own business, Dot, and get on with what you're paid to do."

Dot grinned. She was not in the least offended. "So I'll keep me eyes open, then? See you later, Mrs. M. Don't do anything I wouldn't do."

"Go!" said Lois. Dot went.

Forty-Six

"Morning, Josie! Fancy a ride out to see my new cottage in the country?"

"For heaven's sake! You made me jump out of my skin! Haven't seen you for ages." Josie had been stacking lower shelves with tins of tomatoes and pasta sauce, and had not heard Matthew Vickers come in through the open door of the shop. He was off duty, a pleasant, casual young man. It was a lovely morning, bright sun and a fresh wind blowing through the village.

Josie had been brooding on the row she'd had with Rob before he'd set off for work after breakfast. He'd been asking again about getting engaged, and she had said she was quite happy with things as they were.

"Well," said Matthew, "how's about it? Can you get Gran to cover for you? It's too good a day to be shut up in a shop. And I want your advice about work to be done on the house."

"Haven't you got work to do for the police force and the good people of Tresham?" Josie said. "I thought a policeman's lot was not a happy one. Seems to me it's a doddle. Solve a few minor crimes and take a couple of days off. Help a couple of old ladies across the road, and take half a day to recover from such arduous work. Are you serious?"

He nodded. "Quite serious. Any chance of Gran coming down here? I could go and ask, if you want the might of the law behind you."

"You're very perky this morning, Matthew Vickers! Have you been promoted, or what?"

"As good as," he replied. "Looks like I'll get a permanent transfer to Tresham before Uncle retires, so as he can break me in. It's what I've always wanted, especially lately."

Josie didn't ask him why especially lately. Things were complicated enough. But the idea of being out in the sunshine in the middle of a field, with him, was attractive. "Oh, all right, then. I'll give her a ring. I have to think of a good reason, though. Gran's pretty smart." And she's fond of Rob, she reminded herself.

After taking small liberties with the truth, Josie persuaded her to take over for an hour or so, and she and Matthew set off in his car. "I told her it was to do with Doug and the police," she said, shamefaced. "So how is the police investigation into old Clem's murder going? Mum's been a bit secretive about it all lately. We had a family conference after Doug was questioned again. She didn't give much away, though."

Matthew glanced sympathetically at her. "Not too sure myself," he said. "Except my uncle's been like a bear with a sore head lately. His PA says he's impossible to approach at the moment. The rumour round the station is that your mum and him had a ding-dong and he's suffering withdrawal symptoms." He quickened up on a long narrow lane, and Josie cautioned him that she was carsick at speed.

"What d'you mean by withdrawal symptoms?" she said, as the needle sank back to sixty mph. "There's nothing going on between them! I can assure you of that. So you can squash any rumours of that sort straightaway!"

"Okay, okay. Keep your hair on. It's just that everyone knows he thinks the world of her, probably fancies her, but would never do anything that was out of order."

They turned down the rutted track that led to the cottage. "Is that it? That crumbling heap?" Josie was grumpy, put into a bad mood by Matthew's light-hearted view of her mother's reputation. "You must have been crazy to buy that. It'll cost a mint to put it right."

"I bought it very cheap. Most of the work I can do myself, with one or two mates, and you'll be amazed at the transformation."

"I certainly shall," said Josie, as she stepped out of the car and turned her ankle on a deep rut. "Ouch! Now look what you've done!"

Matthew looked at her face, saw that she was near to tears, and realised that she and probably the whole family were under considerable stress. He walked around to her and picked her up bodily. "Light as a feather," he said, and carried her across to the house.

"Put me down!" she yelled. "Help! I'm being abducted!"

He was relieved to see her smile, and set her down gently at the front door. "Come on in, little one," he said protectively. "Here, sit down here and rest your ankle."

"Not on that flea-ridden settee!" Josie said. "And I'm not

little, and my ankle is fine. Lucky for you it wasn't a real twist. I don't suppose you've got a kettle around?"

"Coffee? Tea?" He disappeared into what she guessed must be the kitchen, and reappeared minutes later with a steaming mug. "Sugar in it, for the shock," he said. Josie was about to say she never had sugar in tea or coffee, but suddenly felt swimmy. She sat down, and accepted it meekly.

"Thanks," she said. "Sorry. It was my fault, not looking where I was going. Sometimes I hear myself sounding exactly like my mother."

"I've noticed," he said. When the coffee was finished, he put out his hand and asked, "Right, are you ready for the guided tour?"

She ignored his hand and stood up. It did not take long to inspect the small rooms, with their peeling paint and worm-eaten floorboards. "The stairs don't look safe to me," Josie said.

"We shall start with those," Matthew said. "It'll be fun doing it. Are you any good at painting? When it's all solid again, I'd love you to come and choose some colours."

"You want Mum's new recruit for that," Josie said. "Andrew thingummy is an interior decorator. Very good, so I'm told."

"And very expensive, I expect. Anyway, I don't fancy Andrew thingummy."

Josie looked at him. "Don't," she said. "You know it's not on, Matthew."

He nodded. "I know. But I'm a patient man. Meanwhile, if you can paint walls, it'd be a lot cheaper than Andrew thingummy."

The tension in the air slowly evaporated, and they returned to the car. Josie was quiet on the way back, and when they stopped outside the shop, he said finally, "Penny for 'em, Josie."

She shook her head. "Most of the time at the moment I'm thinking about Doug and how on earth we're going to take the heat off him."

"Leave it with me," Matthew said quietly. "I'll have a word with Uncle, and see if we can restore normal services between him and your mum. And the minute I hear of any develop-ments, I'll let you know. I do care for you, Josie, but you probably don't want to hear about that at the moment."

"Thanks," she said. "And thanks for taking me out. It was a lovely break, and I know the house is going to be great. Eventually. 'Bye...and take care."

Forty-Seven

"So what's on this morning, Mum?" Jamie said. He was sitting in his dressing gown, hair tousled and face unshaven, eating a mammoth Gran breakfast, while she stood over him, smiling proudly.

"Bet the boy doesn't get good breakfasts when he's on the move all the time. What do you think, Lois?"

"What? What did you say?" Lois was examining the contents of a letter Gran had put beside her plate. It was a letter with a questionnaire from the museum. Had they enjoyed their visit? Was there good accessibility? Were the guides and room stewards helpful and well-informed?

"Do you know about this place, Jamie?" she said. She told him about the WI visit, and Derek supported her in describing the curious and interesting exhibits. Jamie said that he remembered going in a school party. The general consensus then had been that it was a dusty, dreary, boring old place, full of old ladies and waxwork dummies, and you couldn't always tell the difference.

"Museums not in your line, then," Lois said. "I thought you might like to go, but I won't bother to ask. Still, I've got work to do today. I expect you'll be wanting to look up old mates."

"Might even do a bit of ferretin'," he replied. "I've got one or two ideas I want to follow up."

Dear Jamie, thought Lois. He always was a nice, helpful lad, and now here he is, quite confident of solving the Clem Fitch murder in a couple of days. Still, not to discourage him. Any of us could come up with vital information.

"So what are you doing today, me duck?" Derek said. "Apart from work, I mean. Time for a coffee with the girls, or shopping for a new outfit?"

Lois looked at him pityingly. "Poor old Derek," she said. "You must wish you'd married one of those nice normal women."

"Don't fish for compliments," Derek said, smiling lasciviously at her. "You know you're the most fanciable female I ever met, and I wouldn't swap you. Not even for Dot Nimmo," he added, and went off out of the kitchen whistling.

"So who's in for lunch and who isn't?" said Gran impatiently.

"I'm in," Lois said, "but I know Derek's over at Waltonby doing a big job. He'll be gone all day. I shall be out this afternoon." She looked at Jamie, who said better count him out for lunch. He'd probably be tied up somewhere. "An old girlfriend," he said to Gran.

"Huh," she said. "Old girlfriends are more interesting than old grandmothers. I realise that."

"Dunno about that." Jamie smiled. "You know her well. Miss Enid Jacob, my very first piano teacher, and the source of much-needed inspiration and encouragement."

Lois laughed. "One up to Jamie," she said. "I'll leave you two to finish the game. It's work for me, I'm afraid."

She picked up the museum questionnaire and escaped to her office. There was a leaflet enclosed, and she looked through it once more, remembering all the things she had seen that day, but chiefly the room steward. Lois had a clear mental picture of the female steward, wearing a cashmere twinset and a string of pearls, with neat grey hair and a familiar face. It was this nagging memory that decided her to make a second visit to the museum after lunch.

This time the reception area was empty, except for the friendly man behind the desk. He seemed to be a permanent fixture, Lois thought. He'd probably taken early retirement and now found this a congenial way of passing the time. He greeted her cheerfully, making it clear he remembered her with the other WI ladies. "Wasn't it your mother who gave us such a wonderful performance on the pianola? Not with you today?"

"No, she's slaving away at home—at least, that's how she sees it," Lois replied, and added that she'd like to have a wander round on her own if that was allowed. One or two things she'd like to take another look at, she said.

"No problem. There's always someone about if you need help. We have a new caretaker, Mrs. Pat Morne. You may run into her. We are very pleased to get the right person so quickly."

Lois set off, leaving the light, modern reception area, and entering the world of rural Victorian England. She felt quite at home in the parlour, and had a few tentative runs on the pianola. There were no sounds of voices, no unruly parties of schoolchildren. She reckoned she might be the only visitor in the museum. After sticking out her tongue at the predatory hawk, she moved through to the schoolroom. Ah, here was someone, sitting at the teacher's desk, busily writing. "Good afternoon," Lois said politely.

A startled face regarded her. The man stood up and smiled. "You are the new infant teacher, I presume, madam?"

Blimey, thought Lois. Look at him, all dressed up in the right clothes. They do things really well here. She smiled back and said, "Not bloody likely!" She was totally unprepared for what happened next.

"It was like he was beamed up!" she said afterwards to the woman in the next room. "Just disappeared with a horrified look on his face and faded in front of my eyes, and then he wasn't there at all!"

The woman wore a steward's badge, and introduced herself as Maisie Jones. "Never mind, dear," she said, as if it was an everyday occurrence. "He's a friendly ghost. Never seen anywhere else but the schoolroom. Most visitors think he's a steward, playing the part. He doesn't usually disappear until they've gone out of the room. You must have said something to offend him!"

"I did," said Lois, mortified. "Still, I can tell Derek I've seen my first ghost. It's funny it's not more frightening, isn't it? You got any more in the museum? Like a woman in a cashmere twinset and pearls? Very neat-looking. Bit creepy at the same time?"

"Oh, goodness, no! That's not a ghost. It's our new caretaker. She's a bit superior for a caretaker. Probably calls herself site manager or something. She's somewhere around. Do you know her?"

"Not really," said Lois. "She's a friend of a friend. I just thought I'd say hello."

"You're bound to meet her. I'll tell her you're here if she comes through. Would you like me to come along with you, as you're all alone? Some visitors would be screaming their heads off after seeing old Schoolmaster Perkins."

Lois said she would be fine. She thanked Maisie Jones, and walked on. Next she was in the street of shops, and this was where she genuinely wanted to take another look. Each one was so crammed with authentic bits and pieces that she'd not had time with the WI to see it all. She was most interested in the stationery and postal service, but she wandered first around the ironmonger's, full of wonderful tools she'd never seen before, and tins of lethal-looking stuff for killing every pest in the house and garden. Then she entered the Victorian post office, and thought to herself that this was the least changed of all the shops. Perhaps it was the more dignified atmosphere there, indicating clearly that this was not a shop but an important nationwide service. Even now Lois felt slightly intimidated, as if she had joined one of those long, snaking queues in big town post offices, waiting for a free window.

But this postmistress was as still as a waxwork. Or was she another ghost? Lois looked at the woman sitting behind the counter, and realised it was indeed a waxwork, with that nasty pale face. But this one was not dressed in authentic costume. Maybe she was a chuck-out from Madame Tussauds, and they hadn't had time to find her a black bombazine dress. Lois looked again. A neat Liberty print blouse, and at the neck... a string of pearls. A half-finished mug of what looked like cold tea stood on the counter in front of her. Lois's heart quickened. Was it a waxwork? It was certainly very lifelike, but unmoving, and its head had been fixed at a funny angle. As she watched, the figure slid slightly to one side, until it rested against the cupboard beside the high stool. Its arms flopped off its lap.

Lois was rooted to the spot. It was not a waxwork, but a real human being. More deathlike than lifelike. In other words, it was the new caretaker, and she was now a genuine relic of the past.

Forty-Eight

Lois swallowed hard. she felt sick, and her feet were like lumps of lead, unwilling to move and take her flying to fetch help. Common sense told her that this woman was past help.

As she stared, the corpse began to slide again, and Lois almost panicked. But it did not go far before stopping in a slumped position. The face was still visible and Lois realised she could get a good look at it.

She tried to imagine it without the diamanté glasses and grey curls. That neatly waved hair looked like a wig, anyway. And was that a faint blue shadow round the jaw? Still, lots of women of a certain age began to grow vestigial beards and moustaches. She narrowed her eyes so that just the face was in focus.

Oh, God, it's him! It's the skinny man, dressed up as a woman. So that's how he disappeared. Well, it worked. It was not true that she had never suspected, but her suspicions had never gelled into the truth. She turned away, knowing that she must tell the manager before more visitors arrived and were frightened out of their wits. Then she would have to phone Cowgill. Blast! Maybe she could just inform the police in general. But of course that wouldn't work. He would be told, and have the perfect reason for getting in touch with her.

As she began to walk back towards the reception area, a movement caught her eye. She was in the schoolroom, and said in a loud voice, "Bugger off, Mr. Schoolmaster!" The lighting was very low, and she thought the figure went towards the door that she had just been through. She dismissed it from her mind. Something much more important to do now.

The manager was still in reception, and took her news remarkably calmly. "Lead the way, Mrs., er..."

"Meade," said Lois. "We'd better hurry before new visitors arrive. You'll not be able to write this one off as a ghost."

They went through the parlour into the schoolroom. No moving shadows now, and Lois walked on into the street of shops. The post office was about three shops down, and the manager took her by the arm. "Are you all right? I can take a look on my own, if you'd rather."

Lois shook her head. "I'm okay," she said. "It's in here."

She turned into the post office and gasped. "What the hell!" she said, and grabbed the edge of the counter to keep her steady. The manager came up beside her and once more took her arm. "Take it easy," he said. "I'm sure there's some explanation."

They both looked at the stool, still upright but empty. They went behind the counter and found nothing and nobody. Lois was speechless, but not for long. She looked along the counter and said, "Hey! Wait a minute! Look, there's the mug, still half full. No! Don't touch it! And don't let anyone else touch it. Get the police here as soon as possible. I'm going now. I've got a call to make." She took a New Brooms card from her bag and handed it to him. "You can contact me on this number," she said. "The police know it already. And don't look like that! I ain't done nothing wrong. Murder's not in my line. Yet."

Hunter Cowgill sat at his desk, going once more through all the papers relevant to the Clem Fitch case. There must be something here he had missed, and he was desperate to clear up the whole thing. He might then have a chance of putting things right with Lois. It was not until he had seen her reaction to the second bout of questioning inflicted on Douglas that he realised how much he cared for her. In the early days, he just fancied her a lot. He still fancied her a lot. And her feisty spirit amused him. But now he really cared about her and would do everything he could to avoid hurting her or her family.

Damn! he said, when the phone interrupted his thoughts. "Hello? Who is it?"

"It's me," Lois said.

"Lois! What's wrong? Are you all right? Nothing happened to the family?"

"Which of those questions d'you want answered first?"

"None of them. I can tell you're fine now. And I can't tell you how glad I am to hear your voice."

"Well, yeah. Enough of that. There's something important to tell you, otherwise you wouldn't have heard from me. Have you had a call from the museum yet?"

"No. Why?"

"Because they've got a dead postmistress in their shopping street. At least, they did have. She's disappeared. And don't think I've lost my marbles. I saw the body myself, and by the time I got the manager bloke, it had gone. Vanished."

Cowgill said nothing for a few seconds. Then he cleared his throat. "Can you hold on a moment, Lois? Call on another line coming in. Maybe it's the museum."

It was, and by the time he returned to Lois he had had quite a different account from the one she had given him. The manager had even chuckled. He was used to odd visitors, he said. The period atmosphere of the place seemed to unhinge them. And no, they'd never had a waxwork in the post office, sitting on the stool. Sometimes a member of staff would go in to answer questions.

"Lois, are you still there? Good. Now, it is most important that I see you straightaway. Can you meet me at the museum in twenty minutes? Where are you now? In your car, outside the reception area. Right, stay there until I come. And lock yourself in."

"Did he tell you about the mug?" Lois said. "No? Well, better ring him back and tell him not to touch it. If it's still there..."

Cowgill got out of his car in the museum car park and walked towards Lois. He did not smile, but indicated to her to let him in. When he was sitting beside her, he turned to her and said, "Do you trust me, Lois?"

She was taken aback by this, and thought for a second. "Yes, I do," she said, rather to her own surprise. Seeing him again, solid and reliable in the seat beside her, diffused the anger and resentment she had felt. Besides which, she needed him.

"Well, the feeling is reciprocal," he said.

"What?"

"I mean I trust you, too. And now I'll tell you why I needed to say that." He gave her a factual account of what the manager had said, and waited for her reaction. She did not explode, as expected, but nodded.

"I thought so," she said. "I could tell he didn't believe a word I said. Stupid sod! Did you ask about the mug?"

"I did. He said he'd seen no mug, and could think of no reason why there should be one. Staff and visitors are not allowed to eat or drink in the exhibition areas. There is a perfectly good café at the end of the tour, and people respect this."

"He said that, did he? Well, it's his word against mine. Do you still trust me?" Before he could answer, she added, "Oh, and there was something else I forgot to tell you. I wouldn't bother you with ghost rubbish, but I did definitely see a real somebody in the schoolroom as I came through to inform the manager about the dead body. It disappeared fast towards the street."

She told him about the schoolmaster episode and said he could check that with Maisie the steward. Nothing barmy about me there, she said. Maisie said loads of people had seen him.

"Ghosts don't do very well as hard evidence," Cowgill said. "But I will, of course, bear it in mind. Come on, then, girl. Let's go back in time for a bit."

When the manager saw Lois come in with the inspector, he looked embarrassed. As well he might, thought Lois. She kept in the background while the men talked, and then followed them through to the street of shops. "Is it all right if I go and get a coffee?" she said, after hearing Cowgill's conversation with the manager. "I'll be in the café, and won't go away. I promise."

She's up to something, Cowgill thought, but said that was fine, he'd catch up with her in a short while. If Lois was up to something, it was usually useful.

In the café, she said hello to the volunteer woman in mobcap and pinny behind the counter, and ordered a coffee. "By the way," she said, smiling at the woman playing her part with such enthusiasm, "did anyone bring you a dirty mug to wash up in the last hour or so? I saw one somewhere around in the exhibits, and feel guilty that I didn't bring it through to you."

"Don't worry about that, dear," the woman replied. "Our manager brought it back a while ago. He's most particular about that sort of thing, so I won't shop you! Now, I made this lemon sponge first thing this morning, and it's most delicious. Can I tempt you with a slice?"

"Why not? And thanks for keeping my secret. Don't mention my asking about it, else he'll be on my track and I'll end up being locked in your gloomy-looking Victorian cell!"

A very satisfactory conversation followed, with both agreeing on how much better it was in the old days, when every village had its local cop and some even had small lockups where villains could be detained overnight to cool their heels.

Cowgill came in quite soon and sat down with Lois, ordering a coffee for himself. The woman brought it over and winked at Lois. "Here you are, sir," she said. "Are you going to join your wife in having a piece of my lemon cake?"

Lois opened her mouth to deny any possibility or likelihood of being Cowgill's wife, but he got there first.

"Thank you, my dear," he said sweetly. "That will be very nice."

Forty-Nine

"How would they have got the body out?" Derek said, as they sat at the supper table. He had been really worried about Lois's involvement in what was clearly a very dangerous situation. Whoever they were, and whatever they were up to, they were not amateurs. He believed absolutely that Lois had seen a real dead body, and also a half-full mug on the post office counter. He was impressed that she had had the wit to ask the café woman if anyone had brought such a mug in from the museum. He was proud of her presence of mind, but was also extremely anxious at what this gang might do next.

"I know how they would have got the body out," Gran said. She was looking pleased with herself, and waited for somebody to ask for more information. Nobody did. "Well," she continued, "since you're so interested, I'll tell you. When I was a girl I knew the daughter of the farmer who lived there when it was a real farmhouse. She came to my school in Tresham for a while. They owned a lot of land and you could tell they were not short of a bob or two. I used to go and play with the girl, and it was a wonderful place for hide-and-seek an' that. All them barns and dairy buildings and stables were perfect for hiding in."

"But how would they get from the post office into the farmyard?" Lois could see immediately the problem of getting a body into a vehicle without being seen and at speed.

Gran smiled. "Ah, well, there it is, you see. It was a bit like now, with connecting doors between all the yard buildings, so's if it was pouring or snowing, they could still get from the house and round the barns an' that without getting soaked. The farmer's wife was delicate. At least, she said she was, but my mum knew the dairy woman and she'd seen the missus taking regular vigorous exercise up in the hayloft with the young stockman at the time."

"Mum!" Lois said. "That's ancient gossip. What you just

said doesn't explain how they got into the courtyard without being seen."

"Easy peasy," said Gran. "All the buildings also had doors into the yard, o' course. The pretend post office is next to the old store what had double doors for feed being unloaded. It's still used as a storeroom. All the body snatchers had to do was back their van right in through the doors, nip into the PO and do the deed, then whiz the body out into next door, and shove it straight into the van without anybody seeing. You said there were very few people about. It was a bit of a risk, I suppose, but they got away with it."

Derek was looking more and more alarmed. "Now you listen to me," he said to Lois. "These are a desperate lot who obviously think nothing of bumping off anybody who gets in their way. That includes you, and also Douglas. I don't want you havin' anythin' more to do with it. No more heart-to-hearts with Cowgill. No more ferretin', not from any of you. It's police business now, and it's their job to run into danger. They get paid for it. So, family and New Brooms only from now on. An' that's an order."

Even while he was saying it, he knew he was wasting his breath. Snooping was in Lois's bones. She couldn't stop now. And this time it was worse, because her own son was under suspicion. The best he could hope for was that she would be very wary and not do anything really stupid.

"Brilliant deduction, Mum," said Lois, as if Derek had not spoken. "Only one problem: how did they open the double doors? They would certainly have been locked."

"Somebody planted at the museum specially to pinch a key and open the doors for them?"

Derek laughed. "If you remember, Gran dear," he said, "all the stewards are decent retired people with not a stain on their character. You'll have to do better than that."

Lois said nothing, but remembered vividly the slumped figure of a retired grey-haired lady, to most eyes a pillar of respectability, but to Lois a skinny man dressed as a woman, cleverly disguised, and a plant with guaranteed evil intent. If one, why not another?

"Mum might have something there," she said. "There must have been at least three of them to do it so quickly. We need to ask around and see if—"

"Lois!" exclaimed Derek. "What did I just say? Leave it alone! And that goes for you, too, Gran. I don't know what the pair of you think you're doing. There's plenty of work for you to do here, Gran, without wasting time cooking up fairy stories, and as for Lois…"

"Yes?" said Lois.

"I give up," said Derek, and stumped off out of the room.

Silence reigned in the kitchen for a minute or so, and then Lois said, "You're a natural, Mum. Now I know where I get it from."

"Hello, my dear," said the mobcap lady in the café. "Hubby not with you today?"

Lois knew she meant Cowgill, and was tempted to put her right. But then she would probably think Lois was trying to cover her tracks after an illicit lovers' meeting.

"Yep," she said. "Can't resist your lemon drizzle cake. And a nice hot cup of tea, please." She stood at the counter waiting to be served and looked around the big room. One side looked out to the fields beyond, and the other into the farmyard at the back. So Mobcap could have seen something. "I expect you see all kinds of comings and goings in the yard. Must break up the boredom when there's no customers," she said.

"Oh, you'd be surprised! Couples having a quick smooch, men having a pee into the drain in the corner. And we've got smart new toilets! Honestly, people have no shame these days. Mind you, they don't realise I'm looking. The window is quite small, and they'd have trouble seeing me."

"Didn't seem much going on when I was here yesterday," Lois said, taking her tea and cake to her seat. "I reckon I was the only person here for a while."

"Oh, no," said Mobcap, defending the popularity of the museum, "we had quite a few in. And then there are deliveries out in the yard. Vans unload most days. There's a general store over there. There was one yesterday, though you probably didn't see it. But it shows you how much stuff we get through. There's the shop, the café, the offices. We all need supplies."

Lois smiled. "So what did they bring for you?" she said.

"Nothing at all yesterday. Actually, I didn't recognise that van. Couldn't see much. But there were three men, so they must have been delivering something heavy. Probably a new filing cabinet or something like that. Our manager, between you and me, is a bit free with the museum's lolly! Always a new gadget arriving."

"Sounds intriguing," said Lois lightly. "A dirty white van draws up outside the double doors, three men get out, disappear, and are back in minutes. They drive off at speed."

"How did you know all that?" said Mobcap. "All exactly right, except for two things. They didn't go to the double doors—they were backed up close to the door out of the post office—and they weren't gone in minutes. Leastways, the first time I looked they had just arrived. Next time they all came scuttling out again. They sat in the van for a while, and then got out and loaded up something. I couldn't see much, the way they'd parked the van. Then they were off like bats out of hell! Still, you were nearly right. You ought to be a detective," she added, and began to wipe down her surfaces.

Fifty

"So somebody unlocked the yard door of the post office," Josie said.

She and Lois, with Douglas and Susie, were sitting in the Long Farnden kitchen, while Gran was busy with kettle, mugs, and plates of biscuits newly baked that afternoon. Derek was staying late to finish a job over at Ringford. He'd gone to fix a wall heater in Ivy Beasley's bathroom, and she had him more or less at gunpoint to get it finished.

"What about that manager chap, Mum?" Douglas asked. "It was him that took the mug away to the café, didn't you say?"

"So the mobcap woman said. I guess she would know the manager pretty well."

Douglas frowned. "He could have some other reason to take the mug. Supposing he thought he'd left it there himself, thereby breaking the rules. He'd want to keep quiet about it to you and Cowgill, wouldn't he?"

Josie said with a smile, "And I suppose he was scared that Cowgill would cart him off to prison for such a gross offence? Doesn't wash, Douglas."

Douglas looked crestfallen, and Lois interrupted in his defence. "It could be something like Douglas said, but I somehow don't think the manager's involved. For one thing, he would have known who—"

She stopped suddenly. She remembered that she had not yet told them about the victim being Skinny Man in disguise. She could not be absolutely sure until Cowgill let her know once they'd found and examined the body. Then they'd know! The idea that the manager was involved put a whole new complexion on things. It could explain how the skinny man got the job in the first place. On the other hand, the manager could have been very relieved that there was no body and taken the mug against Lois's instructions, just to keep his precious museum blameless.

"Mum?" said Josie. "What were you going to say?"

Lois was saved by Gran officiously plonking down mugs of coffee and handing round biscuits. But Josie did not give up. "Come on, Mum," she said. "Who would he have known?"

"She's not going to tell, Josie," Gran said. "I know that look in her eye."

"Not that," Lois said. "It's just that I've thought of something, and it'll need to be sorted out before I can tell you. Don't want you all going up the wrong track."

"Is it all right if I say something?" said Susie, blushing with nervousness. They all assured her she could say anything she liked, especially if it would help Douglas.

"That's what I'm here for," she said, more confidently. "Well, it was at work, when I was on cigarettes and magazines an' that. That big man, the one I've seen going in to Braeside, came up and bought cigarettes and one of them magazines we keep on top shelves. After he'd paid, he didn't go away. Just stared at me. I was beginning to feel a bit scared, when he said he thought he'd seen me somewhere before. I said probably on another counter. We all change and change about. But he said no, it wasn't at work, it was somewhere else. A sort of look went over his face, as if he'd remembered, and then he was pushed from behind by one of them yobs who spend all day sitting on the window ledges outside causing trouble. I've never seen anybody move s' fast! Big man that he is, he hadn't got the courage to face up to the yob. That's all, really, except I don't like the idea of him recognising me

..."

This was a long speech for Susie, and she trailed off in embarrassment.

Douglas took her hand. "Don't worry, sweetie," he said. "Very useful information. You've done well. He probably did recognise you. Anybody seeing you come out of Clem's house would want a second look!" He squeezed her hand, and she moved closer to him.

And anybody from Braeside seeing Susie with suspect Douglas Meade would be more than interested, thought Lois, and possibly put her on the danger list. But she judged Susie was frightened enough already, and so did not say anything.

Derek came noisily through the back door and into the kitchen. "That old Beasley woman needs putting down!" he said furiously. Then he noticed the group at the table, and looked even crosser. "What on earth's going on here?" he said. "I thought I told you, Lois and Gran, that there was to be no more...Oh, well, forget it. Any more coffee in the pot?" He took a handful of biscuits and sat down. Gran tut-tutted and handed him a plateful of hot food from the oven. "Get that inside you first," she said, with a sideways look at Lois.

They told him what they'd discussed so far, and Josie said that Mum wasn't telling them everything, but she supposed they'd have to get used to that. "She's practically an honorary member of Tresham special branch," she said.

"Did Ivy get her heater working?" Lois said to Derek, patting his hand and changing the subject.

"Yeah. I think she would've locked me in if I hadn't finished."

"I reckon we should be going, Susie," Douglas said.

"And me," said Josie. "Rob will be wondering where I am."

"Don't let me bust up the conference," Derek said, but Lois could tell that was exactly what he wanted. Then the two of them could talk.

After Derek had finished his supper and the washing-up was done, the three of them migrated to the sitting room to watch television. Gran fell asleep almost at once, as usual, and Derek yawned a lot. Lois was wide awake, and watched the moving screen without taking in any of it. She had other pictures before her eyes. The friendly manager, always helpful and kind to old ladies. The WI outing, with the grey-haired woman steward whispering a vague threat. A strange, well-groomed elderly lady going in and out of Braeside. A string of pearls. The same steward, wig askew, lolling sideways against a cupboard door in the museum's post office. The empty stool and a vanishing mug. And the mobcap lady's vivid picture of the body snatchers at work.

She realised with a shock that the moving shadow in the schoolroom must have been a lookout, and it was her approach that disturbed them and sent them fleeing for the van. They'd sat there until she had gone to tell the manager, and then done a lightning snatch and driven away like bats out of hell.

Derek reached for the remote control, and switched off. Gran did not move. She was snoring lightly, and Derek smiled. He turned to Lois and said softly that he thought it was safe to have a little talk.

She sighed. "Yep," she said. "I wondered when you'd get round to it."

"I'll start," said Derek. "All day I've had this rotten feeling that you're gettin' into deep water. Too deep, me duck. There's a lot known now, and for God knows what reason I trust Cowgill to put it all together and get the right answer."

"Sure, we know a lot," replied Lois. "There's Skinny Man, and Braeside and Mrs. Blairgowrie," Lois replied. "And Susie being tied up, and the big man over the road. We know all of that, but we don't know why it's all happening. Surely we ought to have an inkling or two by now? I reckon they've been clever. Mind you, I think Dot Nimmo still knows more than she's telling. We've got to forget the murders for a bit, and find out exactly what they're doing, and why it's worth violent crime to keep it a secret. We should go right from the beginning, when Skinny Man was a recluse, buying lots of food, and living next to Clem."

"What we should do, Lois, is stop now. If you want to know what I think—"

"I know what you think, Derek. You've told me often enough."

"I'll tell you again, then," he said, his voice rising. "You are being very irresponsible. It's not only you that's threatened. It's Douglas, of course, and also Susie, and all of us in the Meade family. And probably New Brooms as well. You said Dot Nimmo knows more than she's tellin'. So it's got to stop!"

His voice had risen to a shout, and Gran woke up with a start. "What's happened?" she said anxiously. "Has somebody been murdered?"

Derek looked at Lois with an angry face. "See? The poor old thing is even dreamin' about it. It's time to stop!"

"Hey, less of the 'poor old thing,' if you don't mind," said Gran, fully awake now. "And if you want to know what I was dreaming, I was back with Lois's dad, standing in the back garden in Tresham, watching the fireworks over the way in the park." Her lip quivered, and she stood up. "If you two could stop shouting at each other, I might get a bit of peace," she said, and almost ran from the room.

Lois sat quite still, looking down at her hands. "Haven't you forgotten something?" she asked quietly.

"What?" said Derek. He was sorry about Gran, but had not relented.

"Don't forget that Douglas is still under suspicion," she said. "Whatever the police say, they haven't taken him off the list. In fact," she said bitterly, "I reckon he's the only one on it so far."

"So?"

"So I intend to do everything I can to help. More than that, I mean to find out what's behind it all. If it means getting back in touch with Cowgill, then I'll do it. I'm sorry, Derek. I know what you're saying. But I can't stop now. Sorry, love."

Fifty-One

Derek sat for a long while in front of the dying fire, thinking about what Lois had said. She had made it sound as if he did not care about Douglas. What rubbish! He knew without any doubt that his son could not have killed a man. He had always been a kind-hearted lad. There was that time when Mrs. Tollervey-Jones had asked him to go and help with the beating on a big shoot on her estate. He'd never been before, and never went again. When he came back, he had been violently sick, and Lois had been all for marching arms akimbo to tackle Mrs. T-J.

No, Douglas would never be charged. The police weren't that stupid, whatever Lois said. He had no love for Inspector Cowgill, but he respected his ability to solve a case, and get it right. He had a new thought. Since Lois had not been in touch with Cowgill for a while, so far as he knew, the police might have a whole lot more evidence and be much nearer sorting it out than Lois and the others thought.

Above all, Derek decided, he had a duty to keep the whole of his family safe. And in his opinion, Lois was heading straight for disaster.

In Sebastopol Street, Dot Nimmo lay stretched out in her new single bed. After both her husband and son had died, she'd gone to pieces and the house became a slum. Then, largely due to her job with Lois, who had given her a chance when nobody else could be bothered with her, she had come to a point where she was herself again and turned out the whole house, cleaned and redecorated it, and bought new furniture throughout. When she had first gone to Braeside, she had been puzzled by the rubbishy look of it all. Her own home was perfect now, but posh Mrs. Blairgowrie's looked like it had been furnished from secondhand shops and jumble sales.

"Of course!" she said aloud. That was just what had happened. Braeside was only temporary accommodation. No doubt they moved around often. She wondered if Mrs. M had spotted it.

Dot had gone to bed early and now could not sleep. The time was surely coming when she would have to tell Lois everything about the abduction and what she was nearly certain was going on. Every time she went to Braeside to clean, Mrs. Blairgowrie stayed out of her way. No more cosy chats over cups of coffee, no more fabricated tales of life in aristocratic Scotland. Dot made sure she had her mobile in her pocket, and got on with her work. The only conversation she had with Mrs. Blairgowrie was to announce her arrival and, in due course, her departure. Dot was not scared of what might happen. She'd been too well trained by the Nimmos in years gone by. But she remained alert. Big Alastair was obviously keeping out of her way. Now, although she overheard no telephone calls or conversations behind closed doors, she sensed a growing tension in the house. It was like a buildup to something big, something dangerous and secret. Or was it her imagination?

No, Dot knew she was not big on imaginative thought, and relied on instinct and experience. She turned over once more, thumping the pillow, which had become a lump of rock, and made a decision. She would tell Lois tomorrow, after her morning at Braeside.

The house in Long Farnden where the Pickerings had spent happy years was now silent, except for the sonorous breathing of Alastair John Smith and the occasional sob from the pregnant woman in the back bedroom. He was unaware of her deep sadness, and even had he been aware, he would not have cared. She was a chattel, a necessary adjunct to the household, whose duties were to clean, cook, wash and iron, and keep out of the way as much as possible. He had, of course, noticed that the small swelling of her stomach, there when he'd first installed her, was now very large.

The foetus was not so active now. The woman put her hands protectively round her stomach and whispered comforting words. Was it a boy or a girl? She had no preference, and was concerned only that it should make an entrance into this hostile world safely. So many unpleasant things had happened to her that she had no longer any idea of the passage of time, and so no notion of a date when the bump would become a squalling infant. She supposed it would be soon, but so far had no plans for what she would do. She sobbed more loudly, and was suddenly silenced by a furious knocking on the wall beside her narrow bed. It was him. She loathed and despised him, and was completely in his power. Unless...She dared not even allow the thought to enter her head. If you cut off the head of a worm, it wriggled away and survived.

Hunter Cowgill also could not sleep. In his lonely bed he thought of Lois. Should he call her tomorrow and ask her officially to meet him at the secret place? She was under no obligation to do so, and he expected that she would more than likely refuse. Still, he had to do something. Information had come his way which implicated Douglas more deeply. It was another anonymous letter, but this time it stated facts and times which required investigation. If he could have rejected them outright, saying he had no intention of following up ridiculous accusations, he would have done so, for Lois's sake. But it was more than his job was worth.

He got out of bed and went down to the kitchen. It was chilly and still dark outside. He put on the kettle and spooned instant coffee into a mug. When he had stirred it and put in two brown sugar lumps, he sat down at the table and tried to think about the new evidence. Instead, he found his thoughts returning to other cases he had worked on with Lois's help. She had always seen through the mass of misinformation, false witness, deliberate red herrings, straight to the heart of the matter. In doing so, she had put herself and her family in danger. No wonder Derek hated the sight of him!

Then he was back with the Clem Fitch murder. Douglas had a father as well as mother. He could talk officially to Derek instead of Lois. What could Cowgill say that would encourage him to help? What would he want most? That his wife and family were well out of it all, that he could get on with a peaceful life and enjoy the lottery money still sitting in the bank, increasing day by day like homemade bread rising with yeast.

That was it, then. Tomorrow he would engineer a casual meeting with Derek Meade. He went back to his bed, his eyelids dropped, and he was asleep in minutes.

In a now silent house, Derek put out the sitting room light and prepared to go upstairs to bed. Perhaps tomorrow things would not look so bad. Maybe Gran could talk some sense into Lois. Some chance! He put out the hall light, and blinked when it was almost immediately switched on again from above. He looked up and saw Lois in her nightdress, staring down sadly at him.

"What's up, me duck?" he whispered, so as not to wake Gran.

"Can't sleep," she replied. "I'll come down for a minute."

Derek stood at the foot of the stairs and held out his arms. Lois came down slowly and stood in front of him. "You need a cuddle an' that," he whispered in her ear, and lifted her up.

She began to giggle. "Put me down!" she spluttered. "Don't want you in a silver frame just yet," she said. But Derek clutched her more tightly and made it to the top of the stairs.

Safe and warm in bed, he held her close. "Give me a minute or two to get me breath back," he said, and added, "then we'll put everything right."

Fifty-Two

Next morning, Lois left early for a meeting with a possible new client, and after that she planned to call in at the office in town. Derek had gone off to a job in Waltonby and Gran was left alone, mug of coffee in hand, taking a short break from housework to watch a quiz show on television.

The telephone rang and she decided not to answer it. Let it ring, she thought, and whoever it is can leave a message. But it rang and rang, and she realised Lois had forgotten to switch on the answer phone. She sighed and muttered, "No peace for the wicked," and got up to answer it.

"Sorry to trouble you, but can you tell me how to get in touch with Derek Meade?" It was an educated woman's voice.

"He's not here," Gran said, instantly suspicious. "What do you want him for?"

"It's an emergency," the woman replied. "I've got no electricity, and we have chicks in an incubator. I've rung the electricity board and they say it must be in our own equipment. No cuts in supply, they said. Mr. Meade has been recommended," she added hopefully.

"Give me your number," Gran said. "I'll give him your message."

"I'm afraid I do need to speak to him urgently." Now the woman's voice was more authoritative. "I am sure he has a mobile."

Gran reluctantly gave her the number, and said that if he hadn't got it switched on, and it really was urgent, she'd be able to find him at the schoolhouse in Waltonby.

With a quick thank-you, the woman rang off. Hope I've done right, thought Gran, and having lost the thread, abandoned the telly.

"All right?" said the policewoman, handing Cowgill a piece of paper with an address and telephone number on it.

"Brilliant," he said, "you should have been an actress."

He put on his jacket and went down to the back of the station to collect his car. As he drove along the familiar road to Waltonby he thought about Derek. Derek Meade had been a patient man, and sometimes a very angry man, and at times

Cowgill had felt sorry for him. If only the two of them had been able to have a drink together in the local pub, talked man to man, he could have explained how valuable Lois's help was to him. He would never have mentioned his undying love for her, because he never intended to do anything about it. Never, he told himself firmly. But he would have told Derek that from what he knew of Lois, she loved what Derek called ferretin' and had a natural aptitude for working out solutions. She certainly didn't do it for the money, as he'd never paid her a bean.

He slowed down obediently at the thirty-mile-limit sign, and cruised along, heading for the school. Sure enough, there was Derek's van parked outside. Cowgill drove past, parked just around the corner, and walked back to the pub. He looked at his watch. Coffee time. He had some notes to write, and he knew the landlord, so he'd be left undisturbed. Sitting by the window, with a good view of the schoolhouse, he greeted the landlord and settled down.

After an hour, his patience was rewarded. Derek came down the garden path and got into his van. Cowgill could see sand-wiches being unwrapped, and got up swiftly. "Back in a minute," he said to the landlord, and ran out. Why shouldn't he and Derek have a drink together? He could only ask, and if Derek refused, then he would have to think of something else.

Derek looked at him with surprise and dislike. Cowgill motioned him to wind down his window, and Derek did so reluctantly. "What d'you want?" he said. "Have you been following me?" he added, frowning.

"Good God, no," Cowgill said. "I've got minions to do that for me. No, I was having a chat with a useful friend in the pub, and saw you come out from the schoolhouse. Fancy a drink?"

"With you?"

"Yes. Why not? I'm off duty. We can talk about football if you like. I know you're a fan."

"Lois told you, did she?" Derek put his sandwiches to one side. "All right, then," he said. He suddenly fancied telling Cowgill a few home truths. "S' long as we don't discuss Lois," he said, and followed his enemy into the pub.

It took a while for the conversation to get going, with Derek answering in monosyllables, but when Cowgill said he hoped to go to the match on Saturday, and what did Derek think of United's chances, it was too much for the team's greatest fan, who gave him a detailed assessment of the possible outcome of the game. After that, they had another half, and the atmosphere warmed up slightly.

Derek looked at his watch. "Time I was getting back to work," he said. He hadn't said any of the rough things he had in store for Cowgill, but now felt mellow and wondered if perhaps he hadn't misjudged the cop. After all, he had a job to do.

"There was one thing I should tell you," Cowgill said, suddenly serious. "It's about Douglas. We've had another anonymous letter, giving more incriminating evidence, and again accusing Douglas of killing Clem Fitch. I was going to tell Lois that we'll have to face him with it, but then I saw you and—well—here we are."

Derek was silent. All his mellow feelings disappeared, and he stared at Cowgill. Then he said, "You didn't just spot me by accident, did you? You were lying in wait for me. Thought you could soften me up with a beer or two. I nearly fell for it," he added loudly, and got up from the table. "You do what you like," he said as a parting shot. "It don't matter what sodding evidence you got, my Douglas would never hurt a fly, and me and Lois will make sure you don't get your lousy fingers on his collar."

And then he was gone.

Cowgill finished his drink and went to the bar to settle up. "Didn't get far with that one, did you, Inspector," the landlord laughed. "Not losing your touch, I hope," he added.

The jokey comment echoed in Cowgill's head as he walked back to his car. He hoped to God he was not losing his touch, or his marbles, or anything else that he valued in his solitary life.

Fifty-Three

Now what to do? Derek drove slowly back to Long Farnden. He had abandoned his sandwiches, told the school headmistress that he had to go for an hour or so to sort out an emergency, and headed for home. Should he tell Lois about the new threat to Douglas? He'd managed to calm her down last night, but this morning she was looking anxious again. Derek remembered with relief that Douglas himself seemed to be treating the whole thing in a very breezy fashion.

He pulled up just in time to avoid a baby rabbit determined to commit suicide under his wheels. As he set off again, he recalled other times he had tried to keep unpleasant facts from Lois. It was impossible. She could worm anything out of him with very little effort. No, he would have to tell her, and probably about the meeting with Cowgill, too.

As he turned the van into the drive, he was relieved to see that the New Brooms vehicle was not there. He knew Dot Nimmo was due to see Lois this afternoon, and so she would soon be back. Meanwhile he could sound out Gran on one or two things.

"Derek? What are you doing back home?" Gran was ironing, with a radio play turned up loud. She lowered the sound, and added, "Did you get the message?"

"What message?"

"From the lady with the chicks. She'd got an emergency and wanted to get in touch urgently. I gave her your mobile number and told her where you were working. Did I do wrong?"

"I knew it!" Derek thumped the table with his fist. Gran looked alarmed and turned off the radio. He saw that he had frightened her, and said, "Nothing to do with you, Gran. You did the right thing. But there was no lady with chicks, and I never got the message." Then he told her about Cowgill, who'd set him up, and pretended to run into him by accident. "He got me in that pub and soft-soaped me until I nearly believed him. All designed to get me on his side, so I could persuade Lois to be nice to him again! Bloody cheek!"

Then he told her about the new anonymous letter, and asked whether he should tell Lois. Gran shrugged and said that he knew Lois as well as she did, probably better, but on balance she thought he should tell. "You know she'll wheedle it out of you if you don't," she said. He nodded sadly. A sharp knock at the door interrupted their conversation and Gran went to admit Dot Nimmo. At the same time the New Brooms van arrived and Lois stepped out.

Derek telephoned the schoolhouse and apologised, but said he couldn't be back until tomorrow morning. It was not a particularly urgent job, and the headmistress was very accommodating. Then he said hello to Lois and said he'd do a spot of gardening while she talked to Dot.

"Is it a bad time, Mrs. M?" Dot said, as Lois took off her jacket and led the way into her office.

"No, not really. What was it you wanted to see me about? Must be something important to bring you all this way from Sebastopol Street!" Lois laughed, but got no answering smile from Dot.

"It is important," she replied. "I just come straight from Braeside to tell you. You'll probably say I should've told you before. But anyway, here goes."

She began at the beginning, when she had found the transvestite magazines in Mrs. Blairgowrie's bedroom, and been caught in the act by Big Alastair. Men dressed as women, Lois thought. How pathetic.

"Well," continued Dot, "Al is big in himself, but small in the brain department." She described how they'd tied her up and were going to keep her a prisoner somewhere with other people. Then she told how she'd got loose, recognised where she was, and done a bunk. "Lucky for me there was a Tresham bus come through an' I was on it like greased lightning."

"But why...how...? How come you're still cleaning at Braeside? You are still cleaning, aren't you? And why don't you go straight to the police? This is very serious, Dot."

"A Nimmo go to the police? You should know me better than that, Mrs. M. An' don't you go tellin' your friend Cowgill. I can handle this." Then Dot told how she had faced them, threatened to tell unless they left her alone, and was confident she had the upper hand.

"Oh, my God, Dot," Lois said, and covered her face with her hands.

Dot waited, and then said, "I was worried that they'd go for you, Mrs. M. Do you want me to tell you what I think their racket is? It's only guesswork, mind."

Lois nodded. "Can it get any worse?" she said.

"Might do. The way they talked, this place they were takin' me wasn't the house across the road, where that foreign woman lives with Alastair. I reckon he was just givin' her instructions when I escaped. We were goin' on somewhere else. If you ask me, Big Al's not big at all. I reckon he's a small part of something big. I bet you a pound to a penny that he's in the white slave trade. Bringin' in illegals and findin' them jobs. Jobs that you wouldn't want your daughter to do. An' there's a sort of clearinghouse somewhere, where they're kept until they move on."

Lois was reeling under all this, and for the moment could only say that the woman he had in his own house was black, and so it couldn't be the white slave trade. But what Dot had said could certainly explain Alastair's offer to find cleaners for her. Why hadn't she thought of it herself?

Dot ploughed on. "You know Alastair used to work up the Job Centre years ago? He got the push under mysterious circumstances, so they say. But if you think about it, Mrs. M, he'd have some good contacts for gettin' people jobs."

"Did you see the woman who lives with him?" Lois said. "I did mention her to Josie, but she says she's never been in the shop. He goes to the supermarket, like most people, and uses the shop just for toothpaste or a newspaper. What about the day you escaped? You said he went in through the back gate of the house."

"I didn't see her at all. I reckon he keeps her chained up in the cellar."

Lois laughed. "Don't let your imagination run away with you! Is that all, then?"

"Yep," Dot said. "Except that now I don't hear nor see nothin' at Braeside. But I reckon something happened that stirred 'em up last time I was there. There was a phone call, an' then a dirty white van drew up outside and Mrs. Blairgowrie rushed out—no stick or dark glasses, mind—an' I saw her look into the back. Then they drove off an' she came in and ran upstairs to the bathroom an' was sick as a dog. I called to her but she said she was all right. Then all the doors was shut and it was quiet as the grave as usual."

"Did anybody visit while you were there? Any do-gooders to bring Mrs. Blairgowrie's shopping? Nobody like that?"

Dot shook her head. "Nope. Nobody except me. Anyway, Mrs. M," she said, looking at her watch, "I must be going, else I'll be late for me next client. I'll see you at the meetin'.

But for God's sake be careful. An' tell your Josie. There's robbery with violence in a lot of village shops these days. I wouldn't trust that Alastair round the corner."

"I'll tell her," Lois answered. "After all you've said, I've a lot to think about. Still, thanks, Dot. You've been a huge help, as always. But please be careful yourself. Maybe I should take you away from Braeside?"

"No, don't do that. It'd look too suspicious. Then they'd know I told you, and might be driven to do somethin' really stupid and dangerous. No, don't worry about me, Mrs. M. It'd take more than the likes of Big Al to frighten a Nimmo. If I hear or see anything else I'll report back. And don't forget, this is between us two."

Fifty-Four

Nearly dark, Lois noticed. she had been so preoccupied since Dot's revelations, she had almost forgotten Jeems's customary last walk of the day. Now she walked with her dog through the quiet lane at the back of the houses in Blackberry Gardens, and looked over the fence at the Pickerings' new house. Not a new house, but new to them. Jeems stopped to produce a couple of neat turds and Lois dutifully bent down with a Dogpoo bag to pick them up. Suddenly Jeems pulled on the lead and began to bark. Lois turned around to see what had started her off, and saw too late a dark shadow behind her. Then Jeems yelped as a boot caught her in the side. She collapsed on the path and Lois fought like a tiger to release herself. But there were hands holding her in an iron grip whilst others tied a hateful-smelling gag around her mouth.

It was all done at great speed and in total silence. Lois was dragged back the way they had come, leaving the little inert body behind, and the next thing she knew she was being bundled into a car and driven off slowly along the main street. Along with others, she and Derek had campaigned against streetlights, and now she realised they could have saved her life.

Although she could not speak, they had not blindfolded her. She could see the two men in front had hoods and silly masks.

She looked out of the window and just made out the dark shapes of houses she recognised. Then they turned off the road, round to the playing fields, and the car cruised silently to a halt. Now she was dragged out again and through a gate. With sinking heart, Lois knew where she was going. To Alastair John Smith's house.

In the small back bedroom, a bare bulb of low wattage shone on the moaning pregnant woman. She stared fearfully at Lois, and rattled off something in a foreign tongue, holding out her hands beseechingly. Then a contraction caught her and she screamed at the top of her voice. One of Lois's captors, now with bare shaved head, reached out and slapped her hard across the face. "Shut up, bitch!" he shouted, and at that point Alastair came through the door. He looked at Lois and smiled triumphantly.

"Well done, lads," he said. "Now then, Mrs. Meade, we require your services. Too late for cleaning services, which you so kindly offered. Midwifery is on the job list for today."

Lois shook her head and made loud noises. Alastair chuckled, walked up to her, and whipped off the gag with rough hands.

"I don't know nothing about being a midwife, you idiot!" she shouted at him, and his henchman stepped forward with clenched fist. Alastair barked out a command to leave her alone. He freed her hands and went to stand by the door. In his hand he held a gun.

"You've had kids yourself," he said. "Three, if I'm not mistaken? There's lovely Josie in the shop, interfering Douglas in Gordon Street, and now a young one who tickles the ivories? All bent on discovering who killed—"

The woman's scream was deafening. She arched her back and looked piteously at Lois. "Plea...ea...se!" she shouted. "Help me!"

"I'll get an ambulance straightaway," Lois said, and walked stiffly towards the door.

Alastair waved his gun at her. "Oh, no, you won't," he said. "This brat is going to be born without anyone knowing. When you've delivered it you can go home. And if you breathe a word about this to your loving husband, children, mother, and especially your cop buddy, the short life of this little black bastard will come to an abrupt end. Not to mention a nasty accident involving one of your loved ones, Mrs. Meade. We are very clever at revenge on people who get in our way. So clever that Tresham plods are still floundering in the dark."

"You don't know that," Lois said. "They could be comin' up those rickety stairs at this very minute."

Alastair half-closed his eyes and smiled. "Get on with it," he said in a whisper. "Or else I'll—"

This sounded so much like a schoolboy threat in the playground that Lois could not help laughing. "You and who else?" she said, and then turned to the weeping woman.

"Let me have a look, dear," she said, and then completely forgot everything except the need to make sure that this baby arrived safely and was protected somehow against the villains surrounding it. She dredged up memories of her mother's tales of births in the old days. "Hot water, clean towels, an' a pair of scissors," she said for a start, and hoped to God that instinct would help her out with the rest.

After what seemed like hours later, Lois saw the top of a tiny head, black-haired and plastered with white streaks, emerging from between the woman's legs.

"Push, dear!" she said for the umpteenth time. "Nearly there!"

An almighty push sent the baby slithering out into Lois's waiting hands. It was not breathing. "Christ! What do I do next?" she said.

"Thump it," said Alastair. The two thugs began to move towards Lois.

"No!" screamed the woman, and tried to sit up.

Lois turned and faced the three men. "If you touch me or this baby, I swear to God I'll see you in hell," she said. "And I always keep my promise."

To her surprise, they stepped back and stood against the wall. Alastair's gun-toting hand dropped to his side, and they stared at her.

She'd done her best with the cord, and now cleared the baby's mouth and nostrils as best as she could. She took hold of it by its heart-breakingly small ankles, tipped it upside down, and smacked its little bottom firmly. The resulting yell brought a seraphic smile to the mother's face, and Lois bit her lip. "It's a lovely boy," she said, and then, seeing her blank look, she repeated, "a boy," and showed his mother the evidence.

"Where on earth is she?" Derek said. "Did she say where she was going?"

Gran shook her head. "Just said she'd take Jeems for a short walk, and would be back in ten minutes."

"And how long ago was that?"

Gran said she wasn't sure. She was pale, and had been feeling guilty since Derek had woken her up and said Lois was not in the house. "I had a rotten headache, and took a pill to sleep it off. I'm still a bit woozy. And anyway," she added defensively, "where have you been?"

"Darts over at Fletching," he said, "as you very well know. We always have a few drinks after the match, and time goes." As he was saying this, he vanished into Lois's study and picked up the telephone. "Cowgill?" he said. Almost immediately Cowgill came on the line, sounding sleepy.

"Derek Meade here. Lois has gone missing. Took the dog for a walk and didn't come back. Gran went to bed and I've just got in. She could've bin missing for several hours."

"There in twenty minutes," Cowgill said, and was gone. As he screeched through the lanes to Long Farnden, he was more awake than he'd ever been. Police work had begun to build a picture of what was going on, and he knew without doubt that Lois was in danger.

Derek came rushing out and got into the car beside Cowgill. "Where is she?" he said. "Where is she?"

"I have to make a call," Cowgill said, and put a number into his mobile. "Dot Nimmo?" he said. "Inspector Cowgill. A man is on the way to pick you up and bring you to Long Farnden. Lois Meade is in trouble. Be ready in five minutes, please."

"Why Dot Nimmo? We're wasting time!" Derek said.

"I have reason to believe—," began Cowgill.

"Oh, God! Can't you talk like a human being?" Derek yelled. "Lois could be dead by now!"

There was a silence, and as Derek realised what he had said, he covered his face with his hands. Then he said, "Why do we need Dot Nimmo? We're wasting time!"

"Try to keep steady," Cowgill answered, knowing that whatever he said would make no difference. At least Derek had a legitimate reason to panic. Cowgill had to keep up a front of professional calm.

"Mrs. Nimmo can give us vital information. She will be here very shortly, and then we'll move," he said, and began to tell Derek what he intended to do.

Fifty-Five

Lois sat on the end of the woman's bed, watching carefully as the baby slept peacefully in his mother's arms. It had not been a difficult birth, thank God, and apart from suspecting that she had made a bodged job of the cord, everything seemed to her to be fine. The woman, too, was dozing, and the room was quiet. Alastair slumped on a rickety wooden chair, but was wide awake, and the other two sat on the floor, legs stretched out and backs to the wall. Every so often one of them nodded off, and his mate dug him in the ribs.

Lois knew she had to stay awake at all costs. For some reason, her threat had kept them at bay for a while, but although they had not replaced the gag or rebound her hands, the odds were against her being able to get help. Three of them, two fit and violent and one flabby and nasty and holding a gun. Her only hope was to be still and hope that all three would fall asleep at the same time. Some hope!

The baby stirred and gave a small cry. Alastair sat up and grasped his gun tightly. Lois smiled, and helped the woman put the little mouth to her breast.

"Isn't it miraculous?" she said conversationally to Alastair. "Every time, a miracle."

"Or a bloody disaster," he grunted.

The other two men were yawning, and one of them asked if they were still needed. "Nothin' we can do now until Terry brings 'em in the minibus," he said. He gave another nudge to his mate. "Him and me could do with a kip before tomorrow. Big day, boss," he reminded Alastair. "What will you do with the brat?" he added. "Why don't we just take it now and get it over with?"

Lois held her breath and they all stared at Alastair. The mother understood enough to fold her arms protectively around the baby.

Alastair stared at the woman who had looked after him so well, in spite of his showing total indifference towards her. "Leave it," he said. "The brat's part of our bargain with Mrs. Meade. Bugger off, both of you. There's those sleeping bags in the big bedroom." He looked at his watch. "You take two hours, and then we'll switch. I don't need much sleep, but there's a lot to do tomorrow. Trust that woman to produce the kid tonight of all nights," he added.

After they had gone, Lois said, "How much English does she understand?"

"More than she lets on. Why?" he said. He looked at her suspiciously. What had she got in mind? He had heard of Lois's reputation but had always dismissed it with a laugh. How could a cleaning woman be useful to the police?

"Good," said Lois. "We need to talk."

"No, we bloody don't!" said Alastair. "Keep your mouth shut, else I'll gag you again."

Splendid, thought Lois, and began to talk. She pretended she knew exactly what he and his associates were doing, hoping that her guesswork would be close to the truth. "One thing I'd like to know from you," she said authoritatively, as if she was not facing a loaded gun. Was it loaded? She had to assume it was.

"Shut up!" said Alastair.

Lois ignored him. "What were you going to do if you'd not been able to get me? Leave this woman to die, and her baby, too? Because that's what would have happened."

"Oh, no," Alastair said, sounding quite offended. "We had it all arranged. Pat—"

"—or Patricia?" interrupted Lois.

"Oh, very clever, Mrs. Meade. Well, we'd got all the gear for Pat to deliver the baby. Instruments, everything. Even a black bag. We were especially proud of the black bag. The woman was going to be safe. She was too useful to me. But then Pat was careless. Had a skinful once too often and blabbed to some of our associates in the pub, boasting about the cushy job at the museum, and other confidential matters. There were listeners there, as usual. I tried to save the stupid idiot, but no chance. They dealt with him. Things were beginning to look dicey for all of us in the trade, and we had one more job to do."

"But why me?"

"The woman going into labour took us by surprise, and you were the only person I could grab locally. At least there's a chance of keeping your mouth shut. And now," he added with menace, "not another word from you."

"So this baby was to be killed," continued Lois. "That tiny little spark of life you saw struggling into the world. What a welcome!" Lois was trembling now as she watched him finally lumber from his seat towards her. He picked up the filthy gag in one hand, and with the other tightened his grip on the gun.

"Get up!" He stood in front of her now, his crotch level with her head. The very thought of what she had to do made her feel sick, but like lightning she butted her head forward straight into his goolies. He doubled up and yelled with pain, dropping gag and gun.

Lois was on the gun in seconds. She gave him an almighty push so that he collapsed on the floor, and held the gun to his temple.

"I know how to use this," she lied. "Stay where you are. It won't be for long. By now they'll be combing the country for me, and the penny's bound to drop soon, even with Cowgill." She stopped, and caught her breath as she remembered Jeems's little body stretched out on the footpath. Derek would find her, but maybe too late.

She controlled herself with difficulty, and said, "And don't try getting those thugs back in here. There's more than one bullet in this, I'm sure. With your organising genius you'll have thought of that. Don't move, Mr. Smith. We must be patient now."

She returned to her seat on the bed, keeping the gun trained on his prone figure. She looked around the room speculatively. High up on a cupboard she saw to her surprise a large fluffy rabbit pyjama case.

"Well, that's a point in your favour," she said. "At least you thought of a toy." She went across and lifted it down. As she did so, the half-open zip disgorged a shower of booklets.

"Put those back!" shouted Alastair from the floor.

Lois picked up one of them, and saw the word Passport.

"Oh, my Lord, you wicked sod!" she yelled at him, and stuck the gun to his head again.

Alastair groaned. "For God's sake, don't shoot," he pleaded, and then Lois knew that it was loaded.

Cowgill, Derek, and Dot moved swiftly and quietly. Cowgill had summoned his troops and they were stationed in the shadows along the High Street.

"You wait here," he said, and stood firm against Derek's protestations that he should be the first to rescue his own wife. As they approached the house where Dot said Lois was sure to be held prisoner, Cowgill heard the sound of a vehicle approaching. It was a dark blue minibus, and it turned down the lane to the playing field.

"Listen!" Dot growled. In a minute or two the engine was shut off, and the village was silent once more.

"Got 'em!" whispered Cowgill. He then became the perfect professional and made sure his men were where they could be ready for anything, but neither seen nor heard. "You wait under that tree," he said to Derek. "And no heroics, please," he added. "You could cost us Lois's life by blundering in."

Now Cowgill glided along the front path and round to the back of the house. He went swiftly past the minibus parked there. Its terrified illegal cargo had been greeted by police, accompanied by Dot Nimmo to guide them, well prepared.

"Now," Cowgill whispered to the man guarding the door.

"What kept you?" said Lois, as Cowgill entered. "There's another couple of charmers in the front," she added. "Pity to spoil their beauty sleep, but they might have guns." She waved hers gaily towards the door, and Cowgill rapidly relieved her of it.

Then he saw the woman and the sweetly snuffling baby, and realised what Lois had been brought here to do. He put his arms around her and held her tight, his face against her hair. She stayed quite still, breathing in the fresh, clean smell of him. Then she gently pulled away and nodded.

"Better send for an ambulance," she said. "I never was much good at first aid, an' there's probably things to be taken care of."

Fifty-Six

Douglas was looking out of the window into dimly lit Gordon Street. Derek had told him that his mother was missing and he had wanted to set out on a search at once. But Derek had said to stay put. Lois might phone him there if she was in trouble. Douglas had said surely if she could phone she would try Derek first. "Don't argue," Derek had said, and Douglas knew from the tone of his voice that he should do as he was told.

Susie sat by his side, holding his hand and occasionally stroking his arm. She could feel the tension in him and wished she could do something more useful to help.

Time passed. Douglas looked at his watch. "Wouldn't you like to get some sleep?" he asked, but Susie shook her head and said she couldn't possibly sleep until Lois was safe. Douglas held her close and the two stared out without talking.

A light snapped on upstairs in Braeside, and Douglas and Susie jumped to attention. They saw a figure silhouetted against the light. "It's her," Susie said. "It's Mrs. Thingummy, in her nightie."

"Blairgowrie," said Douglas. "What the hell's she doing up at this time of night?"

"Going for a pee?" said Susie.

Then the light went out, and Douglas said, "Watch carefully, Susie. Especially the front door."

They did not have long to wait. A police car came slowly down the road and pulled up outside. They saw the policeman walk swiftly to the house, and then another joined him and they gave a great kick to the front door. It splintered open, and they rushed in.

Douglas ran out, followed immediately by Susie. He pushed his way into Braeside and saw Mrs. Blairgowrie—now strangely bald—struggling as a policeman secured her wrists. Her wrists? Douglas gulped. She was a man, he saw with disgust. "Go back, Susie," he said firmly, but she didn't move from his side.

The second policeman came rattling down the stairs. "Nobody else," he said.

"Where's my mother?" shouted Douglas, and he moved threateningly towards the captive. The policeman caught hold of him and said, "Steady now. Your mother's safe at home. She'll be wanting to see you."

"Is she hurt?" Susie said anxiously.

The policeman smiled. "Not so's you'd notice. I'd say she was fighting fit, even after a great night's work."

They were all there. Gran, Lois and Derek, Josie and Rob, and Jamie, and as Douglas and Susie came in, Lois hugged them both. "Sorry about all that," she said. She was holding on to a sleepy Jeems as if she would never let her go.

After Gran had insisted on Horlicks and digestive biscuits— "No coffee at this time of night"—Lois told them as briefly as possible what had happened, how illegal immigrants from several countries had been smuggled in by Alastair and his contacts over a long period. She explained about the woman he had kept for his own use, and the baby now safe from certain death. A knock at the door interrupted her, and she went apprehensively to open it. Cowgill and Dot stood there.

"I'm just checking to make sure you are not in any way hurt," he said in an official voice. "There will be questions and so on, but tomorrow will do for that."

They turned to go, and Lois said, "Dot! Where are you going? Into the kitchen with you. Gran'll kill me if I let you go home without us looking after you."

Dot grinned, gave Cowgill a peck on the cheek, and went through to the kitchen.

Lois looked at him without speaking. After a few seconds she put out her hand and touched his arm. "I'm fine," she said. "They're all here, standing by. I'd ask you in, but..."

Cowgill shook his head. "I quite understand," he said. "So long as you're not hurt. I'll say good night now. Well done, Lois," he added, and turned on his heel. She watched as he got into his car and drove away. Poor old Hunter, she thought, going home to an empty house and a cold bed. She shook herself, shut the door, and returned to her family.

An hour of amiable questions and answers passed, and finally Lois yawned widely. "Time for bed, everyone," she said. "Dot, you're in the spare room. Douglas—um—well, you and Susie..."

Douglas rescued her. "That sounds like the perfect cue," he

said, and stood up. He took Susie's hand and cleared his throat. "I'd like to say that one good thing came out of tonight's dramas. While me and Susie were waiting for something to happen, I asked her to marry me. Not the most romantic venue, I suppose, but she said yes, and I'm the happiest man in the world."

After that, there was no going to bed. Derek found a bottle of bubbly wine, and a toast was drunk. "Well done, Douglas," he said. "And welcome, Susie, to our family. As to the romantic venue, I'll tell you how I proposed to your mother. We were on a day trip to Brighton on my motorbike. We thought we'd go along the coast to have tea at Rottingdean, and on a patch of loose gravel the bike spun and tipped her off. I lifted her up, sat her down on the verge, knelt down on me grazed knee, and asked her to marry me."

Everybody looked at Lois, who was smiling broadly. "And I said yes, more fool me," she said. "Still, I'd do the same today. Your dad, Douglas," she added, "has picked me up from disaster many times since then, and I hope you'll do the same for Susie."

A round of applause drowned Derek's aside to Gran. "I hope the girl won't get hooked on ferretin' like our Lois," he whispered.

"It's Josie I worry about," Gran replied under her breath. "Like mother, like daughter," she added. Derek looked across at Josie sitting next to Rob, and saw him put his hand over hers. With some alarm he watched as she withdrew her hand and turned away to blow Susie a kiss. Rob's a fool, he thought. Should have popped the question months ago. Looks like it's too late now.

Dawn was breaking over Tresham as Cowgill was finally able to drive up to his substantial house in the best part of town. No welcoming lights shone from the windows, there would be no warm gathering in his chilly kitchen. After the death of his wife, his daughter had wanted him to move into a flat, but he had resisted. Now he thought that it might, after all, be the most sensible thing.

He checked his messages. There was one from his nephew Matthew, a bright, confident voice telling him he would be coming at the weekend to work on the cottage and hoped to see him. Oh, and by the way, did he know if Josie Meade was around? Not on holiday or anything like that?

Cowgill smiled to himself. He felt cheered, and went to bed with the memory of a small, bare bedroom in Long Farnden and Lois in his arms.

Fifty-Seven

Next morning, Cowgill was in Long Farnden punctually at ten thirty. Lois saw him park outside the house and approach up the drive. He had a spring in his step, she noticed with amusement. Another case wrapped up, and one step nearer to his retirement. She wondered if they counted up the number of cases solved and adjusted pensions accordingly. Of course not. It would all be part of an elaborate structure, and whatever it was, he would be loaded. What would he do with himself? He was a policeman to his bones, and seemed to have no hobbies or outside interests.

She shook herself. He'd made no mention of retirement lately, and in any case it was no business of hers. She dodged out of her office quickly, before Gran could get to the front door first.

"Morning, Lois," he said. "Is Derek here? I hope this won't take too long, but we do have some sorting out to do."

She led him into the sitting room, called Derek, and asked Gran to bring some coffee.

"I expect you'll want me to answer questions as well?" Gran said, smiling hopefully at Cowgill. He replied that he would be most grateful if she could stick around, so that he could check any points with her. "But for the moment," he said gently, "I'd like to talk to Lois and Derek."

Gran's face fell, and she departed looking huffy.

"I hope you got some sleep, you two," Cowgill began. "I wish we could do this later, but memory is fickle. Some things seem to vanish, and often they are the important links. So here goes."

"Why don't you start?" said Derek grumpily. "You tell us what you think we don't know, and then we'll fill in the rest. Or rather, Lois will. I know very little, as usual," he added sourly.

This was not what Cowgill had planned. He had his questions prepared and would go through them systematically. But he could see that Derek intended to assert his head-of-the-household status, and revised his plan.

"Right. This is the position as we know it. As you will appreciate, there are some things we have not been able to divulge..."

"Well, divulge them now, and get on with it," Derek snapped. Lois grinned and said nothing.

"Right. First of all, this trafficking in illegal immigrants is a much wider organisation than the cell in Tresham. Smith—we'll call him that—was boss of his small outfit, but answerable to higher authority."

"That's not something we don't know," Lois said. "Dot told me that ages ago."

"Ah, well, I'm sorry you neglected to pass that on to me, Lois." He smiled forgivingly at her, and continued. "Anyway, the system gives the likes of Smith a certain amount of freedom to operate. It also helps him with jobs like forging passports and setting up safe houses for the poor sods who've paid thousands to get here. The network uses no-hopers and ex-cons with secrets to hide who won't flinch at theft, violence, and, if necessary, murder."

In Lois's inner eye, a picture of Clem upside down in his toilet was quickly followed by a grey-haired postmistress with her head at a funny angle. She swallowed hard.

"Smith can call on these characters when he needs them," Cowgill continued. "And he'd got your Skinny Man and Mrs. Blairgowrie where he wanted them. Blackmail, not to put too fine a point on it. Smith used the little Gordon Street house for hiding packages of passports, and as a convenient sleepover before the victims got moved on. Hence the sleeping bags," he added with a smile at Lois.

"You have to hand it to Mrs. B and Skinny Man! They made very convincing women. Both of 'em fooled me." Lois laughed.

"Depends how you like your women," Derek muttered, glaring at Lois. "Go on, Inspector."

"They're professionals, Lois," Cowgill said. "Both of those villains were well known to us. The poor old blind lady is actually a hit-and-run merchant. He was speeding in a built-up area of Glasgow, and mowed down a small boy. The child didn't make it. We're very glad to have so-called Blairgowrie in our care."

"And Skinny Man?"

"Scared and inept. He'd been a promising crime writer, but got himself involved in a sex scandal that hit the national press. Wife divorced him, and she had the money. He was more or less destitute and helped himself to cash from a village post office. Wrecked his career. Got the plot wrong in that case." Cowgill smiled, pleased with his bon mot.

"Now," he continued, "first question. What the hell did they think they were doing grabbing you off the footpath, Lois?"

"Why don't you ask them?" Derek said.

"It's all right, Derek," Lois said calmly. She turned to Cowgill. "Big Al's not all that bright, y' know."

"Nor is he a fool," Cowgill said quietly.

"Maybe, but he thought he was clever, cleverer than anybody and especially cleverer than me. Mind you, they didn't plan for me to be midwife. It was Pat the skinny man's job. But he got snuffed out by the heavies, didn't he. Then there wasn't nobody else."

"Rubbish!" Derek said. "You bet they got plenty of women at their beck and call. Your own fault, Lois, for being involved in the first place!"

Cowgill frowned. "If you could just wait a while, Derek," he said. "I promise you shall have your say. Please go on, Lois."

"Well, the poor woman goes into labour unexpectedly, and there I was, living just across the road. Al knows nobody in Farnden except me, the woman is screaming, and he panics. Makes an on-the-spot decision, thinking he can keep me quiet with threats of violence to my family if I talk. Sends those blokes creeping around, and they find me."

She moved closer to Derek, and said, "If you'd seen that woman with her baby, love, you'd be glad I was there. An' I'm safely back, aren't I?"

"Until the next time," Derek grunted.

Gran poked her head round the door. "More coffee anyone?" she said. All shook their heads, and she retreated reluctantly.

The questions went on, and Derek had his say. It was mostly what he had said many times before and he knew it was a waste of breath, but he felt better for saying it.

"This is the last time, Lois," he finally repeated a couple of times, and thumped the coffee table with his fist to make his point. He got up, indicating the interview was at an end, and took the tray of mugs through to Gran in the kitchen.

Lois saw Cowgill to the door. "What will happen to the woman and her baby?" she asked, and he replied that he would personally make sure she was cared for.

"If she's allowed to stay here, d'you reckon she'd be interested in a cleaning job?" Lois said. "Once you've settled her safely?"

Cowgill put out his hand and took hers. He gave it a small squeeze and said, "That's my girl. I'll be in touch."

"Yes," Lois said, and stood at the door watching until he was in his car and driving away.